THE FREEDOM TO LOVE

THE FREEDOM TO LOVE

BY JEZA BELLE

RESOURCE *Publications* · Eugene, Oregon

THE FREEDOM TO LOVE

Resource Publications
An Imprint of Wipf and Stock Publishers
199 W. 8th Ave., Suite 3
Eugene, OR 97401

www.wipfandstock.com

PAPERBACK ISBN: 979-8-3852-3960-3
HARDCOVER ISBN: 979-8-3852-3961-0
EBOOK ISBN: 979-8-3852-3962-7

01/29/25

To my husband and God-given partner in life for over fifteen years. This book was born out of the fact that our relationship would have not have been possible only a short time ago in these United States. Mercifully, love does prevail, even through the most horrific of times and experiences. I am blessed to live when the blood and tears shed by others led to this space where our love can not only exist, but thrive.

"Love knows no color. It has no bounds like time, space, and air.
It is not specific to binaries or man-made labels.
Love exists in its simplest form and it is free."

-JEZA BELLE

Contents

Acknowledgments

Khloe Cain - for being an absolute rock star of an editor.

Thomas Evans Photography - for an amazing press photo.

Wipf and Stock / Resource Publications - for continuing to step out and make a mark.

Prologue

The old, Black man used a cane made of a dark-toned wood to help himself to the ground. It was not one of those canes folks of his kind were forced to whittle for themselves. It was a smooth polished walnut color with a silver handle carved into the shape of a snake; the type that was special ordered and produced with great care for those of some means.

His knees creaked but he made it to the dirt and sat atop a freshly covered grave.

There he took a small chisel out of his gray suit pocket. It couldn't have been more than six inches but it was just enough for him to grip with the whiteness of his palm where the melanin strayed away.

The man held it up with his left hand and pulled yet another tool from his jacket with his right hand, this time a hammer. He lifted its head high into the air and his hand shook violently from the weight. He motioned it downward until its steel hit the butt of the chisel whose basil-shaped blade sliced its first mark into the empty tombstone.

The sound of children's laughter carried high on the wind, so he lifted his head as if to chase the sound. Then the man closed his eyes and remembered.

Separation

With the back of his arm, Arthur pressed his crisp, white linen shirt against his forehead to soak up the beads of sweat forming along his fair brow line. The heat from the late afternoon Kentucky sun had matted his golden tresses against his youthful face. Once his forehead was dry, Arthur leaned over and drew a bird in the dirt with the tip of a carved stick he held in his right hand. It was roughly hewn to resemble a copperhead, its teeth bared and ready to strike.

"Well," Arthur laughed with abandon. "What is it?"

Samson was squatted at his feet; his ragged clothes the color of the dust that his naked toes had scrunched beneath him. "It's a chicken?" the young slave tentatively called back; his brow arched with anticipation.

Arthur slapped his head with his free hand and stood up straight. "A chicken?" His chest shook from giggling. "That definitely is not a chicken!"

"Shaw, pshaw!" Samson cried out.

Arthur reached down again but this time his hand grabbed ahold of Samson's right bicep. With all the force a nine-year-old could muster, he yanked the other boy upright until Arthur could look Samson directly in his eyes.

He smiled at his friend warmly, if you consider someone your family owned a friend. That's who Samson was to Arthur, one of Lanark's slaves, yet they had a friendship.

When time permitted, Arthur would often sneak off to play hide and seek or ham bone with Samson. On occasion, he would even tuck away with the young boy under the porch where they could play ring taw out of sight from the watchful eyes of Athur's mother. There they would shoot the colorfully swirled glass marbles Arthur brought out from a crimson bag he kept in a felt-lined box in his fine bedroom. Samson told Arthur once that the marbles felt like magic and Arthur would watch the way his friend swirled the smooth glass balls between the skin of his rough little fingers.

With the stick extended once more, Arthur scratched again in the dirt. *Surely he will guess it now,* he thought to himself.

"A turkey?" Samson tried one more time with a tightened face.

"No, not a turkey either," Arthur sighed. He put his free arm around Samson's shoulder and squeezed.

"It's a grouse, you silly-billy!" he declared, and they laughed at their play.

After he released Samson from his grip, Arthur ran a finger over the snake's pointed fangs. They were sharp, but not enough to break the skin. "Thanks for the stick, Samson. It's really nice."

"Oh, it's nothin'. Poppa Blue is teachin' me to carve and I thought you'd like it."

"Still, it's appreciated." Arthur studied it hard; his upper teeth biting into his lower lip.

"I'll have to hide it from Mother, as she's certain to go hog if she finds it."

Arthur recalled his mother's twisted face the time she discovered a painted rock under his bed that Mammy Gert gave him for his sixth birthday.

"It'll be black magic cursed!" she screamed before she tore open the window in Arthur's bedroom and tossed it outside.

The slave woman, who had raised and nursed Arthur day and night as if he were her own child, was led off by ropes that next morning. He wondered for a second whatever had happened to Mammy Gert but the attention span of boys was short, so he shrugged the thought off.

"How about later we catch lightning bugs and put them in a mason jar?" Arthur suggested. "I can meet you down by the river after supper."

Samson shrugged. "I'd like that but reckon I have to do my chores first."

Arthur kicked a pebble and it ricocheted off the front porch of his large plantation home. The house was the color of freshly churned butter, each window trimmed in the same milky white. There were even four large pillars Arthur thought were big enough to hold up the sky, or in this case the upper balcony of this two-story behemoth.

The house, like the land, was named after the place where Arthur Buchanan's family immigrated from deep in the Scottish Highlands more than a hundred years ago. His mother would frequently remind Arthur that the Buchanan's name and the Lanark house were things that set him apart and above most other people.

A loud bang rang out as the door to the mansion flew open and hit against its wood siding hard. Arthur's eyes widened as the new house slave,

Hattie, was dragged outside by two men. Her face was the shade of honey and twisted with fear.

"I ain't neva meant to break it," she cried out, but the two men gripped her tighter and pulled her down the steps of the porch.

Their rough handling caused Hattie's large breasts to break free from the top of her coarse cloth dress, which was a step up from the clothing the rest of the Lanark slave women who did not work in the plantation home wore.

Arthur wanted to shield his eyes because he knew it was not nice to look on at a woman's nakedness uninvited, even if she was a slave. But it all happened so quickly and unexpectedly that he could not help but to stare.

Piglet, was a wiry man whose constant snorting giggle led to his name. He latched onto Hattie's right side and looked down and grinned while his beady eyes stared at her bouncing breasts. Even Arthur knew Piglet's peepers were like to never get to see a woman's boobies unless it was by force.

On Hattie's left side, Arthur saw Flicker; a recent hire that Arthur's father, Buck, told him was one of the toughest overseers any plantation could hope to have. *What the big farms like us here allow sets precedence for all the others,* he remembered Buck explaining. *So best our man be full of righteous fire.*

Between Flicker and Piglet, Arthur knew whatever Hattie was headed toward, it was bound to be no good.

Hattie moved her head to and fro as if she was looking for someone, but Arthur wondered who, if anyone, would be bold enough to step forward on her behalf.

As the men dragged her feet right through the grouse Arthur had drawn in the dirt, he turned back to look at the red-haired woman in a pale blue dress who proudly emerged from the Lanark house. This lady swept down the steps a few feet behind the troubled slave and paused.

Mrs. Anna Buchanan's face was hard as stone. Arthur noticed that she, too, was scanning the vast acreage of the estate. *She is probably looking for my father,* Arthur thought to himself.

Hattie squealed with pain causing Arthur to shiver, so he reached over and tapped Anna on her arm. "Mother?" he asked, soft alarm in his voice.

"Shush." She swatted his hand off of her arm. "Your father brought that bitch into our home just two weeks ago and she's already managed to break the serving plate my mother brought over from the continent," she looked down at him, fury in her eyes.

Arthur had rarely seen Hattie before the move, except on occasion when she was coming in from the fields at night if he was still permitted to be outside. That was at least until that one time recently when she and Buck were doing something of a strange dance over by the woodshed. They were rubbing and grunting at each other somehow or another, and his father had a weird expression on his face, almost like when Grandfather Buchanan had one of them seizures, collapsing on the parlor floor two years back. Buck didn't appear to die like Grandfather, though he moaned as if he were about to. When Buck spotted Arthur and Samson, his father yelled out for them to skedaddle, and they did so quickly. Then, poof, Hattie was in the house working alongside Mae in the kitchen the next evening, and Arthur heard his parents in a nearby room hollering back and forth.

"We already have a good cook so why in Sam Hill do I need another?" He heard his mother explode through the wall. "And you didn't even ask me none, you just did it."

"Don't you ever forget a woman's place is to obey her husband," his father had shot back.

"Obey? I'd ask what exactly are you up to, Buck Buchanan, but I think we both know!" One of the two then slammed a door.

Boom. There was a loud crash as Flicker's thick, grizzly beast of a leg swung out; his boot then tore open the barn door.

"No!" Hattie howled as the two men pulled her inside the dark doorway and disappeared. Arthur watched his mother's eyes narrow then she turned back to her son and spotted Samson for the first time.

"Don't you got no work to do?" she scolded.

Samson's eyes hit the dirt.

"I'll have to speak to Master Buchanan about you next. Every time I turn, you are up under Arthur's feet like one of the farm dogs."

Another yelp escaped the barn and Anna hitched her skirts up. She turned back to Arthur and instructed him. "Now, you go wash for supper."

"But Hattie?" Arthur pressed. "Will they hurt her?"

"You're a child, not in the position to question. You do as your mother said. Wash up and pay no mind, y'hear?"

"Yes ma'am," he answered sadly.

With that, Anna marched the distance to the barn and slammed the door shut behind her.

Not wasting a moment, Arthur looked at Samson then nodded. Samson seemed to understand Arthur's silent suggestion, and he followed him as Arthur dropped the snake stick in the dirt and ran around to the back of the barn where a tall ladder led up from its stone foundation into the timber-constructed hay loft.

Quickly, Arthur pulled and pushed himself upward with Samson right on his heels until they plopped in through the hole and landed right on top of a soft bed of hay.

Arthur dared not stand up for fear his mother would see him, so he crawled along the dried grass until his eyes could peer down unseen into the barn below. Samson crept up on his belly beside him.

There, down below, hung Hattie; her arms suspended by a rope that was thrown over one of the wooden rafters. Her tiptoes barely touched the straw beneath her.

Anna walked over to one of the barn walls and pulled a long whip down from a rusty nail. As she handed it to Flicker, she nodded to Piglet, who snorted and licked his lips like it was time for Sunday supper before he stepped forward and tore the back right off of Hattie's dress. The garment split and dropped to the barn floor leaving her naked as a fledgling robin.

Arthur turned back to Samson, who appeared transfixed in fascinated horror at Hattie's situation.

The slave woman appeared to try again to turn her head around, this time it was as if to see what was happening behind her, but the crack of the whip in the air as Flicker tested it out seemed to be enough to answer any question.

"I didn't mean to Missus Anna . . . I's . . . I's be more careful I promise you!" her voice quivered as she begged.

"I can promise you, too, Hattie," Arthur's mother answered icily. "After this, you will never forget that I expect my negroes to be heedful and think only of what would please me when they are in my house, and make no mistake, the Lanark home is *my* domain, and no one else's."

He watched as Anna walked around from behind Hattie and looked up into her eyes. "A broken platter does not make me happy."

Anna's eyes dropped to Hattie's belly that was newly exposed and now visibly curved.

"And neither does that."

A small gasp escaped from Hattie's lips.

Mrs. Buchanan nodded at Flicker and the whip sang out in the air before it sliced into Hattie's back. Arthur flinched as blood flew from her body the way the scream of pain flew out of her mouth.

"Please," her words echoed off the rafters. But Arthur's mother was not known for her mercy so she nodded again to the bear who more than willingly obeyed a second time.

Arthur's shoulders seized with tension each time he saw Flicker raise his hand high, again and again. Tears formed in his eyes and he opened his mouth to call down and beg his mother to stop, but suddenly a muscled arm reached out and grabbed hold of Arthur's shoulder. With a quick jerk, he was yanked to his feet and found himself staring into the cold gray eyes of his father, Buck.

Buck Buchanan's skin was like leather, as tough against the elements on the outside as he was on the inside. He told Arthur that all Buchanans had to be strong because it was a God ordained gift that they possessed 2,500 acres of crops, forest, and animals that worked their fields on both four legs and two.

Arthur tried to look away from Buck's hard stare, so he turned his head aside where he caught sight of Samson's wild eyes. The young slave jumped up and backed away slowly from Arthur and his father until at last, Arthur saw Samson's naked feet had touched the first rung of the ladder. He was gone in a blink, and Arthur couldn't blame him, as everyone knew leather could tan the hide of any negro, grown or small.

Alone, Arthur struggled to get free from his father's grasp so that he, too, could escape. He was certain he was in trouble for snooping and was due for a sermon and a whooping, but Buck seized this particular opportunity like the nape of Arthur's neck.

"Down there," Buck hissed, directing his son's gaze.

Arthur's eyes once again descended the barn to see Hattie's hanging body, which had now gone limp and she was in a state of semi-consciousness.

Buck forcefully squeezed Arthur while he pushed him closer to the edge of the loft so that his toes moved out into the open air.

"Look good and long, son," he growled softly. "And remember this moment."

Arthur wasn't sure he would ever forget the pain of his father's hand on his neck or Hattie's limp body.

"These creatures are to be used hard and trained twice as such," his father continued, his voice a raspy murmur.

Arthur cringed. "Yes, sir," he whispered back. He knew he must agree with whatever his father said, yet Arthur saw no creature. To him, there was just a poor woman whose body shook violently with each humiliating lash of the whip.

Down below, Anna grabbed the half-awakened woman by the jaw and shook her face until she regained full consciousness.

Aware of her situation once again, Hattie raised her eyes into the air and cried for Jesus. Arthur noted that instead her eyes caught Buck's up in the hay loft and she seemed to offer a wordless plea to his father as if he had come to her rescue. But she was answered with only the upturned corners of Buck's mouth like he was a barn cat that had just swallowed the pet goldfinch in front of the farmer's eyes.

His father's face reddened briefly. "Slaves are meant to provide our livelihood, son, but they are also meant to entertain us, as you are likely to learn soon enough." Arthur watched Buck's eyes as they stared down lustily on Hattie's ripe bosom and belly Then he turned back to Arthur and those same eyes bore down on him as if they were meant to pierce his young Christian soul. "But always remember . . . we are meant to tame the beast in them as the Lord has required."

A blood curdling scream rang out and Arthur's body jerked upward, but his father's grip only tightened.

His father at last released his neck and the two of them backed away from the edge of the loft. "Keep them in line, Arthur, or if you don't, they'll be the ruin of you."

Once they were safely away from sight, Buck continued his instruction. "It's my job as your father to bring you up in the Lord the right way, Arthur, and that means making sure that you understand right and wrong."

Arthur wanted to cry, but what good would that have done. His father was not one to spare the rod, especially for being soft. *No,* Arthur thought to himself. *Best to nod and agree,* and he did both.

"Your mother and I only have one child," Buck said. "As such, you have spent your youthful years with that boy, Samson, but I want you to understand, son, he's not one of us, he's one of them." His father pointed back to the loft's edge. "Samson is just like her."

Buck leaned down close to Arthur's height until he could see his father's eyes up close. "But trust and believe my boy," his father's voice deepened into a thundering whisper that flew out of his mouth like a gale force wind. "These niggers are not your friends."

The words hung in the air.

After a few seconds, Buck stood up straight and grinned. "When you are through here, go wash up for supper. Your mother and I have something important to share with you," he said to Arthur, then Buck disappeared down the same ladder Samson had left from only moments ago.

Now alone, Arthur told his feet to leave this barn as well. At the church his parents took him to every Sunday, they talked about evil and he felt it in this place and it made him shiver with a boy's deep fright. But somehow his feet moved away from the ladder and he found himself once again looking back down over the ledge below.

His mother still had Hattie's face in her hand. "And make sure to beat that baby out of her body today, Flicker," Anna spat as she released Hattie's lips that she had smooshed together with her fingers.

Arthur knew Mrs. Buchanan could make Flicker and Piglet seem like the sweet peaches the Lanark's slaves plucked alongside the lower forty each July. They'd be ripe for cobbler in comparison to Anna's ferocious, and at times, cruel behavior when it came to what she called, "my negroes."

Once, Arthur had overheard her say to some women at a party, *"Afri-CANs my ass,"* she mused to shrill laughter. *"It's Afri-WILL-do-what-I-say or I'll tan my negroes raw."*

His mother would think nothing of having one of the slave's fingers cut off for tapping too loudly, or having any one of them flogged publicly for the way they walked. Yet, those benign actions didn't reflect publicly on her or her marriage the way Hattie's proud belly did.

"I'm no fool as to why Mr. Buchanan brought you into my house," she continued.

Hattie's eyes welled up and she sobbed aloud. "No, it's not the baby's fault. No, Missus Anna, no!"

Arthur's mother appeared to have no interest in Hattie's cries. "I won't have a half-breed running around right up under my nose," she spat out.

Anna then walked off toward the barn door as if to leave, but right before she made it to the door, she turned back to Flicker and said, "When it's all done, have Piglet take her down and send her right back up to the house."

Arthur made out Piglet's smile from up in the loft, but his swine like grunt was unmistakable.

"I'll expect supper without delay and she best be prepared to serve it," Anna said. She turned, stepped through the barn door, and slammed it shut.

Once Mrs. Buchanan was gone, Flicker dropped the whip onto the floor and walked around to the front of Hattie's hanging body where he lifted his maw and turned it into a big fist. Arthur cringed with fear as Flicker pulled it back hard and then released it swiftly and directly into Hattie's full stomach.

The potency of the strike caused Hattie's eyes to widen as all the breath inside her lungs flew out of her mouth upon its impact. At last, Arthur looked on as she fainted and laid motionless, her body dangling from the ropes. Steady drops of blood began to plop one by one onto the straw underneath Hattie's legs.

"You heard the Missus. Wake her and send her on up to get back to work," Flicker grunted to Piglet as he, too, walked to the door and exited the barn.

"Alone at last," Piglet giggled, unaware of Arthur's presence.

Unable to move, Arthur stood there looking as Piglet's toothless grin grew bigger the closer he stepped toward Hattie's limp body. The little piggy licked his snout and began unbuckling his pants. Arthur wondered what Piglet could possibly be doing but his thoughts were quickly distracted by Hattie who came to and kicked her legs out wildly behind her to push Piglet away from her.

Hattie's foot connected with Piglet's groin because he yelled out in pain. "You stupid bitch," he cursed, then grabbed her ankle to stop her from kicking him again.

Just at that moment, an old woman's voice could be heard calling from afar. "Hattie! I need your help for supper, Hattie."

Arthur thought to himself that Mae needed Hattie's help like Jesus needed nails in his wrists. She seemed quite angry ever since Hattie was brought into the Lanark home, but here she was calling out for her as if she were her own child lost in the dark.

"Fuck," Piglet whistled through his teeth. Arthur put his hands over his mouth at the word. "Why do I never get me some!" Piglet pouted aloud while he pulled his pants back up around his waist.

Once they were secured, Arthur looked on as he helped Hattie down from the ropes. When her feet were fully on solid ground, poor Hattie looked confused about whether she should clench her stomach or pull her torn dress up from the barn floor to cover her nakedness from Piglet's beady eyes.

"You best go on up or the next time it'll likely be even worse," Piglet told her. He smiled and licked his lips as if Hattie was a piece of one of Mae's stacked sweet potato pies with molasses.

Hattie slowly backed her way to the door. As she moaned, she held one arm around her belly and with the other, she held her shredded dress up over her breasts. Piglet followed behind and Arthur stood there in the silence; his young chest heaved from relief that the current situation was over. He stood there for close to five minutes in an attempt to make sense of what he had witnessed, but eventually Arthur gave up as most of what his parents did when it came to the handling of the men and women of the plantation were beyond his grasp.

As he made his way down the ladder and back up to the house, Arthur felt the same uneasiness hugged the air the closer he got to the Lanark house's sprawling porch.

I'll eat quick, he thought to himself. *Then go back out to play.* Arthur knew there was less chance of being subjected to his mother's harsh words when he was outside of the building, as Anna craved comfort, and the heat of summer was a world she preferred to avoid. So whenever possible, Arthur broke for the fresh air and the chance to get away from her incessant nagging.

When Arthur entered the dining room for supper, Buck and Anna cast uncomfortable glances at each other from where they sat at the heads of the table. It was made from the darkest of Bubinga hardwood that Grandfather Buchanan used to brag about how he had it imported from the Ivory Coast the same way he ordered up men and women from the darkest continent. The table was set with a fine bone China with little pink tea roses that peeked up from inside the soup bowls as if to tease the eater by saying, 'see if you can find me again once I'm covered in rich broth.'

Arthur found his seat in the middle of the table. He had run upstairs quickly and was now freshly dressed after laying on top of the barn's hayloft earlier.

At the far end of the room, on a stool next to the buffet was Basil, Buck's boy, who had more white hair coming out of his ears than on top of his wrinkled old head. Arthur had asked his mother once why they called Basil "boy" when he seemed twice or maybe three times as old as his father, but Anna just shushed him the way she always did when it came to these questions.

Basil sat and tugged this evening at the Shoo Fly Fan, like he had done all of the evenings Arthur could remember. The fan was made of a simple wooden board and it was covered in the same pink damask that decorated the seat cushion that Arthur sat his backside on. Back and forth Basil yanked rhythmically so that the fan swung over the dining table with each pull, and in doing so, it cooled the family from the summer heat while it shooed away the flies that came in from the open windows and away from the food.

The door that was set between two built-in cabinets that were filled with all sorts of breakable dinner and glassware gently creaked open. In hobbled Hattie, a deep soup tureen in her shaking hands. She was followed by the elderly, Mae, who told Arthur she had been working inside the Buchanan's home since she was his age. Arthur knew that as hard to please as his mother was, Mae's good cooking and mild manners kept Anna especially keen to keep Mae around, knowing she had served several generations of Lanark Buchanans already.

Hattie limped up close beside Arthur's father first, her eyes cast downward like she was a dog that had been beaten for destroying her master's favorite set of slippers. Anna had repeatedly directed Hattie these past few weeks that Buck was always to be fed from the dishes first, but Arthur could not believe Hattie was serving at all given what had happened in the barn less than an hour ago.

Mae came up beside Hattie and grabbed the ladle in the tureen and scooped up some of its Pepper Pot soup. She then plopped the mixture of red peppers and tripe that Buck always declared was one of his favorite dishes into his bowl.

The women repeated their dance over the sides of Anna's and finally Arthur's bowl, too, before Hattie unsteadily placed the tureen on the buffet. At last, Mae and Hattie stood with their backs against the wall under the large painting of Grandfather Buchanan, waiting for further instructions. This was the signal to Arthur that he was allowed, or rather, expected to eat.

"What a delightful day this has been," Anna said wistfully, picking up her spoon and swirling it in the soup.

Hattie's legs wobbled and it looked like she was about to fall on the floor.

Anna shot her a stern look and said, "And I expect it to be an even more delightful supper without any distraction," which caused Hattie to scrunch her face slightly in pain then she stood up straight once again.

He didn't understand much of what had taken place today, but from what Arthur could make out, Hattie was with child when she went into the barn. After the punch and the blood, she looked now to be more like someone who had already given birth and was better suited for the bed, not the supper table.

As metal clanked against the sides of fine porcelain, Buck slurped loudly before he smiled widely and shouted, "Mae, you did this here thing once again!"

Mae's sagging shoulders perked up at his father's compliment, and Arthur could have sworn Mae gave Hattie a look as if to say, 'Now this is how you are treated if you behave yourself at Lanark.'

Just yesterday, Arthur had run into the kitchen to grab one of those spice cookies that Mae always had a plate full sat out for him. He could smell the peanuts, cinnamon, and ginger when he pulled one of the treats up to his mouth to sink his teeth into when he heard Mae, who was just outside of the kitchen door, say something.

"E'rebody know you be spreadin' them legs willin'ly else you'd be back in the slave houses wit the rest, stead of up here believin' youse gonna be some kinda Lanark wife."

Hattie's voice replied and it was full of pride and determination. "Just youse watch. Imma have this child and me in a bed in this house's just the beginnin' what gonna come to me."

Mae snorted like someone had told her a funny.

"He done promised," Hattie replied with a touch of anger.

"Promises be the devil," Mae snapped back.

"Speak to me like that again and I's box your ears, old lady," Hattie retorted in anger.

"Or betta yet, I's speak to the Massa and have him sell your wrinkly ass down the river."

Arthur couldn't recall a time that he had ever heard Mae fight or even raise her voice toward anyone with a tone. Ultimately, he was more interested in the cookie, so he took a big bite and ran off to play. Yet, here now, he caught a second glimpse of some kind of feeling that Mae seemed to have about Hattie.

"Thank ya, Massa Buchana,'" Mae said aloud, her shoulders then sunk again and she stood back and faded into the paisley wallpaper.

At last, Buck dropped his spoon into the empty bowl and Hattie stepped forward to retrieve them both.

"Arthur," his father began, his deep voice filled with decisiveness. "Your mother and I have been talking. It's not healthy for a young man to be all on his own with no peers . . ."

Suddenly, Arthur's mother blurted out loudly. "We're sending you to a boarding school in Virginia."

There was a loud clunk as Arthur's spoon hit the table. "Away?" he asked, his eyes widened with terror. He cocked his head to the side to try and make sense out of his mother's words. "From home?" he pressed further.

Buck shot Anna a steely glance. Arthur knew he did not like it when Anna spoke over him. Nevertheless, he spoke to Arthur again, though this time he did not take his eyes off of Anna. "This here plantation is fine right now, Arthur, with your mother and I," he pressed his palms down onto the table like if he was smooshing his mother's face into the wood. "But one day both of us will be gone and it's going to need someone with grit and a keen mind to keep it going."

"I don't want to go away," Arthur started protesting, but his father lifted then slapped one of his hands down so hard that Arthur dared not push him further.

"This here is an opportunity to study at a good school where you can learn proper numbers worthy of an estate such as ours," Buck said, his voice stern in his pronouncement.

Arthur's lower lip trembled and he cast a helpless glance at his mother on the other end of the table hoping she would be more sympathetic.

"But I'll be alone," he whispered to her.

Mae moved in to remove the bowl from in front of Arthur and while she did so, she let her hand brush up against his arm secretly as if to demonstrate sympathy for him. Arthur saw Hattie roll her eyes at Mae before she walked over and pulled Anna's empty bowl.

Tears welled up in Arthur's eyes, so his mother got up from the table and approached him. Arthur hoped Anna would do something she rarely did and hug him and tell him it would be alright, but instead she grabbed hold of him and shook his shoulders violently.

"Mother and father are trying to make a man out of you, Arthur. Don't be ungrateful!"

Arthur knew he was trapped. He choked back his feelings like he choked back his tears and sat there upright and silent.

"Good," Anna said as she made her way back to her seat. "You'll get to go off and see parts of the world that I've never even seen." As she slid back into her chair she continued. "I have heard the Rivington Academy is lovely."

At the name of the school, Arthur could not stop himself from trying one last time so he blurted out loudly. "But I don't want to go to the Rivington Academy . . . and I don't want to go to Virginia! I want to stay here with you, Daddy . . . and Samson!"

Anna sighed and looked over at Buck, her face reddening. "This is why he has got to go," she barked at her husband. "He's naming a damn negro in the same sentence as us as a reason to stay at home, as if the thing that was created to pick up his dirty undergarments was to be in the same breath as two Lanark Buchanans."

"One day you will thank us," Buck said curtly.

Mae and Hattie, who had stepped out unnoticed, returned with three plates filled with pork chops covered in a thick gravy alongside a pile of mash with butter beans in bacon.

Anna turned her head back to Arthur and commanded, "Now, hurry up child. Dry your eyes, eat your supper, then head upstairs. We have a lot of packing to do before your coach arrives in the morning."

"In the morning?" Arthur gasped.

His mother's eyes widened in fury. She pointed her finger at the dining room door.

"Go upstairs right now," she stammered. "I will not have my own child balk and bite over the decisions that his parents wisely made for him. This here food is for those who don't need cow's milk and wheat flour mush before their mammy changes their napkins."

Anna stood up from the table then marched behind Arthur's seat and pulled it out. "You will have to leave here in the morning on an empty stomach as a mere hungry brat and hope to heaven that Mae here will have enough mercy on you to pack a basket for the ride."

Arthur slowly got up from his seat, his head hung so low that his chin touched his chest.

"Why do you always have to open up that mouth and interrupt?" Buck yelled at Anna as Arthur marched to the door.

"Well, if you had been doing your job as a father instead of out there playing hide the slug with these . . ."

Arthur exited the room and his parents' argument faded as he walked up the stairs to his bedroom.

The rest of the evening was spent packing his clothes into a brown chest and two cases. It seemed as if everything he had in the world was ready to be shipped off with him, and he wondered if his parents meant for him to ever come back.

When it was almost pitch dark, Arthur heard his name being called from the open window in his bedroom. He walked over and stuck his head outside to find Samson down below, holding a mason jar up in each of his fists.

"You ready, Artha?" A number of little lights flickered in the air all around Samson.

"They be a'swarmin' tonight and I's reckon our jars be filled to the brim," he continued with a giant smile.

Arthur's face fell as there was nothing he wanted more than to run down those large stairs outside of his bedroom and head straight out the front door to frolic and play in the blinking bug-lighted air. Instead, he frowned and called down, "I can't."

Samson's face fell, too, and he lowered the jars in his hands.

"I am leaving in the morning. Don't know when or if I'll be back," Arthur said sadly.

"But where to?" Samson asked. "And why?"

"My parents are sending me far away to a school," Arthur called back down.

"I's ain't neva heard of a white boy being sent away. Don't they want ya no more?" Samson inquired with the innocence of a child.

All Arthur could do was shrug then he pulled his body back into the window and laid down on his bed.

Arthur lay awake most of the night but at some point, he must have drifted off because when he opened his eyes, sunlight streamed inside his eastern-facing window. Rustling could be heard downstairs so Arthur got himself out of the bed and threw on some pants and shoes before he opened the door. He came out into the hall and looked down over the balcony where he saw the chest that they had packed last night being dragged outside by old Basil.

Resigned to his fate, Arthur approached the winding staircase. All along its curved wall were portraits that ran from the top of the steps to the very bottom. These were the Buchanans of old, both those that lived here in this house themselves, and those whose likeness was brought over when the first of the Buchanans made their trip across the sea. They were said to be lairds and ladies of particular grit, having served the Scottish cause all the way back to Robert the Bruce and the Battle of Bannockburn.

Peppered in between were pictures of Anna's family, their last names being things like Culpepper and Preston-Hilliard as these were fine English families who never knew for want. The first of Anna's ancestors to make the journey to the Americas came after Oliver Cromwell's death and the restoration of the monarchy, having wrongly sided with the Parliamentarian over Charles II. But even they never lost placement in society or suffered financial ruin and in fact, they found themselves even more lauded in this new offshoot of England than they had been in their familial estates of Devonshire.

So steeped were the two sides of Arthur Buchanan's ancestral lines in both their titles and position that it was some selfish wonder that both saw the need to be the aristocrats not just in the old world, but in the new one as well.

Arthur ran his hand along the banister and as he descended, he looked into the faces of every one of these paintings of his family. He wasn't sure if he had ever really studied them before, but he could not help but to notice now how every last one of them had the same look of judgment. Their eyes seemed to follow him from the first step to the last while they looked down their noses at him as if to say, 'You had best go forth from this house and come back as someone who knows and appreciates their station.'

Only, Arthur cared less about station than most so his mind drifted to things like, *what will it be like to sleep someplace new,* and, *who will Samson play with now that I am leaving for good?*

He smelled bacon frying and his mouth watered as he had not eaten since lunch the day prior. As if she read his mind, Mae came out from a door behind the staircase, a basket in her hand that she handed off to Basil saying, "Now make sure this here food gets on the wagon by the young Massa' Artha' as it be a long journey to Virginny, I's be told, and I's can't bear to think he gonna starve."

Just then, Anna came out of the parlor in a dress the color of sweet cream. She hooked her arm into Arthur's with a big smile on her face and walked him to the front door. There was a coach wagon that had his cases tied to the top. A man sat there on the driver's seat with his hands on the reins of two white horses that were ready to pull the wagon along when commanded. Anna led Arthur down the porch stairs where Buck waited next to Basil, who held the door to the coach open.

"Now you write to us once a month," Buck said, reaching out to shake his son's hand like he was making a deal on seed in town. "No point writing more than that as you will have plenty to do in your new life."

Mae and Hattie came out the door and stood on the porch to see Arthur off. Wet drops formed in the corner of Mae's eyes while Hattie's were blank.

Arthur stood frozen for a minute. He looked around to see if Samson had come to see him off too but when he realized he was nowhere in sight, the young Buchanan slowly inched forward to board the wagon.

"Make us proud, Arthur," Anna yelled out as the door to the coach closed. Then before he had even departed, his mother turned around and headed back into the house as if bored from all the fuss.

Buck raised his palm to the driver who then flipped the reins. The horses pulled and the coach bucked forward with all of their power. Arthur turned around inside the passenger's seat and watched the house become smaller as the horses clopped their way down the dirt road.

When they were about halfway down the driveway, Arthur saw Samson, who ran up in a breathless sprint alongside the coach before he tossed something into the open window. Arthur reached down to the floor to pick up what Samson had thrown in and then he lifted hold of the carved snake stick from the day before. He clutched it tightly, turning back and around to look into Samson's smiling eyes before the horses rounded the oak trees at the front of the property and turned.

Arthur sat back in the stagecoach and pulled the stick toward his chest and cried. Never in his life had he felt more alone.

Prodigal

I t had been close to ten years since Arthur had been sent away from his family's plantation in Mason County, Kentucky, to the Rivington Academy in Virginia. Here, he had grown from a thoughtful boy with limited social experience into a surprisingly popular and athletic young man. At Rivington, Arthur had diligently studied accounting, read the works of Virgil, and closely followed the growing political divide that rippled across the United States around the question of slavery.

The subjugation of others was what afforded Arthur Buchannan's parents the money to support Arthur's tuition at this prestigious institution. Yet, the argument over who other than God really dared own another person was one he was not insulated from. For Arthur spent many an hour listening to lectures, reading, and lying in bed thinking about the justifications, or lack thereof, for forced servitude.

In fact, only the week before, Rivington had hosted a debate between the "Rail Splitter," Abraham Lincoln, a lanky but affable country lawyer turned politician and the aristocratic-sounding, Dennis Harrington, president of the Virginia Society for the Continuation of the Slave Trade, and something of a dandy. This was part of a series of speeches the Illinois politician was making around the country met by various challengers as he continued making a name for himself on the national stage.

Arthur got chills when Lincoln stood at the podium and made quick, but sober, work out of the Society's president over the question of the Republican party's platform.

"We should in every way resist it as a wrong, treating it as a wrong, with fixed idea that it must and will come to an end. If we do not allow ourselves to be allured from the strict path of our duty by such a device as shifting our ground and throwing ourselves into the rear of a leader who denies our first principle. Denies that there is an absolute wrong in the institution of slavery,

then the future of the Republican cause is safe and victory is assured," Lincoln said in what was to become part of his pat political speech.

Arthur was lost in deep thought one morning, remembering these words from the Illinois politician, when a group of young men with a rugby ball approached Arthur's bedside in the boy's dormitory. All of them were in their late teenage years, and were an assortment of heirs to industry and agriculture alike from all over the states and territories. Each one primed to step into their father's shoes when the time came for them to assume their places at the heads of their families.

"Let's go, Captain," one of the strapping young men in shorts and a long sleeve shirt called out. Another pulled the covers off of Arthur's bed.

"We need to practice now if we plan to beat those boys at Memorial in next week's championship match," shouted another, as two more boys helped pull Arthur out of his bed.

Arthur laughed at their good-natured tussling, and he quickly got dressed. Then he followed the group out onto a field that overlooked the academy's main brick building. More boys already waited out on the pitch, and they rapidly assembled into a game of fifeteens. Arthur carried the ball and came into contact with a defender that started a maul, when a call was heard from the side of the pitch.

Someone blew a whistle and the game was brought to a halt, as one of the Academy's secretaries walked out onto the field.

"I was told to get this to you immediately," the woman said as she handed Arthur a note and turned to depart.

Arthur stood there. His body, now taut with muscles, was covered in grass and dirt that crisscrossed his white trousers; his black and white striped shirt splashed as well with the verdant color. His face was reddened and though he panted hard from the stalled game play, Arthur unfolded the paper and read the five words that he knew would come one day, though he thought they would still be many years off. "Buck Buchanan dead. Come home."

Numerous thoughts rushed through his head. How could his father who seemed practically unbreakable have submitted to death? Did this mean he was to truly be master of the house at Lanark when he returned to Kentucky? What role would his mother play in all of this?

There was not a lot of time in that moment to sort out the answers because he needed to get cleaned up then pack for the long journey.

His teammates and friends helped him get ready by folding his belongings and patting him on the back every few minutes. Before he knew it, Arthur was seated on a private coach, but this time back to Kentucky for a new life in his old home.

In the years since he originally left, Arthur had only returned to Lanark once. Instead, most holidays he shuffled along with one of his class-
mates to their homes. He was especially partial to those in the north where,
not perfect, a different kind of energy seemed to pulse through places like
New York City, Philadelphia, and even Boston. His only visit back to Mason
County was when he turned thirteen and his mother decided to throw a
party for him at Lanark. It was meant to celebrate his coming of age and
Arthur remembered that she embraced the occasion to put together a *ceil-
idh*, or caylee as she called it in Buck's old Scottish tongue, the likes of which
Mason County had never seen.

Anna arranged for highland dancers, a bagpipe procession, and even
traditional games like a caber toss and a hammer throw. Arthur had to dress
from head to toe in the ancient Buchanan tartan with shades of blue, red,
green, and yellow that were meant to symbolize the clan's connection to nature and the land. The party was not much fun for him as he was essentially
pushed to the side and ordered to stand there on display in itchy wool while
his mother was front and center.

Toward the end of the party, Arthur had gone outside to get some air.
As he stood on the porch, he could just make out the outline of a boy about
his age near the hand water pump over by the chicken coop. Arthur raised
his hand to wave but the whites of the Black kid's eyes faded into the darkness and Arthur was left there just as alone as he had felt throughout the
entire caylee.

The next morning, Anna had him on his way right back to Virginia
bright and early, and Arthur looked around as the carriage pulled away to
see if he would get one more glance at his former friend, but all he saw was
the flitter of a male Rose-breasted Grosbeak in the trees.

Back at Rivington, Arthur wondered if something was not right with
his father as Buck wrote to him not once but twice in the past few months.
Meanwhile, Buck never once penned a single word to his son in the prior
ten years. Both letters contained legal information about the deeds and controlling of the land, but Arthur just assumed at the time that it was because
he had reached the age of accountability and was set to return to Lanark
at the end of this term to take up work alongside his father. In retrospect,
perhaps Buck knew his days were coming to an end.

Arthur sat himself back onto the leather seat of the coach and settled
in to think further on what lay ahead for him at Lanark where he would now
be lord and master of everything the Buchanan's owned.

The miles turned into more miles. Arthur laid his head back and
closed his eyes as the wheels scraped and rattled into an uneasy rhythm.
"Buck Buchanan dead. Come home."

• • • • •

BUCK BUCHANAN WAS DEAD. The news rippled across the fields of cotton so that dang near everyone in Lanark, or rather in all of Mason County, Kentucky, had the news on their lips. Yet likely not one person was as curious as to what the new Massa Buchana' was going to be like than the slave called Samson.

Close to twenty years of age, Samson had been one of the prime hands on the Lanark Plantation for over a decade. He was known to work hard, kept his head down, and most importantly, kept his thoughts to himself, at least around the white folk. Around his own kind, he was as quick to snap back as a possum in a trap but when it came to the Buchanan Massas, for Samson, beatings, dismemberments, and hangings were enough to learn that one was better off simmering on the inside around them than showing what he felt on the outside. And simmer he did. Night and day Samson thought on why some people were born just to live their whole lives under the thumbs of another. "How come me and the others be meant to wipe the asses of the white folk with soft cotton cloth just because they's almost as see through as the bed sheets the house slaves hang up in the sun to dry?" he mumbled aloud to himself. It made no sense.

Samson laid in his bed made of pine board on this morning thinking, too. It was made of the same dry wood that formed the walls of the slaves' cabin in which this bed was set. His head was filled today with questions about Arthur's return such as, *will he be as serious as his daddy been all these years or as mean as his momma?* Minerva hit the bottom of the bedframe with a sage broom, breaking him from his thoughts.

"No time to fiddle. The house done ask for two chickens be brought up," Minerva ordered.

Samson yawned and stretched his muscled limbs hard before he swung out and pushed his strong bare feet down onto the cabin's cold floor made of dirt. One would think it was some kind of fine imported tile like they had in the Lanark home, the way Minerva swept that sage across it night and day.

"Biscuits on the table. Getchaself one then skedaddles yourself to the coop, lest that devil woman call down twice or you more like to wind up on the dinner table for her son's return than them chickens."

Samson walked over to the table, the smell of some kind of gravy wafted out of the oven pit the slaves who lived in this cabin before him and Minerva had built decades ago. He picked a biscuit from a plate and pushed the whole thing into his mouth so that his cheeks bulged out, then he turned around and smiled.

Minerva looked up. "You look more stuffed like a mattress over filled with corn husks than a fool." She laughed so hard that her head scarf shook.

Samson never knew his real mother. The Buchanans sold her just after his birth, but Minerva was said to be her cousin's cousin and she took Samson in as if he had come from her own loins and claimed to be his auntie.

"Now git outta here before I's pluck and stuff you myself," she ordered with a smile. Samson rushed out the door and closed it behind him.

The sun was already breaking through the trees where it dropped its rays on top of the other cabins. Smoke blew out of the chimneys of the dozen or so cabins, some long and thin, others short and wide. The long cabins fit ten to twelve slaves usually made up of an extended family or in one case, a whole bunch of young'uns the Massa had bought a few months back. There, these children were tended to by three old mammies, women who no longer were fit to work the fields and whose sole job now was to grow them babies up strong so the Massa saw a return on his investment.

There was a small cabin next to Minerva and Samson's where the old man named Poppa Blue lived. Poppa was blind for as long as Samson knew him, and he was outside now carving wooden figurines the same way he was when Samson went to sleep the night before. Day or night mattered naught when the light was always kept from him.

Poppa had a particular gift for these carvings that he would do by feeling. Each week ole Mae from up at the house would take a basket of Poppa Blue's creations with her into the town and hand them over to Mr. Hadler, the general store's owner. Hadler would sell them to his customers and split the money with Poppa, though Mrs. Buchanan would always insist that Mae give her most of his earnings so that Poppa Blue usually got just a few cents each week for all of his efforts. Those earnings he used for tobacco and donated the rest to the plantation's church.

The church sat right in the middle of all of the cabins. It was a small but cavernous building where the sounds of the plantation preacher and the singing of the choir ricocheted through the rafters.

Poppa Blue had an affinity for the little church so he would tell Samson to bring his coins there each Sunday and place them in the plate that he could not see. "The lawd knows betta how to use these pennies than an old blind fool," he would say each time.

Samson never understood how the Buchanans left Poppa Blue to his cabin to whittle the days away. Seemed like with everyone else they'd have sold them off or likely killed them rather than have them sit idle and be another mouth to feed. But Poppa Blue was still here when way too many than Samson could remember had come and gone in the years he was alive so he just shrugged, called out good morning to Poppa, and marched himself up to the coop.

With much effort, Samson managed to capture the two biggest meat hens, and before long he had swung the axe and left their heads on the ground for one of the barn rats to savor over for their own supper.

After each bird was plucked, Samson headed around to the back of the big house and knocked on the back door that led to the kitchen.

"Well come on in, this ain't no fancy 'stablishment,'" a woman with a deep voice yelled out. "It's a damn kitchen," she continued.

So, Samson, who had a bird in each hand, grabbed both by the neck with his right fist and pulled the door open with his left.

As he stepped inside, he saw three women in various forms of preparation hard at work. Ole Mae stood over a large bowl that sat on top of a high work table. She was mixing something up by hand with a large wooden spoon. Mae nodded to him but kept at her task.

Right next to her, the young woman named Bess with the smoothest almond skin Samson ever did see, kneaded dough on a breadboard. The girl put one hand up to her face to cover her smile and giggled at the sight of Samson. The flour from her hand left white dust all over her lips.

Bess had only recently moved to Lanark but all the slaves had known of Bess before she ever was brought here from a neighboring farm for her dimwits. She was said to be so dumb that she laid with any man that showed her his jingling Johnny. Samson felt kind of bad for Bess as he knew she was likely to have been bought on account of this fact and brought to the house for the Massa before he went and died, so he smiled back, though he personally had no intention of showing her his diddlestick.

Over the stove stood the third woman, her hips as wide as a hay wagon. She turned around and pulled a finger out of her mouth that she had just stuck into a pot on the stove and bellowed, "This here needs more salt, Mae!"

Mae just rolled her eyes at Samson.

Hattie had filled out in the years since she'd lost her baby. Her once narrow frame was gone and had been replaced by a thick one after years of tasting the fine foods of Lanark before they were laid out on the Buchanans' dinner table. But with her size, her presence also grew, so much so that she was now considered the head slave of the Lanark home. Everyone knew that Hattie never gave any more problems to Missus Anna once the whole affair over the baby and the platter were sorted out. Instead, she ran the other house slaves like she was Flicker inside these fine walls. She barked out orders from morning till night and poor Mae, who had worked in the kitchen for decades before Hattie ever spread her legs for the Massa, told

Samson she acted like she owned Mae and all the other house slaves more than Missus Anna herself.

Samson watched as Hattie walked over to inspect Bess' kneading. "I's don't need tell you that the Missus will 'pect this dinner to be near perfect with her only son comin' home to run this here land now that the Massa's passed on to glory."

Hattie moved toward the door and pulled both the chickens out of Samson's hands.

"Best skedaddle 'fore the Missus see you," Hattie said.

"Well, I's had to bring them here personally, as the chickens weren't gonna fly themselves into your oven," Samson answered.

"Youse save that sass for Minerva. Youse know Missus Anna don't like none but her house negroes round the home lest she accuse youse of stealin' something or another." Hattie flicked her head and neck at the door that she expected Samson to go out of and close behind him.

As she did so, her eyes looked past Samson and widened. Then she turned and threw the birds down on the table before she swung back and nearly knocked Samson out of the way.

Samson turned to see Hattie put a hand up over her eyes to shade them from the morning sun. Behind her, a plume of dust kicked up off in the distance. Samson backed up this time as Hattie turned back and rushed at the table.

"Bess, hurry up now and tell Missus Anna that the carriage is a' come," she commanded the young woman.

Bess giggled and kept on kneading till Hattie came around and slapped her.

"Stupid bitch. No wonder they sold you from the farm, cause youse dumber than a Holstein cow who just stands around shootin' milk out her teats all damn day."

Tears welled up in Bess' eyes. She dropped her dough onto the board and wiped her hands onto her apron.

"I's said go and tell the Missus!" Hattie said again loudly.

Mae looked at Samson and rolled her eyes at Hattie's attitude.

Just as she finished speaking, the kitchen door swung open and a woman in a pink dress walked in.

"Tell me what?" she asked.

Anna, as always, looked positively stately; her smooth face as pristine as her hair that was piled up on top of her head. Samson thought it odd that, with Massa Buchanan only dead but a few days, Missus Anna was dressed in such a bright color, but for fear of the woman's well-earned reputation as a hot-headed hornet, he just lowered his eyes rather than attract her interest.

"The coach be a comin', Missus Anna," Hattie informed her.

From the corner of his eyes, Samson saw that Anna's face hardly moved. Certainly not the joyous reaction one might expect when one's only child has returned, but then again, Anna generally had two expressions when it came to her negroes' entreaties—fury or a blank stare. The latter won out upon this news.

"What time will dinner be ready this evening?" was all she asked.

Hattie informed her that the plan was "half-five," if that was to the Missus' liking, and Anna nodded in approval.

Before she turned to depart though, she noticed Samson by the door.

"What is he doing in here?" she inquired through gritted teeth.

"He be leavin' just now on account he already done brought us the birds we asked foe," Hattie stated as she shooed Samson toward the door with one of her hands flapping at the wrist.

Missus Anna sighed, then looked around the kitchen at the others and hollered, "Well, don't just stand there you lazy asses, get cleaned up and come out on the porch to welcome your new master home!"

Her order caused a torrent of movement as each of the ladies stopped what they were doing, tore off their aprons, and prettied themselves up by tucking loose hairs into their scarves before they followed the Missus out of the kitchen door into the main house.

Samson seized the opportunity to turn tail. He planned to high step it right on back to the cabins before Arthur came home as he had no need of looking on the new Massa until he must.

While he used to love to run and play with Arthur as a boy, there was always a line of separation, and none could be clearer now than the fact that Arthur was returning to Lanark the owner of not just himself, but dozens of other slaves.

How did I eva think I was friends with one of them white devils? he thought to himself. *They do nothing but use us up and cause us harm.*

Sure, children are mostly blind to the limitations that control most grownups, but with age came wisdom and Samson knew his station was not equal and therefore wanted to avoid the humiliation he was oblivious to in his youth for as long as possible by avoiding Arthur until he must.

However, his brain said one thing but it could not overcome his eyes' curiosity, so as he rounded the house, he found himself creeping up alongside the porch, his head just under the footboards.

I remember that one time he did come home them years back and the way he just ignored me. Samson thought of the Caylee for Arthur's thirteenth birthday and his hands shook with anger at Arthur's rudeness toward him.

Afterall, he waited by the coop for his friend to come and at least say hello, but Arthur didn't so much as return Samson's hand wave.

These thoughts and others filled Samson's head, until at last the sounds of horse hooves clopped so loudly in his ears that he could hear his own notions no longer. He skulked down low and peered out along the ground as the wagon came to a full stop in front of the Lanark home.

The coach door opened and out stepped Arthur, who seemed to gleam in the sunlight. Samson gasped at the sight of his old friend. Somewhere in his belly he felt a strange stirring as if someone had stuck him with a pin. Arthur was nothing short of beautiful, like the picture of the angel that stood behind the baby Jesus that hung in the plantation's church. Arthur's blonde hair blew lightly in the breeze and his shirt seemed to cling to thick biceps that had grown wildly on Arthur's arms in the years he had been away. When Samson realized he had stopped breathing, he let out a long exhale then backed away from the porch.

That boy be white and your Massa, Samson thought angrily to himself. *Why the look of that boy cause me such excitement?* he yelled to himself inside, but no answer came except for the strangle tickle that would not go away. Once again, he crept back for another peek.

Missus Anna rushed forward and hugged her child shouting for all to hear, "Welcome home, Arthur." She had a smile as wide as a Sunday bonnet, but then she dropped it from her face and lowered her voice to continue. "Even if it is under such terrible circumstances."

Samson pondered her actions as nothing about Missus Anna seemed to display someone feeling a terrible loss, but most white folks were plum strange anyways.

Samson watched Arthur walk up the steps of the Lanark house.

"I would have waited until the end of the semester to call you home," he heard Missus Anna declare. "But your father left the entire estate in your name and well, there's just too much to learn and too quickly now that your daddy is gone."

"Father lived a good life and there's nothing for us to do now but look to the future," Arthur replied.

"Oh, and it is bright in you, my son," his mother responded, perhaps a little too happily in Samson's mind. She reached out and put her hand on Arthur's cheek then she turned around quickly and pointed at Nelson, Basil's replacement.

"Nelson, what in the hell is taking you so long to get Master Arthur's bags down off the wagon and into this house?" she demanded to know.

Nelson, who was not much younger than Basil had been, was brought over in the same exchange that brought Bess. He hurried at Missus Anna's command but that did not stop her from continuing to rail at him and the others.

"I swear to Jesus, nothing would get done around here if it weren't for me telling each and every one of you what to do minute by minute!" she exclaimed before she changed her scowl back into a smile and locked her arm into Arthur's.

"It's so good to have you home at last," she said.

It was a well-known fact that Anna never showed Arthur any kind of warmth when he was a boy, so why now? *Whatever does she have in mind?* Samson wondered to himself, but a look at Arthur's legs and backside distracted him from any further thoughts until mother and son shut the door to the home behind them.

Samson wanted to clear his mind and his body of the weird feeling that seeing Arthur again had produced, so he ran back to the cabins with all his might as if he fled the hounds for fear of death, until at last he was too tired for words when he reached his own cabin.

"Massa come?" Poppa Blue shouted out. "You seem awfully flushed." Though he could not see a thing, Poppa was more aware of what was happening around him than most.

"Yessuh," Samson replied in between huffed breaths.

"Hmmm," was all Poppa Blue murmured to himself before he went back to whittling on a stick.

Samson decided not to go inside and tell Minerva that Arthur had arrived, so instead he walked down to the pond where he planned to check his gill net for fish.

Samson was more of a jack of all trades than most of the other Lanark slaves. While everybody else was assigned to either the fields or the house, Samson had been fortunate enough to fill in day to day wherever he was needed. Therefore, he didn't have the same assignment each morning and instead found himself following the orders of Flicker, who followed the orders of the Massa that were ever changing.

For a week he might fill in for someone in the field, then the next he could be sawing and dragging trees out of the forest to be cut up for firewood for the big house and all the cabins. This meant that Samson knew how to do just about everything, but also that he knew just about everyone's business, as he worked from one end of the acreage to the other doing tasks both high and low till each and every slave on the plantation had done told him their secrets and whatnot over time.

But Samson had secrets, too. Only he never let them past his lips. No, not ever. Samson had that same feeling he had for Arthur just now as he did for one of the older slave men named Tobias. Samson just let the thought of Tobias' strong hands rest beneath the surface when he was alone at night where no one could see but himself. More than once, he swore Tobias caught him staring at those hands whenever he had fortune to work alongside him in the fields. Tobias had scars on his arms where thorns had eaten at his brown flesh. One time, Samson had passed the cabin where Tobias slept in and saw him naked as at birth while he sponged himself down with hot water from a large, heated pot. He stood there and stared until Tobias caught his eye and walked over dripping to the door and closed it.

He had heard about a slave man who was brought up from Jamaica that got caught with a batty boy sucking on his pole like it was buttered cob but they were both said to have been treated awful. The other slave men were said to have raped the one doing the sucking and the Jamaican was ridden so hard that he eventually tried to run but was brought back in bits by the owner's dogs.

"Stop it . . . no," Samson chastised himself aloud. "They be boys," he said as he approached the pond, but it didn't stop him from sitting his back against a tree in the long grass where he reached down into his pants to pull on himself. The more he thought about Arthur, the angrier he became. The angrier he became, the harder he tugged, until at last, when he was done, Samson stood up and vowed, "That's the last time I'm gonna think on that damn Artha' Buchana' like that again . . . forever." Samson meant what he said, but "forever" was a funny word, as it had a way of changing based on circumstance, and circumstance lay just around the bend.

To Market

Arthur came down for breakfast to find his mother was already enjoying her soft-boiled eggs. *The last time I sat in this chair*, he thought to himself, as Anna dipped a toast point into some yolk, *was when my parents had told me I was to leave for Virginia.*

Anna did not look up from her food but popped the wet morsel into her mouth and informed her son with lips full, "I figured you would want to inspect the land this morning." She followed her chewing up with a sip of tea from a dainty blue cup then put the cup back down onto the saucer and rang a little brass bell that sat next to her plate. "I've arranged for Flicker and Piglet to take you out early so best get your breakfast attended to quickly?"

Anna rang the bell again, only this time louder and with more rapidity.

"That would be fine," Arthur replied, though what he wanted to do was to shout for his mother to stop that damn racket, but Bess entered the room and Anna mercifully put the bell down.

"You are in charge now, Arthur," Anna continued. "It's not a small task to run a property as great as Lanark."

Bess grabbed Anna's empty plate and scurried off quickly through the door.

"You have Flicker and Piglet to direct. There's feeding of mouths, market price for cotton, upkeep of the house and the barn, and so on and so on." She picked up a paper fan from off the table and snapped it open so that it cracked like a whip. Then Anna fanned her face and her breast that heaved with the yellow washi paper. It had a white crane painted across its face so that the bird's wings spread out when the fan was fully opened.

"Just the thought of everything involved is enough to make one anxious," Anna panted.

"I am anxious but to learn about it, though," Arthur replied, which caused Anna to fold her fan back up and she placed it in her lap.

"Arthur," her voice softened. "All I mean to say is that if you decide it is too much, especially since you really have no working knowledge of this plantation, that I can help."

Anna leaned forward so that her breasts now touched the table and then she put an arm out and extended it across the surface toward her son. "I could even have the lawyers amend the documents so that I run Lanark for a few years."

Arthur looked down at his mother's outreached hand. He did not know whether to take it or run from it, as so rarely in his life had it been offered.

"That would give you time to settle in, see what it is all about, maybe explore other interests, such as finding a wife," she cooed.

There was awkward silence.

"Well, just think on it," Anna said, then she shrugged, pulled her arm back to her body, and sat up straight.

After a moment, she grabbed the bell and shook it even harder than before until at last, Bess reemerged; her eyes wide and full of wonder.

"Bess, Master Buchanan is ready for his food. Stop standing around gawking at him like he's a creature in a petting zoo and go fetch his plate!" Anna bellowed.

Bess nodded and quickly left the room.

"That girl is dumber than a sack of grain," Anna howled. "To think that some folk say those damn negroes are our equal." She chuckled as she picked up her empty tea cup. "We are no more alike to them than we are to this here porcelain," she continued laughing while she turned the empty cup upside down and plopped it down on top of the saucer.

Arthur shook his head. *She does not seem to have changed much,* he thought.

Bess returned with a plate of biscuits covered in a thick gravy with chunks of pork sausage that she placed in front of Arthur.

"Thank you," he said simply.

Anna, who had briefly leaned over to fix her shoe shot back up in the seat. She cleared her throat loudly. "That will be all, Bess."

Bess froze.

His mother picked her cloth napkin up from off of her lap and rolled it into a ball. "I said get out, you stupid cow!" she yelled as she threw the napkin across the table where it bounced off of Bess' face and landed onto the floor.

The slave gasped then bent down and swooped the napkin up from the ground before she ran out of the room in tears.

"What did you do that for?" Arthur asked in disbelief.

"You think you will be able to run this farm and turn a profit with thank yous and smiles?" his mother asked.

"Did I do something wrong?" Arthur was confused.

"One never thanks their slaves. It's their damn jobs, and they should be happy to do it," his mother continued, her voice rising.

"Nothing wrong with showing a little gratitude, I reckon."

"Gratitude gets you a heap of those Nat Turner negroes. Next your throat will be slit in your sleep," she spat.

"I hardly think a thank you is going to lead to my death," Arthur replied.

"This is exactly what I meant by your lack of knowledge, Arthur." She stood up and pushed her chair back from the table. "You haven't been here but for mere hours and yet, you have already proved your father was an idiot for naming you as heir when you are clearly not ready!"

His mother rushed for the door.

Before she exited, she stopped and turned around. "It was never supposed to be you," she whispered through gritted teeth.

"Never supposed to be me?" Arthur was confused by his mother's words.

"But your damn father insisted." She turned and stormed out.

Anna's strange departure took her son's appetite with her.

• • • • •

Anna sat on the rose-colored cushion in front of her large vanity mirror. The flesh from the top of her breasts that peeked out over her crimson dress heaved with anger. She had aged but a little since Arthur had been away. True, her hair had some light streaks of gray, but overall, the lotions and potions she bought at Hadler's store in town seemed to keep a lot of the wrinkles at bay. She brushed her long hair using the ivory hair set Buck had bought her one Christmas and stared at her reflection.

I should not have exploded like that, she thought to herself. She didn't have much of a frame of reference for who Arthur was, beyond when he was as a boy, and even then, she had pushed him out her lap and into the professors' at Rivington with a hope they could stamp out the weak, almost disgustingly kindhearted feelings he seemed to have toward her Lanark negroes. Though she had some measure of expectation, Arthur did not seem to resemble either his father, or frankly, Anna herself. But here he was nonetheless, and Anna needed to figure out how to deal with him, as she regretted turning from sickly sweet to bared fangs all too quickly this morning.

The only thing that breakfast this morning had taught her was that she would need to keep a close eye on both her son and her temper. She would need to be just firm enough to keep things running at Lanark until the time she could push him aside and do it her damn self like it should have been the case anyway.

As she continued brushing her hair, she felt a tinge of her anger now shifting toward Buck for leaving her a widow. "That sonabitch was hell as a husband," she whispered through gritted teeth.

Like how he brought all those Black bitches into her home to have relations. True, she had disappointed Buck once in their younger years when she was a new bride before she herself knew the ways of the world. But Buck did as all men wanted to do . . . whatever they wanted, and she had been forced to shut up and turn her head. After all, women from counties far and wide all would have gladly stepped in to become Mrs. Buchanan and all that came with both the name and prestige of the Lanark Plantation if she were to be somehow set aside. Equally true, Buck lifted the skirts of many of the negro bitches, but he left her to run the house as she saw fit. They had a loveless marriage and a lifetime of bitterness, but bitterness could be sweetened with jewelry and fine garments.

As much as Anna could not really stand her husband when he was alive, the thought of no longer being somewhat of an equal to the Mason County community, even if they didn't know it was only on paper, was just the kind of thing that damn man would do to her. She frankly didn't much care if the cancer had eaten him up alive slowly and over many more years so much as she cared that as long as he was alive, she was still the sole woman of the Lanark house and of all of its land. Now, she was forced to watch as everything she helped to build got handed off to her weakling of a son just because he had a damn willie between his legs

The door to the bedroom flew opened and Anna saw in the mirror that Bess had entered her room uninvited.

"I've come to . . ." Bess began.

Anna turned and leapt up at Bess in a flash then began to beat her legs and buttocks with the back of her brush.

"Don't you ever walk into my room without first knocking!" she screamed in between swats.

Bess cowered and cried out, but nothing would slow Anna's fury.

A blood curdling scream escaped Anna's lips when she noticed the handle to the ivory brush had broken with the force of the beating.

"You broke it!" she howled. "Now get out of here before I choke the life out of you from your throat, you noodle-brained, fusty lugg with your famously spread legs!"

Once Bess crawled out, Anna sat back down. She placed the pieces of the brush on the table then she looked up at her reflection in the mirror and smiled.

•••••

AFTER BREAKFAST, Arthur made his way to the stables.

Inside, Flicker sat atop a horse while Piglet had two more by the reins.

"The Belgian is for you," Flicker said, and he nodded at Piglet who handed the brown beast off to Arthur before he squirmed up onto his horse's back.

Arthur put his left foot in the stirrups then swung his right leg over the mare and off the three of them rode. They spent the morning inspecting the various fields, crops, and human chattel of the plantation.

The sun was high over the land when they passed dozens of slaves with burlap sacks across their shoulders, reaching out to pull the fuzz off the shrub. Every few minutes, the sound of the lash could be heard cutting the warm air, as a team of slave drivers that worked under Flicker trotted along the sides of the field, where they surveyed the work and administered whatever they deemed was the appropriate source of motivation for a good harvest. Flicker, Piglet, and Arthur rode on, but Arthur turned his head back to take in the scene as it had been a decade since he'd seen any of this firsthand.

When the three men reached the slaves' cabins on their way back in, they passed Poppa Blue who sat in front of his shack and whittled away at some wood.

"You remember Poppa Blue?" Flicker asked.

When Arthur nodded, Piglet grinned and explained, "He's still blind as a rock."

"I expect there's been lots of other changes in the years you have been gone," Flicker continued.

Arthur noticed that Poppa Blue's head tilted upward at the men as if he were able to surmise who they were, what they said, and even what they wore. They rode on past and rounded the woodshed where Samson stood shirtless with an axe held over his head; his broad shoulders covered in sweat.

"That'd be Samson," Flicker stated.

The chopper came down hard and split the wood in two, but Arthur only noticed that Samson's firm muscles hardly moved from the swing as his torso and arms were so tightly formed.

"That boy that used to chase you around the farm like a loyal bull dog but now he's grown into a fine bull of a man you can see," Flicker continued.

Piglet giggled. "Yeah, and time's come to breed him up and get a few more sows and cubs to market."

Arthur noticed Samson didn't even look up. *Guess he doesn't even remember me,* he thought to himself. *Probably for the best.* Arthur realized he was like to get caught staring at Samson's abdomen, where he noted the light line of fine dark hair that trailed from his firm belly until it disappeared beneath his trousers.

Flicker kicked his heels into his horse and it sped forward, which caused Piglet and Arthur's horses to follow suit.

As they trotted away, Arthur turned back to look one last time at Samson and as he did so, Samson's head lifted and the two locked eyes briefly. Samson threw the axe up over his head once more and forcefully brought it down on top of a new log while his eyes never moved from Arthur's.

Once away from the cabins, the group entered the barn, and Flicker told Arthur of the recent happenings from over at a neighboring farm.

"After that, them boys over at Clarkson's damn near came close to a full uprising . . . that is until Mr. Clarkson sent for your daddy—"

"And the dogs," Piglet interrupted with a guffaw.

"They caught that bastard not but three miles from the Ohio border. But good ole Buck made sure Clarkson drug his body right through our fields too so that every slave in Mason County would be afeared about what happens when you run."

"—Skin peeled right off his body like a boiled potato," Piglet cut in again with a snort this time.

"Clarkson insisted that me and the boys have a go at that boy's woman, too," Flicker finished.

Piglet pressed his fingers up to his lips and kissed them. "Hot damn if that peart gal wasn't sweet."

Arthur listened quietly; his face like stone.

They dismounted and the stable boy, Ellis, came over and took the reins from Flicker's hands.

"Wagon all set and ready, sir," Ellis addressed him while his eyes never left the ground.

Flicker pulled a long thin sheet of paper out of his shirt pocket. "You'll have to excuse me, young Mister Buchanan. I'm fixing to head into town and pick up some supplies we are in need of."

Arthur stepped toward Flicker and lifted the list out of his hands.

"Actually, if you don't mind, Flicker, I'll go in your stead. I've not been into town in an age and it will be good for me to practice riding the wagon," Arthur said.

Flicker put his hands up in the air and took a step back. "Suit yourself." He smiled. "But you will need some help," he said, pointing to Ellis. "He can go with you and then you'll need another."

"I'll take Samson with me," Arthur informed them to which Flicker nodded.

"Good choice. He can carry much and won't embarrass you none in town on account he's generally a good boy."

Ellis led Arthur to the wagon, where he climbed into the spring seat up front. Arthur then waited while Ellis piled into the open back and when he tapped one hand on the side of the wagon once he was safely situated, off they went.

• • • • •

SAMSON PICKED UP TWO PIECES of wood that he had just split and placed them neatly on top of a pile under the woodshed awning. There they would be safe from the elements and ready to use in a few months, once they got good and dry.

The wagon rolled into his view.

"I's can't escape that man today, can I?" Samson muttered to himself angrily.

"We going to town!" Ellis yelled out and waved his hand for Samson to join.

"Damn," he said under his breath, but Samson did what he always did. Obeyed.

After he climbed in next to Ellis, they rode along with nothing but the sounds of wagon wheels that rumbled over roughhewn roads. Samson's body jerked to and fro from the uneven patches and deep ruts that had become repeatedly soft with rain then re-baked in the Kentucky sun over generations, until at last Arthur heeled the horses and pulled the hand brake in front of Mr. Hadler's General Store.

Arthur went inside the building and returned a short time later followed closely by Mr. Hadler who waved his arm in the air to beckon Ellis and Samson to come collect Arthur's purchases.

Samson followed Ellis and Hadler into the store three times, each time coming out with a heavy wooden box and other items that he secured into the back of the wagon's body.

On his fourth trip, he noticed Arthur's eyes that stared across the road, so Samson put the crate down and followed Arthur's gaze with his own. His eyes settled upon the small wooden stage with some strange words painted in white on a sign that hung above. Though Samson like most slaves could not read nor write, one did not need to know their ABCs to figure out this was the slave auctioneer's block.

As if on cue, a Barker jumped up on the platform. He was dressed in dusty black boots, beige trousers, a white shirt, a red tailcoat with big golden buttons, and a tall black top hat. *One could almost think this was funny if he weren't fixin' to sell souls for cents,* Samson thought to himself.

"Up next we have this family of four just brought over from the darkest African continent," the Barker announced loudly so that his voice carried over hooves and wagon wheels.

Samson watched Arthur make his way across the street toward the stage, so he followed behind.

A boxy African woman in her twenties was prodded out onto the stage. She had a toddler boy on her hip and on either side of her stood two little girls, each of who attempted to hide up in their mama's skirt.

The mother's face was full of fear for the unknown. She did not appear to know where she was and what was about to happen. With unease, she shuffled her feet from side to side and bounced her fussing boy on her hip in order to soothe him, though it was her uncertainty that needed to be lulled.

"Let's start with the boy," the Auctioneer yelled out.

A white man hopped up onto the stage and pulled the boy from his nervous mother's arms. While she reached her arms out to retrieve her son back from the stranger, the man lifted the boy up high for all of the crowd to see.

"This here young'un male will make a nice field worker as he grows," the Barker enticed the crowd with his description.

The boy's mother became frantic once calls from the crowd were heard and hands were raised to claim him one by one, as the realization of what was happening crystalized across her pained face.

"I hear five hundred from the woman in yellow. Who will give me five twenty-five?" the Auctioneer beckoned.

"I will," came a voice from the crowd.

"Five twenty and five from the man in black," the seller declared. "Do I hear five fifty? Going once . . . going twice . . . sold to the man in black for five twenty-five."

The man in black came forward and the white man leaned down and handed the child straight into his buyer's arms. At this, the mother screamed and rushed forward for her child.

The Barker in turn rushed at her and he tried to grab the woman by the arms, but she flailed them in every direction. One of her hands smacked the white man in the lip who had just given her child away. As she lunged for the edge of the stage to reach her child, that white man recovered from the woman's strike and punched her square in the face.

The mother fell to the floor in a heap. Her two girls clung to each other and cried at the sight of their mother who was knocked out cold.

At that moment, Arthur moved toward the stage, but Samson stepped in front of him to block his path.

The two locked eyes.

Samson shook his head no at Arthur. He wanted to caution him against making any kind of foolish move that could jeopardize all of their safety. It was best for him to mind his business in these situations, but Arthur only glared at Samson with fury then stepped around him.

"Wait," Arthur called out to the Auctioneer as he approached the stage. "He offered you five twenty-five, I'll give you five fifty."

The man in black looked over at Arthur. "Piss off," he said.

"He's right," the Barker replied. "Once the sale is complete, I can't take no more offers."

Samson edged closer to Arthur. *What the hell is he doing?* he asked himself.

"I'll give you the five fifty yourself then," Arthur offered to the man in black.

"Forget it," the man replied. Then he turned and started to walk away with the boy who cried loudly for his mother.

"Come on." Arthur followed behind him. "That's a twenty-five dollar profit you will have made in mere seconds."

The man kept walking. Samson followed Arthur closely who was right behind the man in black until they reached the man's wagon, where he threw the toddler into the arms of a male slave that sat in the back.

"Six hundred," Arthur said.

The man turned back around and faced Arthur.

"Eight hundred," he said bluntly.

Surely this folly is over? Samson thought to himself.

Twenty minutes later, Samson rode in the back of the wagon over the same tracks that had led them into town. Only this time, he was crammed in not just with Ellis, but with only half of the other goods Arthur had been sent to town to purchase. Leaned up against Samson, a toddler boy slept in the arms of his African mother, who was nestled on her flanks by two girls that snuggled up against her legs.

•••••

As they pulled up to the stable, Flicker and Piglet came out.

"Young Mister Buchanan," Flicker said as he tipped his hat. "I expect you were able to pick everything up from the town with no problem?"

Piglet came around to the back of the wagon where Samson noted his normally beady eyes were now wide as two harvest moons.

"Get them boys, Piglet, and y'all start unloading," Flicker called from the front.

When Piglet didn't move, but stood there dumbfounded, Flicker came to the back of the wagon as well.

"Who are they, and where the hell are the rest of the supplies?" he asked in shock.

Arthur, who came down from the seat, joined them in the back. "Had to buy something else," he said, opening the back up so that all of the people could climb out.

"Looks like several somethings!" Flicker spat. "We needed those goods!"

"Mr. Hadler is holding it all for pick up tomorrow. You can go back in and get it then, but this was an immediate necessity," Arthur explained as he helped the little girls down.

"Necessity?" Flicker asked. "We didn't got no necessity for more slaves. We got immediate necessity for grain and bailing twine."

The woman passed her baby to Samson then got down carefully from the wagon. She smiled wide at Arthur then took her baby back.

"Samson, you show them to their quarters now, please," Arthur directed Samson. Arthur turned back to Flicker. "Besides, I got an excellent deal. Two and a half thousand for the four."

Flicker let out a loud curse that near to burst Samson's ear, as he was closest to him.

"We can't afford two and a half thousand, especially for a sow and three useless cubs!" he screamed.

"Nevertheless," Arthur replied coolly.

Samson did not stick around to hear the rest of the words exchanged as he thought it best to get himself and these new folks away from Flicker as fast as possible.

"This way," he whispered to the woman, who, while she spoke another language, was fluent in "move quickly," and they all did just that. An angry Flicker was something no person with any darkening of their skin wanted to be near at no cost, so Samson did his damnedest to usher them all to a safe distance as rapidly as possible.

Well, this been some strange day, he thought to himself as they passed under the yellow-poplar trees whose spring tulip buds had long since dried out and fallen to the ground.

The mammies who tended to the young'uns came out and helped the new woman and her children to get settled. Samson left them to be placed in an appropriate long house and went back to his own, his head aching from the long day.

When he explained all that had happened to Minerva as she served supper, she put her hands on her hips and said, "That new Massa Buchana' sound to be a curious creature."

Curiously foolish, Samson thought but did not say it aloud.

It was dark when they finished their food, so Samson laid down in his bed where he tried to close his eyes. However, he could not get the image of Arthur from his mind, so he opened them and sat up straight.

Why did that man go and buy those slaves? All he did was anger Flicka! he wondered moodily. "He be getting under my skin like someone done turned over a settled cart of pawpaw fruit!" he huffed then pulled a thin cover over his shoulders and slammed his body back onto the bed with a pout.

There, he thought on Arthur's eyes and the way those blue pools stared at him when he cut the wood earlier. "It's like them things could snatch your soul, they's so pretty," Samson mused, as his jaw unclenched.

"I's ought not to," Samson confessed to himself where no one else could hear him. "But I do wonder what that boy be doing now." And Samson watched Arthur over and over again in his mind before at last he fell into a deep slumber.

• • • • •

ARTHUR SAT IN HIS DRESSING gown at a small desk in front of his bedroom window. He was reading Walt Whitman's *Song of Myself* for what had to be the hundredth time. Deep into section ten, his mind scanned the pages while his mouth moved silently to the words. "*The runaway slave came to my house and stopt outside, I heard his motions crackling the twigs of the woodpile, Through the swung half-door of the kitchen I saw him limpsy and weak, And went where he sat on a log and led him in and assured him . . .*" He could not help but to think of Samson as he read these words, though Samson looked anything but limpsy and weak. He could feel his limpness hardening at the thought of Samson splitting wood earlier. It was the same reaction his body had to the first time one of the new players put their lips on his appendage as part of the hazing process. Each fall new recruits would be forced to pledge obedience to the senior players with a silly rite they called "kiss the tip," but unlike most of his other teammates, Arthur found the horseplay something he liked to experience year-round.

He sat back in his chair and let the image of Samson as a new recruit run through his mind. He pictured his full beautiful lips and imagined them as they bent forward for the initiation, but mid-thought, Nelson suddenly burst into the room.

"Fire, Massa Buchana'. Fire!" he screamed.

Arthur leapt from his desk and leaned over it to look out the window. To his left he saw flames shooting into the air, though he could not tell from what. He ran to a hook and pulled down a pair of pants that he hurriedly shoved each leg into. Arthur then tucked his nightshirt in at the waist and threw a robe across his body.

As he exited into the hall, Anna emerged from her room. "Oh Lord, let it not be the barn," she cried, as she tied her own robe close around her waist. "Your daddy just had it filled with hay for the winter before he passed."

Arthur ran past her and down the stairs.

Once outside of the house, he sprinted across the property for the barn where, through the smoke, he could make out a row of slaves who passed buckets of water to each other along a line.

"It's the chicken coop, Massa," an unfamiliar slave informed him.

Just then Samson and Ellis appeared and Arthur turned and commanded them. "You two come with me. We'll head it off before it gets to the barn then."

They ran off to a shed where they passed around shovels and a pitchfork. They then ran out and started to dig up the ground that ran in between the chicken coop and the barn, and in doing so they created a small firewall. They then tossed the gathered dirt onto the raging fire.

By now there were about a dozen people who doused the flames with buckets until at last, the blaze appeared to abate.

Arthur mopped the sweat from the heat and labor off of his head with the back of his sleeve. Flicker then appeared in the waning smoke. He dragged a young slave boy with him by the arm.

"It was a mistake," the boy cried out as he tried to dig his feet into the ground. "A mistake!"

The overseer tugged harder. "A mistake that could have cost this farm mighty, you Black plug-ugly!"

Piglet came along and shoved the boy until his feet were loosened. The two men together then delivered the child up to Arthur quickly.

"Here's the little shit," Flicker said through panted breaths.

Arthur leaned over until he could look the boy directly in his watery eyes.

"You know something of this here fire?" he asked not unkindly.

Frightened, the boy nodded. "Yes, Massa."

"Now go ahead and tell me what happened," Arthur pressed.

The child stood there silent, until Flicker whacked him across the back of his head with his open palm. "Speak!" he growled.

"Now, now," Arthur cautioned the overseer. "Go on, child," he coaxed.

"I's . . . I's was closin' up the coop fo' the night, that'd be all I's know, Massa," the boy shivered.

Piglet stepped to the boy to take his turn at striking him, but Arthur held up his hand to stop him.

"Go on," Arthur pushed the child again.

"I's put my lantern down to lock the cock into the coop when it tip right ova. That's when the coop catch fire, but it was an accident, Massa Buchana'. I's didn't mean to . . ." The boy broke down again. His body shook with sobs and his head practically touched the ground, it was bent so low with grief and fear.

Arthur raised his hand and everyone around stopped to watch. Arthur knew that they all expected him to reach out and strike this boy here and now, so he was not surprised when gasps were heard when instead he used his hand to lift the boy's head up rather than to beat him. As he held the young slave's chin steady, he looked the child in his eyes and said softly, "That sounds like an honest enough mistake to me."

Then Arthur stood up and glared at Flicker and Piglet. "Now doesn't it sound just so to you two as well?" he asked.

The boy stopped crying and looked over at Flicker's face.

Flicker looked back and forth between the boy and Lanark's new master. "I reckon so," he said apprehensively then he spit on the ground near the boy's feet before he turned and walked away.

Piglet, who had been standing behind the boy ready to drag him away to any decided punishment, followed after the bear of a man in a huff.

"Go on and head to bed, young man," Arthur looked back down and said kindly. "There will be plenty of work to do in the morning to build a new coop for the chickens. I expect you will be more careful in the future with your lantern."

"Oh yessuh," the boy said through a smile. "Yessuh!" He ran off in the direction of the slaves' cabins.

The men returned to the shed and stowed away their shovels and pitchfork. Ellis said his goodbyes then left Arthur and Samson unattended.

Alone for the first time, an awkward silence hung in the air

Nervously, Arthur twitched his feet until at last Samson said to him, "That was a mighty nice thing you did back in town and here with this young'un."

"You think?" Arthur responded with a smile.

"I . . ." Samson began to say something but then clearly thought the better and just lowered his head instead.

"Go on," Arthur pressed him. "No point thinking something if you don't say what you mean."

Samson looked up at Arthur.

"If you really mean it, then I's think it be nice, but only, now Flicka'll be mad as a March hare since youse done made him look seven by nine in front of a heap of negroes not once but twice. I's reckon tomorrow they gonna whip more hides in the fields than if you'd just let 'em beat that boy."

Arthur's face scrunched. "Oh," his voiced softened. "Guess I didn't think none too hard about that." He considered what Samson meant for a moment then he shrugged. "Anyways, what's the point of being the man of the house if you can't make decisions to do right by some people?"

Worry spread across Samson's face. "Careful now, that's mighty dangerous talk around here," he whispered.

"Dangerous talk?" Arthur was confused by Samson's response.

Samson rushed over and stuck his head out of the shed. He looked both ways then he brought it back inside. "Calling that boy "people" might get you in a lot more trouble than stopping the beatin' of one po' slave, or even buyin' a family of four of 'em"

"What kind of trouble?" Arthur said angrily. "You act like I done something wrong by being kind."

"I's best say naught else," Samson sighed. "I's already spoke my mind too much and I's sorry, Massa."

"Oh, shaw pshaw!" Arthur responded. "Just because my daddy's dead doesn't mean you have to call me Massa, Samson. We been friends from birth."

Samson snorted unexpectedly. "Is something wrong with youse? Youse be some kind of daft fool or something? Fall on youse head in 'Ginny?"

Samson's eyes widened at his over familiarity.

Most slaves would be wiser than to call any white man foolish, nevertheless their master, at least to their face, so the words hung in the air.

"I's sorry," Samson said meekly. "I's overstepped. It won't happen again, none, please believe me."

Arthur studied Samson for a minute then smiled.

"It really is so good to see you, Samson. It's been far too many years," he chuckled. "I think we can be good friends once more."

Samson's face turned to stone.

"We be grown men now and though we mighta been carefree youth once, I's know my place. I'll do better to hold my tongue, sir." He then turned to leave.

As he started walking away, Arthur reached out and touched Samson on his arm.

"Wait," Arthur begged.

Samson stopped abruptly.

He then turned his head to look down at where Arthur's flesh touched his.

Slowly, Arthur watched Samson's eyes as they moved back up and into his own. There they stood for a few seconds. Arthur could have sworn he saw terror and excitement in Samson's eyes.

"I have something to show you," Arthur said softly at last to break the silence.

"Show me?" Samson asked with confusion in his voice.

"Yes!" Arthur smiled widely. "It's up at the house."

Invigorated by the exchange, Arthur ran out of the shed quickly.

Samson slowly followed him out the door.

"Come on!" Arthur commanded through a wide grin as he waved his arm in welcome.

"Missus Anna don't like none of us up at the home . . . none save the house slaves," he responded with trepidation. "Especially at night."

Arthur noticed the quiver in Samson's voice, but he insisted. "Oh, come on," he pressed and he rushed forward with excited steps.

After he plodded up the steps and across the porch, he realized Samson followed too slowly, so he sought to assuage his fears. "I'll make sure everyone is settled for the night first, then I'll bring you inside if you're so afeared of my mother," he teased his childhood friend.

Samson's shoulders relaxed some, so Arthur felt it must be fine to continue. "Just wait on the porch here for a couple of quick minutes and I'll be back for you."

"Yessuh," Samson replied.

"Oh, for goodness sakes, don't call me sir," Arthur insisted. "Call me Arthur!" He reached for the door and threw it open.

Inside, Anna stood in her robe. Behind her was Nelson, Hattie, Bess, and Mae each with a lighted candlestick in their hands.

The door shut and Anna begged for information. "Well? Was it the barn?"

"It's okay, mother, it was just the coop. Go on back to bed as all is fine now."

There were sighs of relief from all.

"Thank the lawd," Hattie yelled out, as she slapped ole Mae on the back, causing her to stumble slightly forward.

Arthur continued. "In fact, y'all go rest now. No need for anyone to lose another minute of slumber or to be agitated over this any longer."

"Well, youse heard the Massa," Hattie snapped at Mae and Bess.

The slaves turned and departed in various directions, while Mrs. Buchanan made her way up the stairs to her room. Once her bedroom door closed, Arthur turned and opened the front door of the house quietly.

"Come on in," he whispered.

Samson cautiously stepped inside; his head moving to and fro as if to ensure they were truly alone.

"It's fine, Samson. Everybody's gone back to bed," Arthur assured him before he closed the door gently.

As Arthur led Samson across the vestibule and toward the stairs, Bess crept out from under the steps, where her small room was located.

She had her candle in one hand and she shielded the flame with the other that she pointed out in the direction of the two men.

"Go on to bed now, Bess," Arthur said when he saw her standing there with blank eyes.

He watched as she slowly slid like a ghost back under the stairs until he heard her door click shut.

Confident that she was finally gone, Arthur approached the stairs. He turned only to wave his hand for Samson to follow until at last, they were up the steps and at his bedroom door.

He turned the knob and gestured for Samson to go in first.

Just as he was about to follow behind himself, he heard a small scraping noise and turned his head to see one of Bess' eyes that peeked out from the stairwell.

She must have crawled up the steps silently to figure out what was going on with me and Samson, Arthur laughed to himself.

She gasped at Arthur's gaze. Now caught, her head disappeared once more, this time for good. Arthur waited one more second to be sure then he followed Samson at last and closed the bedroom door.

Once inside, Arthur noticed that the candle on his desk he had used to read by earlier was almost burned down to the base, so he went to a drawer and fetched another made of the paraffin wax that Anna imported from Derbyshire. He pushed it down into a silver holder, then leaned it over so that its wick caught flame from the dying candle.

The shadows of the room retreated and Arthur noticed Samson's eyes, which darted around in every direction, as if to take in the full details of Arthur's bedroom.

"Wow," Samson exclaimed in a whisper of wonder.

"I forget you have never been up here before," Arthur said, as he walked over to a tall bureau and opened its top drawer.

"No, but I's imagined it plenty. Especially all them times that I's called up to you from the outside," Samson responded to him. "Waitin' on youse to come outside and catch fireflies at dusk."

Arthur smiled at the memory then he reached into the bureau and pulled out a long rolled up piece of cloth that he passed to Samson.

"What is this?" Samson asked him.

He hesitated to take hold of it, so Arthur stuck his hand out with more urgency. "Open it, silly-billy, or you will never know," he insisted.

The slave man followed orders and took it from Arthur's hands then unwrapped it gently until he held up the very snake stick that Samson had thrown into Arthur's departing wagon many years ago.

"Well, I's be . . ." Samson said with wonder in his voice.

"I've kept it with me all these years, never once forgetting the friend who gave it to me," Arthur said softly. Then he reached his hand out toward Samson and waited for a response. His hand stood there alone in the naked air until at last, Samson reached out with his own empty palm and took a hold of Arthur's.

Arthur squeezed with all his might.

They stood there, hand in hand, for a moment, until the awkwardness swallowed them whole. Samson at last coughed as a means of escape and retreated.

"Um, 'scuse me," Samson stuttered. "But I's best get to sleep fore the morn' creep up on me."

Arthur replied, "Of course." He led Samson out the bedroom door and down the steps.

"Oh, uh, here's the stick," Samson said quietly. When he handed it back to Arthur, their fingers briefly brushed each other's.

"It was nice just for us to finally be alone again after all this time, Samson." Arthur smiled then slowly closed the door in Samson's somewhat unsteady face.

He closed his eyes and listened to Samson's soft footsteps retreat from the porch then Arthur turned back around just in time to see the hem of Bess' nightgown disappear behind the stairs yet again.

Perhaps she is a tad daft after all, Arthur thought to himself before he once again ascended the stairs silently.

Once alone, Arthur laid there.

He could still feel the place where their fingers touched moments ago. He then took those fingers and pressed them against his nose to smell.

There was a slight scent of sweat and woodchips.

Arthur inhaled deeply then he plunged his fingers into his mouth and sucked on them slowly as if they were a mother's teat.

• • • • •

TOO MUCH UNCERTAINTY MEANT ANNA could not sleep. *Arthur has managed to handle the fire, but what if things had gone worse?* Anna fretted in her mind, gazing out her window onto the smoldering ash heap that was the chicken coop hours ago.

"Not much I can do about it tonight," she sighed. Then as she was about to turn around and head back to her bed, she saw movement down below.

"What in holy hell?" she inhaled her words while she moved her body just to the side of the curtains so that she was able to see outside but if the skulker turned back, it was doubtful they would be able to see her own face.

And they did turn around.

In the moonlight, Anna recognized Samson clear as day. He stopped briefly to face the Lanark home and smiled before he turned and snuck away in the direction of the slaves' cabins.

"I suppose Arthur wasted no time in getting reacquainted," she hissed bitterly. "Next thing he'll have them all sleeping up at the house!"

Anna knew that something odd must be afoot or why else would that boy creep away in darkness. "He knows better than to come near this house and if he did so, especially at night, it was by invitation."

Anna sat down on the bed and put her legs under the light cotton covers.

She had to find a way to get Arthur to step aside. She would just double down on his lack of experience. What else did she have? Double down and bide her time if that didn't work. Something was bound to present itself if she was patient enough.

• • • • •

IT FELT LIKE MERE MINUTES had passed before Arthur was sat at the breakfast table, his meal already finished. He tossed his napkin onto his plate and his mother looked up from her tea.

"Going somewhere so early?" she inquired.

"I have some things to attend to," he said as he got up from the table.

"What kind of things does one who knows practically nothing at all have to attend to?" she mused.

"Our conversation yesterday had this same tone and that one didn't seem to end too well."

"Arthur," she insisted. "I'm only trying to point out what is obvious. You are not tough enough yet to handle this plantation! Leave it to me. I can have the lawyer here this afternoon and sort it all out easily."

"Let's just leave it all be for now," Arthur reprimanded her. He felt suffocated between the paisley walls and his mother's nags that he made a break for the door.

"I've got to get out of this house. Perhaps you sending me off to Rivington as a child was a bigger blessing than I realized."

He felt Anna's eyes as they bored a hole through the back of his head on his way out the room.

I expect I'll be having a lot of these sentimental one on one's today, he laughed to himself once he was outside of the house and felt the fresh air hit his lungs.

Arthur knew who he must talk to next, so he made his way over to the stables, where he found Flicker inside feeding a lone horse from a bag of oats.

"Young Mister Buchanan," Flicker said in acknowledgment, though he hardly looked up.

"Well go ahead, Flicker." Arthur approached the overseer. "I know you have some things to say that you are holding back on, so let's just get them out right now."

"Planned to hold my tongue, truth be told." Flicker shrugged.

"Why does everyone but my momma feel the need to choke on their words," he said in frustration. Then Arthur sighed. "Sorry, go head, Flicker. Share with me your thoughts."

Flicker pulled the sack from the horse's mouth. "Since you asked, I feel obliged, especially on account of your father, Buck."

Arthur stood there and waited.

"Well, I'm not the owner of this here plantation, but your daddy did hire me for a purpose, and that purpose is to keep order."

Arthur nodded. "Continue."

"I know you've been away at some fancy school for a few years now, but letting that boy go last night without so much as a thrashing? Well, that's just plain shortsighted."

"How is there weakness in the choice not beat a child?"

"One thing your daddy asked me 'fore he died was to remind you of your place in this world. That you were put here by God. Now, I don't know much about no Bible ways myself, but I know your daddy was right. He knew just as he did with yourself that the key to keeping on the right path was a firm hand. It's the same with the rest around here. They're all children. Stupid, selfish, unruly children who need the whip to keep them on the path of righteousness like your daddy Buck would say."

Arthur chewed on Flicker's words for a few seconds.

"I thank you, Flicker, for your honesty, and for all your years of service to my father," Arthur responded. "But, as you said first, you are not the owner here at Lanark and as is obvious already, I am not my daddy."

"Burning down the coop be the least of your worries if you let these pickaninnies get a taste of anything but your whip, son," Flicker cautioned strongly.

"I'll consider your advice," Arthur responded, though he neither intended to consider one word shared nor did he believe what Flicker said to be true.

His assurance though seemed to calm Flicker's waters enough for now, as he nodded and said, "That's fair and to be frank more than I expected."

Satisfied that Arthur had provided Flicker with the space to share, he took two saddles down off of hooks on the stable wall and then summoned Ellis to help him gear up a pair of horses.

Once they were ready, Arthur hopped up on one and led the other by the reins out of the stable door. Over to the slaves' cabins he trotted, where he found Samson once again by the woodshed. There the strong slave had already stacked a large mountain of wood into a neat pile even though the day had barely begun for Arthur.

I wonder what he thinks about last night? Arthur thought to himself as he approached Samson on horseback. The perplexed look on Samson's face when Arthur slowly shut the door on him a few hours back stayed imprinted on Arthur's mind. He imagined if he could have seen his own face from Samson's eyes, he might have found he had a similar look of confusion and excitement. Though his stomach was full of nerves he called out, "What do you say we call it quits on chopping and stacking wood and go for a ride this morning like old times?"

An icy frost had settled into Samson's tone in the hours they were apart. "This ain't old times, and I's ain't rode no horse in years," he responded, though he did not look up at Arthur and kept stacking the logs.

Arthur's heart fell into his stomach. He slowed to a stop then got down from his horse.

"No, I suppose they are not. But, there's good cause to make the new ones better," he said through a smile, approaching Samson and reaching out to hand him the set of reins from the second horse.

Samson put his palms in the air to deny the handover. "I's gotta get this wood stacked then head over to the shed up by the big house or Flicker will whip my hide from haunch to cleft."

A sly grin moved across Arthur's face. "Why don't you let me worry about both Flicker and your hide," he said.

Samson stopped working and looked at Arthur with uncertainty.

"Not sure that's a good idea," he whispered.

"Well don't look so Catawamptiously chewed up," Arthur joked. "It's not like I asked you to kill someone? It's just a ride around the farm. What's the harm in that?"

"I's suppose you are the Massa," Samson replied with a shrug, and grabbed the reins to climb up on the horse.

Arthur returned to his and the two men rode off between the slaves' cabins, where the few slaves who were present looked up at their passing. Even Poppa Blue raised his head and waved his hand to the sound of the hooves.

Once they cleared the cabins, they trotted along the fields where men and women bent over as they plucked their way through rows of fibrous white.

"*I want to be ready*," a caller sang out.

"*To walk in Jerusalem*," harmonious voices replied throughout the field.

"*John said the city was just four-square*," he led alone again.

"*Walk in Jerusalem just like John*," came their response.

"*And he declared he'd meet me there*."

"*Walk in Jerusalem just like John*."

"*I want to be ready*," he called again.

"*To walk in Jerusalem*," they concluded with glorious sounds through labored breaths that, though filled with exhaustion and pain, brought the hairs up on Arthur's arms.

He let it seep through his skin and wondered at what cost all of this hardship came? All the suffering endured so that he, and those like him, could live like lords over others. Arthur didn't know how to change things, or make them better for anyone really, but he knew that the way things were did not feel right.

I don't want to be the reason someone loses family members, limbs, or lives, he thought to himself as their horses trotted away. *But what good can I do when that's just the way it all is set up to be?*

They rode on and the slaves lifted their heads to stare. Arthur knew it was not every day that a negro slave rode with his master on his own horse, but Samson was never just a negro to Arthur. For as far back as he could remember, Samson was someone who mattered to him, even if they hadn't exchanged more than a few words in the past decade.

"It's an amazing thing how some time alone in the sun can take a simple seed and turn it into bur, ripe for picking," he said at last to Samson as they edged the cotton field.

"I reckon it's one of the Lawd's wonders," Samson replied.

"True, but from sprout to stand and from bud to bracht, a man's got to be the one to know when the time is right for the harvest, doesn't he?" Arthur asked.

"The Lawd put many a stumblin' block in a man's way though. Drought. Blazin' sun on his back," Samson thought aloud. "No, a man's at the mercy of his maker," he concluded with certainty.

They rode on in silence again for a minute.

"You know . . ." Arthur began. "It would be much cooler up at the house instead of toiling in those hot fields."

Arthur slowed his horse to a stop, and Samson followed suit.

"Would you like to move up to the house then, Samson?" Arthur asked.

Icy coolness returned to Samson's tone. "I's don't think so."

"What if I insisted?" Arthur teased.

"You the Massa."

"No," Arthur insisted solemnly. "I want you to decide."

"I's know nothing of no choices," Samson replied through gritted teeth. "I's wouldn't even know how to start with one."

"Do you like to labor in the sun, or do you prefer to take some shade and work in the house instead?" Arthur asked again.

"It ain't that easy," Samson answered.

"It is now. Think on it and let me know what you decide," Arthur told him, then he dug his heels into his horse's flanks and it cantered forward.

Sweet Tea

T he sun was about to set when Samson told Minerva he was moving up to the house.

"What for?" Minerva asked with deep suspicion.

"Massa Artha asked me," was all that Samson could reply.

"I rememba youse was friends as boys but didn't think none about him asking you to the house when he moved back home," she pondered. "But, I 'pect it's all the same as work be work, and youse still come get your Sunday suppa down here with your old Auntie Minerva, or I'll come getcha behind from out that house, Missus Anna or no!"

Samson laughed and felt relief at Minerva's support. He'd lived too long by now not to know that the rest of the slaves didn't always take kindly to the house slaves. They were seen as uppity though he couldn't remember ole Mae ever looking down her nose at one of them. But that was the way it was on a plantation, one pitted against another, so Samson wasn't going into this blindly. He expected pushback. Hell, he was giving himself plenty of it on the inside.

Me choosing to work in the house? he asked himself. "If this don't beat the devil," he responded aloud in disbelief at his own decision.

After he hugged Minerva goodbye, he stepped outside to find Poppa Blue in the fading twilight. He sat on his log as per usual and whittled away at a small block of wood.

"Is that Samson's feet I hears scurryin' by?" he called out.

"How do, Poppa Blue?" Samson replied. "What youse whittling today?"

Poppa Blue held up the piece of wood and Samson could see the faint outline of a wing.

"'Tis a jay?" Samson inquired.

"No, a robin," Poppa Blue explained. "I remember 'em clearly as a boy near the farm I grown up at, 'fore I's sold to the Buchanas."

"Really?" Samson leaned down toward Poppa as he rarely said much about anything from before his blindness.

"E'ry autumn, right after the corn stalks been harvested, it'd be a sea of red come from the heavens and descend 'pon the ground, pluckin' kernels straight from the dead ears that fell from the wagons," his voice was filled with the wonder of yesteryears.

"Mind if I take a closer look," Samson asked. Poppa Blue held up the carving and passed it off to Samson who explored it curiously.

"I hear tale young Massa Buchana' seems to rememba a soft spot from when youse was chil'en."

"Ah, we was close when we was kids. Tis true, but . . ." Samson began but Poppa Blue cut him off.

"But nothing, boy." Samson looked up from the carving. "Don't you be snared by the devil, chile. Lawd knows I learned the hard way, the white man's a cruel breed."

Samson had never heard such passionate words from Poppa Blue, so he inquired more and asked, "what do you mean?"

"Best be you rememba your place no matter the sweetly kind words they shower you with one minute cause like to be the back of their hand or the barn rafter the next . . . or even worse," he said as he pointed to his eyes.

No one ever talked about how Poppa Blue went blind, so Samson had always assumed it was from a sickness or due to his age. He was confused by what Poppa was trying to say to him.

"But Artha's asked me to move up to the house," he tried to explain.

"No good can come outta that," Poppa replied. "No good."

"Something be different about Artha though, Poppa Blue. It's as curious to me as anybody, but like I's said, he different," Samson insisted. "You know how he buyed those slaves in town, then what he did with the young'un with the coop—"

"It's the bee that make the honey who sting you the mightiest, boy," Poppa Blue cut him off again, then he reached up and snatched the jay back out of Samson's hands.

As he walked away Samson thought to himself, *Maybe Poppa Blue be right? I'll go see what it's like and if something feels funny, I'll just turn tail.* He put one foot in front of the other till he found himself on the front porch. "After all, Artha did say that I could decide myself."

He stood on the porch for what seemed like eternity, and repeatedly rapped his fingers on his thigh until at last Samson gathered up the courage to ring the bell. His head throbbed when the door opened and Nelson stood there wide-eyed at the unexpected guest.

"Boy, you lost your mind?" Nelson asked.

"I's here to see Artha . . ." Samson began.

"Whatever you here for, get your Black ass to the back door in the kitchen, 'fore the Missus have it whooped right here on the porch," Nelson whispered strongly at him then mumbled to himself. "Negro must have lost his mind ringing the front door like he's the damn county commissioner!"

"What's happening, Nelson?" a woman's voice called from inside. Missus Anna approached the door. "Who is it?"

Nelson rolled his eyes at Samson then opened the door fully to reveal him to Mrs. Buchanan.

"I's sorry, Missus Anna, but this here boy musta done lost his mind. He's asking for the Massa," Nelson informed her.

"And you rang the bell?" Missus Anna asked, her voice began rising. "On the front porch?"

Samson nodded sheepishly. "Yes ma'am. Massa Artha told me to come . . ."

At once, Hattie, Mae, and Bess all appeared behind Anna. Ole Mae's eyes looked as if they were about to water; Bess' eyes looked as if they'd seen a butterfly for the first time; but Hattie's eyes looked like she'd have beaten the devil outta Samson herself if she could have, as she stood there hands on hips and her head shaking back and forth.

Samson wondered at his foolishness in coming up here to the house. This decision looked like it was going to come at the end of a whip if Missus Anna's face was true to tell. He was about to apologize for the mistake, turn tail, and run after all when Arthur's head appeared from the parlor.

"What is all the fuss out there?" he asked. Samons's eyes locked with Arthur's.

"Ah, yes," Arthur called then he came to the door.

The young Master Buchanan raised his brow to Samson slowly. "It's a yes then?"

Samson nodded.

"In that case." He turned to Nelson. "Take Samson inside, Nelson. He will need some proper clothing."

"What's that, Massa Buchana'?" Nelson appeared bewildered by the directive.

"Samson's going to be helping up at the house going forward," Arthur announced to everyone.

"Yessuh," Nelson answered though his tone suggested anything but quiet obedience.

"This way," he growled at Samson as he pointed at the kitchen and started to walk away.

"Hold it right there, Nelson," Missus Anna barked. "We don't have need for another boy in this house!"

"Yes. I say we do, mother," Arthur replied coolly and he nodded at Nelson, who after a brief hesitation, resumed his journey and led Samson out of the vestibule.

As they crossed the threshold to the next room, Samson heard Missus Anna yell at the women. "I'm still the mistress of this house! Leave me and my son alone and mind to your tasks at once!"

Off from the side of the kitchen was a small room with two beds. Nelson opened a closet and pulled out a stack of clothing.

"These will have to fit," he said coldly, handing them to Samson. "Well go ahead and put the damn things on 'fore Christ comes back." Then he mumbled under his breath. "I don't know why Massa Arthur need anotha but I reckon he must have some use."

Samson quickly changed out of his torn course clothes into a clean white shirt and pants.

Nelson took out a pair of shoes and handed them to Samson.

"I don't reckon I even know how to put these on." Samson stared at them in wonder.

Nelson sucked his teeth in loudly. "Oh hell with it," he growled. Then he bent over and pulled Samson's feet off the floor one at a time, and forced each shoe over his toes and heels.

"Don't get too comft'ble, mind youse. Youse may be a house slave today, but I's been working in the white man's homes since 'fore you sucklin' your momma's teat. One thing I knows is not many a boy from the field can come from outside and last more than a hot minute. I 'pect you be back pickin' cotton 'fore Mae set the first Sunday suppa on the table. But it won't be on accounta me. Now 'hep to and I's show you 'round the place."

The older man led Samson back out into the kitchen where the women waited.

"Why'd he ask youse to the house?" Hattie asked with suspicion. "He have youse spyin' for Missus Anna to catch us outta turn?"

"Course not." Samson clicked his tongue on the roof of his mouth.

"Tis not ever' day, or fo' no reason a field slave a'come to the home." Mae looked at him with great concern. "So, he's gots to have a reason."

Bess giggled at Samson as if she'd found a pet mouse.

"Oh damn this girl." Hattie rolled her eyes. "Neva'mind her. She's simple as a cornhusk doll." She turned to Bess. "This boy ain't got eyes or time for youse." She swatted her out of the kitchen. "Youse gots cleaning to do and no time to be making sweet faces to Samson or youse both be on the rafter 'fore mornin'."

Once Bess left, Mae continued as before. "Always be a reason."

"Yeah?" Hattie asked. "What was yours?"

"Ole Daddy Buchana' had a thing for my sweet tea," Mae said innocently.

"Is that what they called it back then?" Hattie raised her eyebrows. Mae glared at her for a second, and then suddenly the two ladies laughed heartily. This was the first time Samson had ever seen them so much as smile at each other.

"Well in this case, I do rememba how young Massa and this boy used to run 'round this place like wild goats 'fore he went away."

Bess stuck her head back in the door and bleated like a goat, and this time, even Nelson and Samson laughed.

"Come on then," Nelson ordered Samson with more kindness. "Since you are here, may as well show youse how to get to work."

Samson learned lots in the short time before supper. Nelson quickly showed him how to open the door for the Missus, set out clothes for Arthur for the different meals, and how to keep account of each day's plan. He explained that in the morning, he would teach Samson how to drive the carriage to and from town whenever one of the white folks wanted to go off the plantation.

The time moved quickly in the minutes Samson joined the house, and it was supper before long. Nelson showed Samson how to assist the women waiting on the Buchanans at the table while he took the privileged spot at the fan.

It seemed all was smooth until Samson clumsily knocked a bowl of fruit onto the floor. Arthur got up to help him collect the items.

"What in the world are you doing, Arthur?" Missus Anna asked with incredulity in her voice. "You let the slaves pick things up. That's what we buy them for." She pointed to Nelson and commanded him, "And you, Nelson . . ."

"Yes ma'am?" Nelson said with a question.

"No food for him tonight." She shifted her pointed finger at Samson on the ground.

"Drop food once, you don't eat. Drop food again, and it is Flicker and the whip, boy," she threatened.

Samson's hands shook as he put a cluster of grapes into the bowl.

"Moth—" Arthur started to protest.

"Mother nothing," she cut him off. "I've trained enough of my negroes in my own damn house to know you have got to be stern, and right from the start." Missus Anna turned back to Nelson. "Just take this boy out of here. I think he's shown us enough of what he is capable of for today."

Samson felt heat and redness coming to his cheeks as he got up off the floor. But he quietly followed Nelson out of the dining room.

Hold your tongue, Samson said to himself through gritted teeth.

"I'm surprised she waited this long to find something to chastise you about," Nelson confessed as he led Samson into the kitchen. "Just be sure not to drop anything further." He opened the back door and reached outside. When his arms returned, they each held the edges of two large empty pots. "Meantime, start to fillin' each of these up and set 'em on the stove to boil." He handed the pots to Samson. "Massa Buchana' say he want a bath after suppa, and bath means lot of time heatin' water." He pointed toward the door again. "They be six more where these others come from. I'll be back to check in a bit."

Alone, Samson spent what felt like hours going back and forth to and from the water pump and the stove. Once the water was heated, he and Nelson would carry the full pots up the stairs and pour the steaming liquid into a copper bathtub that was lined on the outside with hardwood that had been painted a pretty shade of moss green. The tub sat in the middle of Arthur's bedroom on top of a heap of towels to catch any water that might splash out.

After the tub was filled, Arthur entered the room and disrobed. Samson couldn't help but to catch a glimpse of Arthur's bare buttocks that were curiously whiter than the rest of his pale skin before he put both legs into the tub and sat down. Nelson got down on his knees alongside the tub and showed Samson how to scrub Arthur's back with a bar of olive soap Missus Anna had imported from Spain. He foamed the skin back and forth with a soft wash cloth.

Once Arthur was good and soapy, he turned his head around to Nelson. "I need another pot or two of hot water," Arthur said to him.

The senior slave turned to Samson and shot the direction over to him. "Youse heard the Massa. Two more pots worth." But Arthur put his hand up to stop Nelson from continuing.

"I'd like for you to get them, Nelson," he directed. Samson looked at Nelson's face, which twisted up with questions. But he was given a directive and had no choice but to relent. He stammered and stumbled to get up and he did as told. Nelson exited the room with a "yessuh" and some kind of a bow.

"You can continue where Nelson left off," Arthur said to Samson, who then picked up the soap and cloth. His hands shook as he rubbed the bar into the soft fabric and then pressed it against Arthur's bare skin on his back.

"Why'd youse bring me up here?" Samson whispered with a hiss of discomfort.

"Cause I need a bath," Arthur replied coolly.

"Not here," Samson said as he hit the water with his hand. "Here," he continued, lifting it up toward the room. "Here to the house?"

"I gave you the choice if you remember."

"But why? I's just don't understand."

"Gives us reason to be closer without raising suspicions," Arthur explained. "I saw the way they looked at you out in the fields earlier when we were riding."

Samson looked down at Arthur's bare shoulders that broke through the steaming water. That feeling he had before was back again and he couldn't tell if he wanted to lean over and press his lips against Arthur's neck or wrap his hands around it for him ever suggesting he come tend to him in the Lanark house.

"Up here in the room alone with a naked Massa might raise more 'spicions than naught!" Samson cut in with quiet fury that won out the debate that raged in his head.

Arthur laughed. "It's perfectly natural for a master to have a slave that cares for him in the home. Nobody's gonna think a thing." He paused then gently cocked his head. "Unless, my nakedness makes you nervous," he teased and Samson felt more anger rising in his throat the way his diddle started to grow when he saw Arthur's bare behind a few minutes back. He was about to say something biting when Arthur burst into laughter.

"Relax, Samson," he roared. When his chortles faded, he continued. "We have got all the time in the world together from now on and I look forward to rekindling our friendship."

"Who eva hear of a massa and a slave that be friends?" Samson's voice strained just as Nelson reappeared with a bucket of hot water in each hand.

"Fresh hot water for young Massa Buchana.' Samson and I will have you all nice and clean for the party," he said, as he poured each one at a time into Arthur's tub.

"What party?" Arthur's voice raised.

"The one Missus Anna be fixin' for you tomorrow night!"

The room was plunged into silence.

Nelson got down on his knees and grabbed the washcloth firmly out of Samson's hands and scowled at him. Samson decided it was best to stay out of Nelson's way, so he watched as the old slave dutifully scrubbed his master's body.

• • • • •

THE DAY WAS FILLED WITH bustle as Arthur's mother never took her hostess duties lightly. He had barely seen Samson since early in the morning beyond a brief second as he passed by frantically from here to there. Anna had employed her staff to do everything from rearranging furniture to hot ironing drapery. Not a thread on a rug was out of place nor a flower not pristinely glistened by the time evening had arrived.

At last, the two slaves finished dressing Arthur. All the way up in his room, he could smell the aroma of the boiled pigeon legs glazed with bourbon peaches Anna had Mae prepare as pass around finger food. He inhaled deep as the thoughts of sinking his teeth into a dozen or two made Arthur smile on the inside, then he stepped back from the mirror to take in his look.

Arthur wore a knee length frock coat in a light beige color that had dark brown checks. His trousers were cut from the same fabric, as was with the three-button vest that went over his shirt that was crisp and white. Around his neck was a bowtie in a solid brown that matched the shade, which boxed the beige checks on his coat and trousers.

"Mmm-mmm," Nelson hummed. "Youse sho' gonna make your momma proud and the ladies go wild t'night, Massa Buchana,'" he declared with a smile as he stepped forward and straightened Arthur's bowtie.

"I hadn't planned to be put on display so quickly," Arthur confessed. "But best to get this over with and then hopefully Mrs. Buchanan will leave me in peace for a good long time."

Arthur sighed then he headed for the door.

"At least there's pigeon," he joked. He exited into the hall where he could hear the bows of the quartet rippling across their strings from below. The din of clinking champagne flutes perked his ears further as he made his way down the stairs. He continued across the vestibule then into the parlor until at last he was finally through to the adjoining ballroom. Inside, forty or fifty people stood around the pale blue room wearing dresses and coats cut in the latest styles of fashion. He glanced the room quickly and saw Hattie and Bess as they ran to and fro to serve dainties off of tiered serving trays with sweet treats such as delicate shaped meringues Mae must have prepared for at least the last two days.

Once Arthur caught his mother's eyes, he watched as she nodded to the quartet leader as the strings in the corner of the room picked up their pace. A number of men grabbed the hands of various women who they twirled out onto the floor and then around and around, their hooped skirts spun like ballerinas in a music box.

"Oh, Arthur," Anna said approaching her son. She was flanked by Mr. Gideon Clarkson, the neighboring plantation owner. Clarkson had the look of a New England puritan; his plain black suit and hat showed little warmth or personality and they matched Clarkson's permanent scowl etched in disapproval.

"Your mother tells me you had quite an experience at Rivington, son," he stated dryly. "I hope you are ready to put that learning to work and make your daddy, Buck, proud of what he left behind for you."

"Yes sir," Arthur replied.

A full figured, red haired young lady came up alongside Clarkson, and Arthur thought she was every bit of sunshine to her father's midnight darkness.

"Hello there," she interjected. "I am pleased to finally meet once again the infamously handsome and all grown up Arthur Buchanan."

"I am unsure about handsome or grown up for that matter, but you are?" Arthur asked.

"Arthur, you don't recall Gillie, Mr. Clarkson's daughter," Mrs. Buchanan rebuked her son with a playful slap on the arm.

"I recall a little girl in ringlets, though before me there appears a woman of poise," Arthur responded. He grabbed hold of Gillie's white-gloved hand and kissed it ever so gently. Gillie laughed coquettishly and batted her eyes at Arthur.

"Well now, I already like this version of Arthur better than the one that used to play in the dirt with his pet negro," she joked.

Arthur took her humor in stride, though on the inside he thought it poorly of her to remake his acquaintance with such a lowbrow remark.

"Be a dear, Arthur, and take Gillie to get some punch," his mother urged, so Arthur held out his arm and Gillie grabbed ahold of it before they walked toward the punchbowl together.

"Daddy tells me you've been away learning for all these years somewhere in Virginia," Gillie asked with interest.

"That's right. Rivington," Arthur answered.

"How on earth did you survive at an all-boys academy? I really have to know." She laughed aloud.

"You wouldn't believe how I managed to entertain myself with all of those other young men, rolling around in the dirt and wrestling in the showers," Arthur joked, and for a second Gillie looked confused by the confession, but she recovered quickly and laughed her head off as if she'd just heard the funniest thing in the world.

"Ah, it wasn't all that bad," Arthur continued.

"Nothing like coming home though they say."

Arthur noticed that Samson entered the room with a tray of tea sandwiches. As he made his way closer to Arthur, Mrs. Buchanan and Mr. Clarkson reemerged and joined the young pair.

"Mr. Clarkson would like another glass of some more champagne, Samson," she directed him.

"Yes ma'am," he replied and he passed his tray to Nelson and then went to fetch the bottle. Arthur watched Samson leave and return while Gillie prattled on about her dress.

I'd as soon spend my time passing out the hors d'oeuvres with Samson, then do this small talk, he thought to himself, but he only smiled blankly at Gillie until her father interrupted.

"That one's a strong stag, Mrs. Buchanan," he began. "Why keep such a one in the house when he could sure pick loads of cotton every day? Seems neither pennywise nor pound foolish."

"Samson was Arthur's childhood playmate and as you can see, Arthur has a soft spot for the boy. Takes someone of fine disposition to know how to pick and choose from amongst the pool to serve faithfully up at the house, doesn't it, Mr. Clarkson?" Anna smoothed.

Arthur laughed to himself at how calculated his mother could be as it was clear she was never going to allow anyone, nevertheless a dour old widower, to outflank her when it came to social politics. Arthur may have asked Samson to come inside, and Samson may even have made the choice, but damn it to hell if Anna Buchanan was not going to spin it into an act of her incredible parenting.

"Besides, I've always said to Arthur, when you train one who is partial to you, you don't have to worry as much about them thieving and taking advantage behind your back," she explained.

"Now that's good thinking, Mrs. Buchanan," Mr. Clarkson agreed. "Train him up in these walls where he'll remember he's out of the harsh and hot sun. As such, he's more likely to remember he owes you his life not once but twice over. Perhaps you can even trust him to keep an eye on all the others for you," Mr. Clarkson suggested.

"Trust?" Anna raised her eyebrow. "Now that's a peculiar choice of words, Mr. Clarkson. I think you of all people would have learned from that little rebellion you had that it's never good to trust any negro, regardless of how docile you think they might be. Dogs bite as an act of nature, no matter how long you stroke and feed them."

When Samson returned with the drink, Anna took it from him and handed it to Mr. Clarkson.

"That'll be all, boy," she said sternly, and Samson turned to leave the room. Arthur fidgeted his fingers along his glass and looked up periodically at the doorway that Samson had exited while the conversation continued.

He and Gillie walked the room, though her mouth seemed to move more to Arthur than her feet.

". . . and that's why I could never dream of going off to someplace like Rivington," her words brought Arthur back to the conversation. "Daddy says there's too many uppity Black freemen who cross into Virginia while doing business from the north."

"Oh, how frightening." Arthur threw his hands in the air and feigned terror.

"Surely you don't believe that Blacks and whites are equal, now do you, Arthur?"

Arthur paused. "I'm still working out what exactly I believe, if I'm honest with you, Gillie. I just know there is a moral dilemma in owning another person."

"Ah," Gillie cooed. "And there lies the question of the forward-thinking Rivingtoners. Are slaves people?"

He put the glass he had been carrying down onto a small round table then rubbed his eyes with his fingers for a moment. "In my eyes, yes."

At that, Gillie let out a howl of laughter then she put her own glass down and wrapped her arm into Arthur's and squeezed. "I find you incredibly intriguing to say the least now that you are all grown up, Arthur," she giggled.

For the rest of the evening, Gillie was by Arthur's side as if she were his shadow. When he spoke, she laughed. When the trays passed, she would grab him the best bits of food. Arthur couldn't help but admit that Gillie was attentive and at times funny, if nothing else.

Yet, no matter how much Gillie worked to remain in Arthur's line of sight, he could not help but to shift his eyes in an endless search to see where Samson was or to watch him anytime he did come in and out of the room.

He noted that his mother spent most of her evening engaged in what appeared to be a more serious conversation with Gillie's father, but even Anna Buchanan could not stop time, so that at last, all the food had been served, all the champagne had been poured, and all the feet had shuffled to their last dance. Though they were the last to go, even the Clarksons eventually waved goodbye while Anna and Arthur stood on the porch and waved back at them.

"Thanks for a wonderful evening," Gillie called out as her carriage pulled off into the night.

As mother and son reentered the house, Anna placed a hand on Arthur's shoulder.

"Well, that was a highly successful evening," Anna said while Bess ran around her so that she could wipe down the nearby wooden furniture with a damp cloth.

"If you define success as hosting a bunch of genteel folks who make a living using other men to do their hard work," Arthur sighed with exhaustion. He was so happy these snobby people were gone and that he could finally relax without any more discussion about buying and selling men by the bushel.

"Really, Arthur," Anna scolded. "I am beginning to worry that sending you away was a grave error. What you need is a good woman to take your mind off any of these liberal sentiments you brought back with you from Virginia."

Arthur seemed startled. "A good woman?"

"Well, Gillie for one seems nice," Anna prodded as she led Arthur to the parlor where they both sat down in velvet chairs facing one another.

Samson entered and picked up empty champagne glasses one by one that he placed onto a tray.

"I suppose Gillie is nice enough," he ceded as he locked eyes with Samson.

"Reckon you were even quite surprised to see what a pretty thing she grew up to be, now weren't you?" she pushed.

As Samson passed by, Arthur grabbed an empty glass off of the side table closest to him and handed it to Samson. Samson reached out and their fingers touched at the exchange. Arthur held his breath as he recognized the same fear and attraction that burned in his body as it did the first time they touched. His feelings were clearly reflected in the wide brown eyes that briefly looked back at him as if they were the only two in the world and not that Arthur was sat here inches away from his mother.

"Um, yes, um pretty," Arthur said as he took his eyes away from Samson's before their fingers separated.

"That's why I arranged for you to take her on a romantic picnic tomorrow," she continued.

"Wait. What?!" Arthur exclaimed.

Arthur immediately looked back to see Samson's mouth was now pinched at the sides as if to control a smile or stifle a laugh before he scurried out of the room, presumably to find the next champagne flute, leaving Arthur to sort out his mother's mess.

"Already spoke with Hattie to make up a special basket with Mae's chicken, some fried okra, and even . . ."

"What the hell did you go and do that for?" Arthur yelled out then stood up from his seat.

"Well, you can't likely court a young lady if you don't spend time with her alone," Anna insisted. "And mind your mouth around your mother, this isn't the rugby field at Rivington."

Arthur rubbed his head and sighed. "It's been a long day." He started walking to the parlor door. "I'm going to retire for the evening and talk about this fiasco tomorrow."

"Fiasco?" Anna said as she too stood up, her voice raised. "Honestly, Arthur, you act like you are not even interested in that beautiful woman!"

"Good night, Mother," Arthur said as he approached his mother and kissed her on the cheek. "We have to do better than fighting each time we speak to one another."

"I just don't know how you could do much better than Gillie Clarkson," Anna sighed.

His shoulders slumped from exhaustion; Arthur left the room.

He pouted his way up the stairs while he removed the bowtie from around his neck.

One thing was for certain, Arthur had never even contemplated the idea of a wife up until now. True, men were expected to marry, but it had been the furthest thing from his mind because at the Rivington Academy he was surrounded by men day and night. They did joke and tease about girls, sex, and female anatomy like all boys did, but they just as much joked and teased about their own bodies. Only since they were the ones there at Rivington, they showed off, and they touched each other innocently, and in some cases intimately, so Arthur was insulated from all thoughts of women and spent little time contemplating his lack of desire for them over the boys he interacted with daily.

Arthur knew he would have to at least go to the picnic with Gillie but he was terrified by the idea of what that might signal. Sure, Gillie wasn't bad. She was pretty and funny, but Arthur had no interest in Gillie becoming his wife. Yet, he wondered, *will I be forced to make someone my spouse? And if so, would Gillie Clarkson be any worse than another?*

Arthur went into his room and slammed his door, and his mind shut for the night.

• • • • •

AS SHE SLIPPED INTO THE **SHEETS**, Anna recalled her conversation with Buck's lawyer the day before Arthur's return. Mr. Landow informed her that although Buck had legally left the farm to his son, if Arthur chose to live elsewhere, it would be considered some form of abandonment, which would mean the full rights of ownership over Lanark would become hers.

That was why she had been to see Mr. Clarkson with such urgency the day before Arthur arrived back home. She didn't divulge all of her reasons, but she did make a deal with Gideon Clarkson, who happened to have no son himself. Clarkson only had that one simple daughter of his whom Anna knew she could easily control. So, Gideon and Anna agreed that if Arthur was to marry Gillie, Mr. Clarkson would make him heir apparent and that Arthur would live on the Clarkson's farm as something of an apprentice to his new father-in-law. In exchange, Anna would gift Clarkson thirty acres of land and five slaves of his choosing as some sort of reverse dowry.

Arthur was too much of a sugar snap to run Lanark, but Anna could not possibly care less if he failed miserably over at the Clarkson's because she would be lord and lady of her own estate for good. The minute he moved over to Gillie's as her husband, she would have her lawyer strike.

"Yes, this is a brilliant move," she declared. She kicked her feet back and forth under the covers that today's soiree had set things into motion just as she had planned.

Now all that she needed to do was to make sure that love ignited between Arthur and Gillie long enough for a wedding. Even if she had to coach that girl herself, or drag Arthur to the altar, she would see to it that this plan was executed and it all would need to start with the perfect picnic. While Anna could not be there herself, as that's not how courting worked, she would make sure they had everything they needed for the most romantic outing ever.

"I will be the owner of Lanark," she told herself as she placed her head down on her pillow. "Not just in name, but this time, without Buck or Arthur, I will be mistress to no one other than myself."

Burly, Burly, Blackbird

I t was a beautiful day. The kind where the sun shone so hard that even the painted turtles down in the pond left the cool water and climbed up on logs to soak in its warmth.

Large cellophane bees buzzed by Samson's head on their way to pollinate the black-eyed Susans who had only recently burst their bright yellow flowers into this same light.

Hattie emerged from the Lanark house with a large picnic basket that she handed to him from the porch steps.

"Is ole Mae in this here thing?" he asked with a laugh as he struggled to lift it over the side of the wagon.

Arthur came outside alongside Missus Buchanan, who held a large blanket in her hands that she forced at her son.

"Be sure to have Samson lay this out. A lady does not want her dress to dampen in the soil."

Samson couldn't help but chuckle to himself on the inside. *That Missus, she never give up when she want something.*

"Oh!" she yelled out. "Don't forget to present her with these flowers." Anna pointed to her side as Bess arrived with a large yellow bouquet of begonias and daylilies.

Once Arthur had climbed up on the seat, Bess passed him the arrangement. Then Samson hopped up alongside of Arthur. He grabbed the reins of the horses and urged them forward.

"Y'all enjoy!" Anna yelled with great excitement. Arthur's face twisted like he had just ate a whole heap of the mineral syrup Minerva would force into Samson's mouth whenever he complained of a sore throat.

After a quick stop at the Clarkson's, Samson set up the blanket and food alongside a small river.

"That'll be all," Gillie directed him. Samson's face flushed.

Why after a lifetime of doing the bidding of white folk, do this one dismissal seem to get under my skin in a particular way? he wondered. She was just a silly woman who meant little harm beyond her belief that she was somehow better than him. But her ordering him in front of Arthur felt like he stepped on a cockspur bush with their spiky thorns jabbing into his soles.

He stood by the wagon and waited while Gillie and Arthur sipped lemonade from the fine glasses Missus Buchanan insisted were packed for this picnic.

"What did you say your boy's name was again?" she inquired though Samson was only a few feet away.

She could have just asked me her damn self, he fumed like a storm inside but on the outside, he stood there with a smile like a still wind.

"Samson," Arthur replied as he picked up a rock alongside the blanket and flung it into the slow-moving waters.

"Right," she mused before she raised her glass and yelled out, "Samson! Samson!"

This sow thinks I's deaf or something? Samson thought, but he grinned and responded joyfully. "Yes ma'am?"

"Samson, I have already run out of lemonade in my glass. Fetch the pitcher and refill both Mr. Buchanan and my glasses, then prepare us each a plate of food."

Though he wanted to pour the lemonade right over Gillie's head, Samson came back over to the blanket and filled both of their glasses before he set the pitcher down onto the ground.

"Oh," she exclaimed. "Don't put it there or it's like to fall." Then she turned back to Arthur and giggled. "If it weren't for us women, all men, white or colored alike, wouldn't last long."

Arthur's mouth moved into an uncomfortable smile.

"The food now," she commanded back at Samson who knelt down to grab a plate from the blanket.

"No," Arthur interrupted and he took the plate from Samson's hands. "That'll be all, Samson. Go sit a spell in the wagon, Miss Gillie and I will be just fine on our own for a bit."

Samson nodded then walked over to the wagon and sat himself down on the ground to listen to the ongoing conversation.

"I can fix my own plate," Arthur said to Gillie. "The Lord gave me two hands and I aim to use them not someone else's."

A peel of laughter erupted from Gillie.

"So intriguing!" she howled. "I'll make my own plate, too," she said through a large smile as she spooned some venison and cabbage burgoo onto a plate. "This seems so modern and dangerously bohemian."

In between her bites, Samson heard Gillie question Arthur on everything from what the fashions were like when he visited New York City, to how many children he thought was the right number for a married couple to have. Each time Arthur spoke, she cooed with the same responses such as *interesting* or *intriguing*. She would punctuate the end of each discussion with shrill laughter where she insisted that Arthur was *so well-traveled* and *brilliant like she heard all of the Buchanans were.*

When more than enough red-headed shit had been shoveled to fertilize the entirety of Clarkson's wheat fields, Samson packed up the remnants of the picnic before he delivered Gillie back to her father who waited on the porch with his weathered scowl.

"Oh Daddy," Gillie exclaimed as she ran into his arms. "Arthur is simply charming!" She ran inside leaving Mr. Clarkson to tip his hat and nod as Samson drove the wagon toward the Lanark plantation.

• • • • •

UP IN ARTHUR'S ROOM a little while later, Samson was setting out Arthur's clothes for dinner while Arthur sat and wrote something in a journal.

"So intriguing . . ." Samson teased as he walked behind Arthur and pretended to read over his shoulder. "So interesting," he cooed and giggled in a high voice like Gillie's.

"I don't think she means no harm." Arthur laughed as he put the pen down.

"Just like the sound of her own voice, I's 'spect," Samson replied. "I's also 'spect she be eyin' herself a groom." He laughed.

Arthur pushed his chair back and stood up. "In that case, I'm afraid she'll come up a few horse nails too few for the bargain as after very little thought I've decided that this groom is not for sale." He laughed back.

Samson folded some pants onto the bed when he suddenly felt Arthur come up and stand behind him.

"I'd rather talk less about Gillie and more about when our hands touched yesterday during the party."

He could feel the pulse in his neck twitch at the warmth of Arthur's breath. Samson's hands shook as he laid the pants down and without turning around, he responded with a faint tremble in his voice, "Been a long day. I's be thinkin' tomorra be jus' as busy. If you don't need me anymore, I's tired."

Arthur did not back away from Samson but whispered, "I told you. You've got choices now."

Not knowing what else to do, Samson moved swiftly for the door without turning around to look at Arthur.

"G'night," he said. He shut the door and his chest heaved with the thought of how he escaped Arthur's intimate proximity when he came up so closely behind him.

"What is he askin' of me?" Samson said to himself aloud as he pressed the back of his head against the closed door.

He sighed and opened his eyes to find Bess mere feet away with some linen in her hands. She stared at Samson for a moment then descended the stairs silently.

• • • • •

SEVERAL DAYS HAD PASSED SINCE Arthur was forced to have lunch with Gillie by the river, but thankfully his mother had not said another word about the event. Anna wasn't the only one silent as Arthur could not help but notice Samson seemed to put distance between them. He conducted all of his duties of course, but Samson would find an excuse to leave the room whenever Arthur entered.

After some thought, Arthur decided it was best not to push the matter so he focused instead on learning all he could about the planting and harvesting cycles of the crops as well as the money and account books for the farm. If this place was his inheritance, he at least needed to know about it so as to not leave future decisions to ignorance or solely to the advice of others such as his mother and Flicker.

Then, one evening, Arthur had entered the dining room for his dinner but noticed that instead of its usual two plates set for himself and his mother, there were four settings.

"Why the additional plates, Mother?" he asked.

"We have guests this evening, Arthur," she replied plainly just as Nelson entered and announced the visitors.

"Mista Clarkson and Missus Gillie," he trumpeted as if royalty had arrived.

Arthur forced a smile as he stepped forward and kissed Gillie's white-gloved hand that she presented. He shook Mr. Clarkson's hand as well while he glared at his mother.

Anna jumped up from the table. "Do come in, do come in," she sang before she warmly exchanged a hug with Gillie.

"Now, Gillie, you sit over here by Arthur," she directed. "He told me he had the most wonderful time picnicking with you last week."

Samson entered with a pitcher of water.

Arthur pulled out Gillie's chair; she smiled at him and cooed.

"It was delightful, and I found Arthur's conversation most intriguing," she said as she sat down.

Arthur felt Samson's laughing eyes dance on the back of his head at Gillie's chosen words, but he pushed Gillie's chair in without skipping a beat and then found his own.

Samson leaned in front of Arthur to pour the clear liquid into his glass, and Arthur became distracted by his musky smell of manual labor mixed with oak ash and lye. He was startled back to his surroundings when Bess, who had entered silently, placed a basket of rolls on the table in front of him.

"To what do we owe the honor of this dinner visit?" Arthur asked with mild strain in his voice.

Anna picked up the little brass bell by her plate and rang it twice. Hattie and Mae appeared with bowls of soup that they placed in front of each of the Buchanans and the Clarksons.

"I thought perhaps Mr. Clarkson here could serve as something of a mentor to you now that your daddy's passed on," Anna began while she picked up her spoon and dipped it into the bowl of boiled cow brains and madeira wine. "Especially as you and Gillie are becoming so closely reacquainted." She chuckled before she ladled the food into her mouth.

Clarkson slurped loudly and then said, "Any questions or concerns you may have, my boy, let me know."

"We will have to get this recipe for Molly," Gillie interjected. "She makes her own mock turtle soup but with tail bones and star anise. I've never been partial to that style of food she brought with her from the islands."

"Oh heavens," Anna pinched her face and exclaimed. "No, Mae only uses the recipe of my English forebears, of course."

"My wife insisted that having a Caribbean girl was going to help her with all the other Mason County ladies in running a fine home, just as you are known to do here at Lanark, Mrs. Buchanan," Clarkson said without a smile. "It's been the insufferable talk of all the addle-brained women of Kentucky I know for as long as I care to recall."

"Oh, Daddy," Gillie huffed. "Now you know Molly was a present from Grandmother to Momma. She was not nearly as calculating as you insinuate."

She turned to Arthur. "Have a listen to him and you will think all us Clarkson women are after is domestic glory," she chortled. Arthur feigned a laugh though his mind was really on watching the way that Samson walked in and out of the dining room.

Those trousers grip his buttocks so that they seem like firm peaches, he thought to himself as Samson passed by on the other side of the room.

"Arthur?" He heard Anna scold him.

"Oh sorry. Yes?" Arthur looked back over at his visitors.

"I was saying that I know quite a bit about raising negroes, Arthur, and that's why your mother suggested I take you under my wing for a bit until you figure out your own way to keep them productive and out of trouble."

"Now that you mention it, Mr. Clarkson," Arthur responded with a furrowed brow. "I did wonder would it not be easier to get more productivity from our workers if they were given better conditions?'

Hattie dropped the serving spoon loudly into the bowl and Anna glared at her.

"Beg pardon, it slipped," Hattie apologized. Arthur caught her shoot Mae a look of surprise before the women left the room.

Arthur continued. "They do say the human spirit rises when one can reap the benefits of their own hard day's labor."

"Really, Arthur," Anna angrily sighed.

"Oh, Daddy, don't you just love the way he's so forward thinking?"

Mr. Clarkson put his spoon down and snapped his fingers at Bess who stood along the wall.

"Take this bowl, girl," he ordered.

Mrs. Buchanan turned to Samson who was nearby. "That'll be all for the both of you for now." When Samson looked up at Arthur with uncertainty, Anna yelled. "Don't look to him when I already told you to skedaddle!"

Arthur watched as Samson followed Bess hurriedly out of the swinging door, though he noted it slowly and quietly slipped back open a hair as if someone had pushed it open slightly to listen from the other side.

"You will give them all kinds of wild ideas, Arthur!" Anna scolded. "Not to mention what an embarrassment you are being to me here in front of Mr. Clarkson and Gillie."

Mr. Clarkson cleared his throat. "Son, as one who has seen first-hand the consequences of permitting their negroes to think, if we can call it such, I can assure you they care naught for conditions, as you call them, but respond only to the tail of your whip, same as your oxen do."

"This is exactly why you need a mentor like Mr. Clarkson," Anna followed up firmly.

"But Mr. Clarkson." Arthur leaned closer from across the table. "What makes a white man a human but naught a Black man one? Don't the Black walk and talk just like the white?"

Anna began laughing nervously. "Oh Arthur," she giggled." I thought you were being serious right up until now. You pulled one right over on me." She dabbed the upturned corners of her mouth then placed her white cloth on her lap and picked up her bell. "He really can be a hoot sometimes." She chuckled in an effort to make the Clarksons believe this was all planned entertainment.

"I am being serious, though," Arthur insisted.

Gillie interjected. "Oh, say more, Arthur. I want to hear more of what you think, I really do!"

He looked back and forth between the table's occupants. Though Gillie smiled a little too hard, Anna looked frightened. Mr. Clarkson sat still with the same stoic look he was like to have had at both his wedding and his wife's funeral.

"It's just that I am really struggling to understand why either one is any better than the other. Aren't we all just exactly the same?"

"Enough!" Anna stood up and threw her napkin down onto her bowl. She turned to Mr. Clarkson. "My apologies, Mr. Clarkson. Arthur had a bit of heat stroke today working outside. He's not used to these conditions after so many years away. I should have rescheduled once I realized he was burning up with fever earlier, but I did not want to inconvenience you both . . ."

Mr. Clarkson raised his palm up toward Anna in an effort to calm her before he addressed Arthur. "Son, I can see that the years away have done you a disservice. Ole Buck failed to realize that too much reading can make one romanticize the world . . ."

The hairs on Arthur's arms stood up so high that they pushed an angry response right out of his throat.

"Romanticize?" he snarled at Clarkson. "And I do not have a fever!" he shouted at his mother.

"Now I don't blame you for these northern thoughts, son, but I aim to offer you my wisdom to help you reacclimate, as it were, back to the real world down here in Mason County, Kentucky. The kindness of slavery. The opportunity and expectation that we bring lift these lowly beasts out of the dirt. That's what us true, God-fearing protestants know and do."

Anna implored, "Listen to him, Arthur, for the love of God."

"Even a feral dog can walk upright on its hinds but one does not foster obedience from the pack save by the stick. So, trust me when I say I know more than most that you would be far better served threatening your slaves with worse conditions than offering them better."

"This is so exciting!" Gillie laughed out. Arthur found her voice as irritating as when the boys at Rivington used to tease each other by sneaking up behind one another and running their nails down over their slates.

"There ain't nothing like watching the lynching of one of your own to help increase productivity tenfold," Clarkson said as he patted his stomach. "Now, I'd sure like to find out if the next course can top that incredible soup!" he laughed.

Arthur— his appetite lost— stood up.

"If you will excuse me. I think perhaps my mother was right after all." He narrowed his eyes on Anna. "I did take on too much sun today and I am feeling a bit unwell," he spat out.

Anna smiled and cooed sweetly. "Of course, darling." She then turned to the Gideon and Gillie. "Arthur really is not himself as you can see and I must apologize for subjecting you to his behaviors tonight. I'll send for the doctor after you all leave. I am certain that a tonic and some rest will bring him back to his health and senses in no time."

"Enjoy the rest of your dinner," Arthur said with exhaustion in his voice. He could just make out Gillie's plea for him to feel better as he stormed out from the room.

• • • • •

SAMSON HAD FINISHED DINNER SERVICE in silence as was expected from Missus Anna then attended to the Clarksons in the parlor after Arthur left the dining table. It was a tense two and a half hours as Arthur's liberal words and sudden departure had left them each in a sullen mood.

Samson could only hear parts of their conversation. He needed to keep going in and out of the room to get more thirst-quencher for Mr. Clarkson's glass. For someone who fashioned themselves such an upright Protestant, Samson couldn't help but to notice Mr. Clarkson never said no to another glass of any libation. Thus, Samson's limited time in the parlor was filled with Missus Buchanan's apologies to the Clarksons mixed in with her harshly barked orders to Samson and her other negroes. Then there were Gillie's endlessly whined question over when she could see Arthur again as well as Mr. Clarkson's mumbled statements about religion and rebellion in between sips of sherry, port, and brandy.

Whenever Samson was out of the parlor, his ears were filled with Hattie's deep voice that went on and on in an excited fuss about how, "Massa Buchana' fixin' to make his momma show her sting and it'll be set right on us, him speakin' crazy and all."

Samson couldn't agree more that Arthur continued to run a dangerous course each time he said things about conditions and men being the same. He had a bad feeling that started all the way in his toes that none of this talk was going to do anything but cause harm and hurt. And Samson knew, harm and hurt was naught to come to the white men and women.

When the Clarksons finally left, he went right upstairs to attend to his nightly duties, which included setting out Arthur's chamber pot and stoking the fire for the night. It was September, and though the days were still warm, the nights began to show the first signs of chill.

With a tray in his hands, he pushed it against his body to hold it steady then he knocked once and opened the door with one hand. When Samson entered, he found Arthur laid out on top of his bed in the same dinner clothes he had marched out of the dining room in earlier.

"Thought you might be hungry after skippin' out on the meal like that," Samson said as he walked across the room and put the tray on Arthur's desk.

"Thanks," Arthur responded and he sat upright in the bed.

"Why you say all that down there?" Samson asked suddenly.

"Say all what?" Arthur replied.

Samson took the glass of lemonade from the tray in one hand and the plate of bread in another, handing them to Arthur. "'Bout spirit and conditions."

Arthur took what was offered. He placed the plate in his lap then took a long drink from the glass.

"Cause it's true," he said as he came up for air.

"Youse mighty strange. They don't got no slaves in 'ginia?" Samson inquired.

Arthur laughed. "Of course they do, but . . ." His voice trailed off and they stood in the silence for a few seconds.

"Well anyways, all your crazy talk got me thinkin'," Samson said at last before he walked to a corner of the room and picked up the piss pot that he returned to the bedside with.

"About?"

"When we's boys, youse always treat me kindly. Like I's an equal," Samson said as he bent down and put the pot under the bed.

Arthur sighed. "Hard to treat someone equal when they're forced to put a bowl under my bed so that I can piss in the comfort of my room each night."

They laughed.

"True, but seems naught much has changed about you now that youse a man after all now that I's think on it more . . . 'xcept now youse a lot more talkative about how youse think and feels about things. Back then, youse both, your momma and your daddy, kept your tongue in its place."

Arthur grunted. "True."

Samson became serious. "I's said it after the coop fire, and I's say it again now, Artha, be careful." To which the young Massa cocked his head then nodded.

Samson felt contented by the fact that Arthur acknowledged his words rather than being dismissive like white men were anytime he spoke, even when he said something important.

Good, he thought to himself. *Maybe everything he say and do be forgotten in a few weeks.*

"G'night," Samson said then he departed.

Kindness was unfamiliar territory for Samson. Massa Buck and Missus Anna were notoriously tough owners and he had precious few other glimpses of white folk outside of Lanark to go by. Those he did have were usually limited to when he was brought along to help pick up bags of grain for feed or crates of goods that Missus Anna had ordered from Hadler's. But back at the cabins, tales ran far and wide about the doings and misdoings of the whites.

I guess he's just a kindly soul. Samson thought about Arthur as he made his way down the stairs and into the small room he shared with Nelson where he got undressed and crawled into bed for the night.

• • • • •

THE NEXT DAY, ARTHUR TOOK a walk in the woods alone to clear his mind. He would save his thoughts on the status of the farm for another time, but today he was simply determined to just enjoy the peaceful, "churry, churry, churry," and "cheep, cheep, cheep," of the yellow Kentucky warblers that flitted from branch to branch.

As he neared the edge of the trees, the bird calls were replaced by the sounds of splashing water. He cleared the woods and came upon a gentle stream. Slightly downhill, the water pooled up to form a large pond where Samson sat naked along its edge and bathed.

Arthur slid back to hide behind one of the pine trees for a moment. He watched as Samson lathered up his chest and arms with lye soap. A smile came across Arthur's face when an idea sprung to light.

He disrobed quickly and ran with all his might toward the pond. All he could see was the white of Samson's wide eyes as he flew in the air past him and landed in the water in a great big cannonball splash.

Arthur came up from the deep to find Samson completely soaked from his explosion into the water nearby.

"What in the hell?" Samson called out in disbelief.

Arthur laughed thunderously then flipped his hands into the water and sent another giant wave of water up that crashed onto Samson's head.

"Come on!" Arthur encouraged him with small playful splashes. "Remember what we used to play when we were boys?" he asked as he treaded the water with his hands and feet to stay afloat.

Arthur threw his head up into the air and called out, "Burly, burly, black bird! I see a lemon curd." Then he sprang his hand forth from the water where he was and it landed near Samson's body. Quickly, he slapped on his slave's bare thigh. "You're it!" he screamed.

The two stared at each other for a moment then Arthur saw a smile creep over Samson's face as he reached out quick as a flash and tagged Arthur right back on his wet shoulder.

Arthur wasted no time and leapt fully out of the water. He stood over him completely naked and slapped Samson on his head then propelled his feet forward and ran along the edge of the pond.

Samson jumped up and ran after him and the two ran around the pond's edge naked as birth as they slapped each other back and forth on various body parts so that the other was "it." They stared one another down and faced off while their feet turned in a circle until at last, Arthur sprung forward and tackled Samson to the ground. The two wrestled, a mass of heaving laughter and dripping body parts.

It was all a twirl of childlike fun until Samson pinned Arthur to the ground by his shoulders and sat atop him; his darkened member pressed across Arthur's chest that heaved with heavy breaths. Their eyes widened and their cheeks blushed at their nakedness and position, but they remained in that position until at last Arthur freed one of his hands and slowly lifted it till it touched Samson's face.

Arthur used his fingers to then gently feel along Samson's cheek and chiseled jaw line until they came to rest on Samson's lips. Unable to control what he felt any longer, Arthur threw his hand behind Samson's neck and pulled his head forward with great urgency until their lips made contact.

Their lips touched softly and then with great passion, their tongues burst into each other's open mouths and explored one another in between shaky breaths. He could feel Samson's organ growing as it pressed against his bare skin.

Suddenly, Samson pulled away. Arthur noted the terror that was now in Samson's eyes as he pushed off of him, jumped up, and ran away. Arthur watched as Samson, in short order, had reached the place where he was bathing before Arthur had arrived, and he knelt down to grab his clothing off of the ground before he ran off into the woods in a dash.

Arthur was left alone. He lay there for a moment; his chest panting from a strange mixture of fear and excitement until at last, he leapt and ran off after Samson. He stopped briefly for his clothes that he haphazardly pulled on.

"Samson," he called out as he ran toward the house following the sounds of running feet and breaking twigs.

When he broke through the forest and the Lanark home came into view, he caught a glimpse of Samson's fleeing figure before his body turned the corner.

He must be going through the kitchen, Arthur thought to himself, so he ran as fast as he could in an effort to catch Samson before he went inside.

The door to the kitchen slammed shut as Arthur approached, but he flung it open without thought and stepped inside to find a dripping Samson. In front of him stood an angry Hattie, her back to the door but her hands on her hips.

"What in Satan's hell?" she yelled at Samson. "Youse dripping water all ova my damn floor!"

"Ahem," Mae, who stirred something in a pot on the stove, said to Hattie as she motioned her neck toward Arthur.

Hattie turned around and her face dropped.

"Pardon, Massa, but you too?" she said as her apology faded to concern for both of the young men before her. "Youse both betta get out those wet clothes 'fo youse catch the 'monia!" she commanded each. "And what were youse thinkin' bringin' all this water and fury in here?"

Arthur, whose clothes were half on and completely soaked, shuffled his feet then looked at Mae and said, "Oh, Mae. I just came in here to ask if you could make me a jar of that special tea you used to brew for me when I was a boy. You know, the kind with the honey in it?"

There was an awkward pause.

"Oh, um, yessuh," she responded. "You Buchana' men always do like youse tea nice and sweet," she said coyly. Arthur saw Hattie shoot her a look of stone as if to warn her off of saying anything further.

"Go on na," Hattie urged. "Get some fresh clothes on quick."

Arthur followed Samson out of the kitchen and into his small room.

"I'm sorry," Arthur whispered.

Samson ripped his wet clothes off and slammed them into a basket.

"I thought you felt something, too," Arthur continued in hushed tones, but Samson ignored him and pulled fresh pants on one leg at a time. "I saw it in your eyes . . . and then when we kissed."

Samson took a shirt out of a drawer and slammed it shut.

"What is all this racket, boy?" Nelson scolded as he entered the room. He looked back and forth in surprise to the disheveled and wet Arthur and the half-undressed slave.

"Oh, um, 'cuse me Massa Artha," he stammered. "I didn't see you none in here." Nelson backed out of the room and left them.

Samson pulled the shirt up over his head and onto his arms.

Arthur's shoulders slumped. "I guess I misunderstood," he sighed. "I guess you don't feel nothing."

Samson's eyes nearly burst from his head.

"Feel nothing?" he whispered back at Arthur in a rage.

Samson let out a sigh and turned away from Arthur and seemed to look out his bedroom window.

His voice sounded as if it shook but Arthur listened closely as he continued. "My white Massa kissed me. Don't talk about how I's don't be feelin' nothin', Artha', cause I's know a slave ain't got the privilege to feel nothin' but afraid."

Arthur reached out and put his hands on Samson's shoulders then gently guided his body around until they faced each other.

"Do you feel this?" Arthur whispered softly then he leaned in and kissed Samson on his neck right below his ear.

Samson let out a small moan.

"The moment I got back home and saw you lifting that axe over your shoulders, I knew . . ." Arthur said as he ran his lips along Samson's jawline.

Samson pulled his face away. "I's can't . . . I's Black . . . youse white . . . we be men," he stammered. "Youse are my Massa!"

Those words hung in the air for a moment.

"No matter," Arthur finally responded as he took hold of Samson's hands and squeezed them tightly. "Feelings are all the same on the inside."

"Same on the inside matters naught. If we get caught there's only one of us fit to be sold down the river," Samson declared then he pushed past Arthur and left.

Arthur decided to leave it be for now, so he headed to his room to change out of the soaked clothing.

What am I thinking? he wondered to himself, but Samson did something to him that no one else ever had. Sure, others were attractive, and Samson definitely was that, but it was more than that. The intensity of his eyes. The way he challenged Arthur's thinking sometimes in subtle and other times in incendiary ways. The strength of his jaw and of his spirit. He knew underneath that hard exterior was someone warm. A friend. Whatever it was; however difficult it was to put into words, he felt that Samson was the type of person he would want to be with. Not just be with once as he had done with some of the boys back at Rivington. Sure, there was more than one occasion where Arthur would sneak out of his room in the middle of the night and slip into one of his classmate's covers. He chuckled in his mind over the time he and Hammoth Wordly were almost caught in the equipment room in an uncompromising position after rugby practice one afternoon.

But he was not interested in just a roll around with Samson. No. Samson was someone he wanted to nurture and do right by. *But how?* he wondered.

He would save that worry for another day just as he did the farm's priorities earlier. Instead, he would remember the warmth of Samson's lips on his and the taste of his tongue as their bodies had pressed against one another.

So, Arthur laid in his bed and let thoughts of Samson's taut body that glistened in the sun while he ran around the pond linger in his mind. He simmered on how Samson's manhood felt when it rested on his chest. Arthur warmed himself with the fire of these memories until his body was spent and he then napped until it was suppertime.

•••••

AFTER DINNER THAT NIGHT, SAMSON brought the dirty plates into the kitchen for Mae to wash off and for Bess to dry. Afterward, as was her usual habit, Hattie inspected and put each plate, glass, and cutlery piece away.

Nelson came in behind Samson and announced, "I've got to go get water for the Massa's basin," before he went out the door.

Samson stood there in deep thought for a minute. Then his right foot started to tap on the ground.

"Boy, you gon' give me a headache if youse don't stop that toe tappin'," Hattie scolded.

"Here," Samson said as he forcefully passed her the dirty glass that was still in his hand.

"I've got something to do."

Samson rushed out the back door and over to the pump where he found Nelson as he furiously moved the lever to and fro to fill the bucket.

"I'll take that," Samson demanded once the bucket was filled.

Nelson looked confused. "Youse don't have to do this, boy. I've got it handled for tonight."

Samson stuck his hand out more forcefully. Nelson looked at it, sighed, and gave him the bucket.

"Ok. If youse want more work than what youse already had for the day, I's am not fixin' to protest," he called after Samson as he splashed the water in the bucket from side to side on his walk back to the house.

Minutes later, he was up the steps. Samson knew he had to face this head on or else things could get bad and quick. *I'll just tell him no. He said I got choices, so let's see. If naught, best to get my lynching over now, as I don't think I can stand the 'tiscipation of it all,* he told himself. His face fell when he realized Arthur was not in his bedroom.

Damn, he said to himself. He walked over to the empty water jug on top of the bureau and tipped some water inside until it filled up. He did the same to the deep-water basin that sat next to the jar.

When Samson turned around, he found himself face to face with Arthur who had crept up silently behind him. All of Samon's resolve to tell Arthur no poured out of him the way the water inside the bucket he carried did when it dropped to his feet. Samson felt himself lean into Arthur's body with abandon and they kissed there in Arthur's bedroom with all of their might.

Before Samson had time to think on what he was doing, he had already pulled off his clothes and was locked in Arthur's arms as they both fell onto the bed.

Their tongues once again invaded each other's mouths with great intensity. By instinct, as Samson had no real working knowledge of how or why beyond his imagination, he found Arthur on his back and himself standing on his knees where he threw Arthur's legs up over his shoulders. Samson stared into Arthur's eyes deeply while he guided his tool into his lover's eager and waiting pale abyss.

Samson rocked his body to rhythmic beats he heard in his head, and then as his motions and their pace quickened, he threw his neck back in ecstasy. Arthur reached up and ran his fingers over Samson's throat just as his insides exploded outward and he became one with Arthur. In that same exact moment, Arthur's love burst into the air and landed across both of their chests.

Samson collapsed on top of Arthur and the two laid there in the smoldering afterglow without a word. He felt contented in a way he had never been before, and the intimacy and closeness of it all left him feeling safe and satiated, so Samson closed his eyes to relish in the moment.

When he opened them back up, a thin ray of sunshine peeked through the corner of Arthur's bedroom window and fell across his face. Samson laid there for a minute, unsure of what that feeling was in his belly until suddenly he shot up in the bed. Arthur was startled awake beside him.

"What is it?" Arthur asked with great alarm.

Samson threw his legs off of the side of the bed and rushed to recover his clothes, which he pulled onto himself in a flurry.

"Shhh," he whispered with a finger over his mouth. "I's best get down those stairs 'fore anyone sees I's never made it to my bed last night. Nelson may sleep like a dead man in darkness, but once the slightest hint of dawn comes through the window, he's up and scurryin'"

He tiptoed as gently as he could out the bedroom door and down the steps though he near to panicked when the last one creaked loudly and broke the silence.

When Samson reached the room he shared with Nelson, he floated inside then slid into his bed quietly and pulled the thin cover all the way up over his head. It wasn't but a minute later before Nelson poked him in his ribs.

"Time to get up," Nelson instructed. The older man's eyes stared down at him when he pulled back his covers. They exchanged looks for a brief moment then Samson got up out of the bed, which forced Nelson to step aside.

"You weren't in your bed when I's went to sleep last night," Nelson stated plainly. "Fact, I's didn't hear you come in 'tall."

"I's came in a little afta and youse was sleepin' sound," Samson lied before he changed his shirt and headed out the door, not waiting for any further discussion.

When he came out of the room, Bess stood there in his way between him and the kitchen.

She batted her lashes and smiled at Samson.

"Um, excuse me," Samson said before he gently nudged her to the side with his right arm.

This one still think she has a chance? he laughed to himself as he walked in to find Mae frying up some eggs on the stove next to Hattie, who was pouring freshly brewed coffee into a container.

"Set yourself down," Hattie instructed, and Samson took one of the seats at the small table behind the door.

There, he inhaled three of Mae's eggs in a matter of seconds.

"Whoa!" Hattie yelled out when she brought over a plate of biscuits. "You eat like youse already worked a full day or somethin'." She sat the plate down in front of him.

When Samson reached out his hand to grab one, she slapped it.

"Just one, and I'll get it for you, seeing's youse actin' like ain't none of the rest of us got to eat this mornin.'"

Then she grabbed a solitary biscuit and dropped it onto his plate.

Samson tore at the flaky dough like he was a bear tearing at a spring fawn's flesh.

"Once you finished, Flicker left a basket of 'tatoes out back that be too heavy for me to lift. I's needs you to take it down to the root cella' right way 'fore they get spoilt in the heat afta daybreak."

Samson got up from the table and went outside. Hattie followed behind as she wiped her hands on the bottom of her apron.

"Those be them right there." She pointed just as Arthur rounded the corner from the front of the house.

"Ready to go?" he asked Samson.

Samson looked at the potatoes, then to Arthur, then to Hattie.

"Afraid I've got tasks to attend to." He shrugged.

"What tasks?" Arthur asked.

"Good morning, Massa Buchana,' I's needs Samson to store these 'tatoes for me, if youse don't mind," Hattie interjected.

"Don't mind at all," Arthur said through a smile. "In fact, I'll help."

Samson saw Hattie's jaw fall to her chest. "Help?"

"Sure," Arthur said then he came and grabbed the basket right out of Samson's hands.

Samson looked at Hattie and shrugged again.

"In fact, after that, it's fixin' to be too nice a day to worry about anymore work," Arthur announced. "Why don't you take the day to go down and visit at the cabins . . . put your feet up a bit."

"Put my feet up?" Hattie asked with great confusion.

"Yes ma'am," Arthur continued as he headed for the root cellar. "I'll let my mother know I've given you the day off and you will be back in time for supper," he declared and then he disappeared down the steps that led to the root cellar buried in the ground.

Samson had pulled open the wooden doors and light streamed into the hole in the ground that was deep in the dirt and lined with wooden shelves filled with all sorts of pickles, preserves, and vegetables such as potatoes and carrots, many brined or salted so that they wouldn't decay in sunlight nor the heat up above.

"Let me help your crazy ass," Samson said as he took the basket from Arthur's hands and huffed it onto a shelf in the dark narrow space. "I's think you gone and done broke Hattie's brain." He laughed heartily.

"Well, let's go now before all of my momma's hellfire breaks loose." Arthur laughed as he ran up the steps and Samson followed him back up into the now bursting morning light.

The two ran off into the woods behind the house as if they were boys again. They spent the day talking and laughing. Every once in a while, Samson couldn't help but to look over his shoulder to make sure they were not seen.

Sometime in the afternoon, they laid down alongside a fallen tree limb. There they kissed; Samson's head pressed down heavy into the coolness of the grass. At last, the urge could not be repressed any longer so they each pulled their clothes off and tossed them to the side. Samson leaned his back against the branch as Arthur sat on his lap and mounted him so that Samson could see the deep blue pools that were his eyes.

They said nothing with words but let their stares and moans speak for them. Samson let the air out of his lungs and relaxed his shoulders as Arthur moved his hips to and fro until the tension rose back up and out with a great groan of pleasure that caused his toes to curl up in excited ecstasy.

"I's choose more of this," Samson said as he held Arthur in his arms afterward. He closed his eyes and listened to the ticks and whines of the cicadas in the hickory trees.

"We best get back before supper," Arthur said at last.

Once they were dressed, they walked on in silence until Samson couldn't help but to ask, "How do we continue this?"

Arthur stopped and looked at Samson. "I don't know, but we will find a way." Then he began to walk again, so Samson followed after him. There was a little bit of a burning in his chest.

"I's mean, can we?" Samson asked, and this time with more concern. "Youse can't go decidin' each mornin' that no one hasta work or I's really dunno what would happen round here to be fair."

"I've been thinking on that," Arthur explained while he walked. "I have to have someone attend to me, that's just expected. So, our spending so much time together day and night shouldn't be too suspect."

"I's suppose," Samson said though he wasn't quite convinced it was that simple. *Then again, maybe it is,* he thought to himself.

As they approached the house, Samson's nose was filled with the smell of fried catfish. Once inside the kitchen, he peered into a pan and was about to take a little spec of some spoonbread off of the side when Mae entered from the dining room. "Youse betta get away from that there food," she scolded. "It's for Missus Anna, she loves her some catfish and spoonbread and I's aims to cool her temper with her favorites tonight."

Samson shrugged then washed up and changed before he headed to the dining room.

Once inside, Missus Anna and Arthur— now freshly dressed— entered one at a time and took their seats. Samson began pouring sweet tea into the glasses on the table.

"I just don't understand what you could possibly be thinking giving one of my own damn negroes the day off!" Missus Anna shouted.

"It was only a few hours," Arthur said calmly. "You won't have hardly noticed her missing."

The dining door swung open and in came Hattie and Mae, each with a plate in their hands. Hattie placed hers in front of Anna, who scowled at her but when she looked down and saw what was on her plate, her face softened.

"You will have to work part of the day on Sunday to make it up," Anna said as she picked up her fork and tore a piece of fish off from the filet.

"Yes, Missus Anna," Hattie said softly then she exited the way she had come in.

Anna's squealed a little as she chewed. "Mae always did know how to soften me," she said in between bites. "They're not as stupid as one thinks, Arthur," she continued as she plopped some spoonbread into her mouth. "I see now that I have no choice but to be more involved in your decisions," she said with her mouth full. "Or they are going to stampede right over your gentle disposition."

After she gulped some tea, she gasped. "Oh, that reminds me. The fair is tomorrow and I've purchased tickets for us to go."

Arthur looked up from his food. "I have not been to the fair since I was a child, that does sound fun. Let's bring along Bess and Samson to attend to us," Arthur suggested.

Anna smiled. "For once you sound like an actual slave owner, Arthur."

Samson had never been to no fair and he was happy Arthur suggested he come along. The rest of the meal was eaten in silence and Samson brought the dirty plates into the kitchen the minute they left the room.

"We bes' head to bed now," Nelson said to Samson as he entered.

"Now? They just finished eatin'." Samson was confused by Nelson's orders.

"Son, tomorrow is the first Friday of the month. We always take all the rugs out and beat 'em clean on the first Friday of the month. To do that, we's got to move all of the furniture 'round, and none of it is light. Tis hard labor and you'll thank me tomorra youse took some extra rest tonight."

Samson rubbed his head as he thought on it. "Nawl. Youse go ahead, Nelson. I'm gonna sit out back for a lil bit. All that time outside today reminded me that I'm not used to not havin' fresh air. I 's reckon I'll watch the fireflies a bit 'fore I's head in to sleep."

"If ya must, boy," Nelson shook his head in disapproval. "But, I's don't 'xpect to hear no words of misery tomorra, cause youse won't find no sympathy from this old goat."

Samson went outside just like he said and there he sat in the fading light until it was fully dark out. He then turned his face to the house and found that none of the rooms inside were lit up so he got up off of the log he sat on and crept around to the front door on the porch. He slowly opened it, stepped inside and ever so quietly closed it before he crept his way up the stairs and into Arthur's bedroom.

"I wasn't sure you would come tonight," Arthur said with relief in his voice.

Samson was about to cross the room when he heard a noise behind the closed door.

"Shhh," he whispered softly. He looked down at his feet and saw a shallow glow under the threshold of the door. *That's candlelight,* he thought to himself. *Someone is out there.*

The light lingered for a second or two before it receded along with the soft patter of feet.

"Whoever it was, they are gone now," Arthur called out softly then Samson saw where Arthur had pulled his covers back so he crept over to the bed and hopped inside.

• • • • •

ANNA WRAPPED HER ARM AROUND Arthur's and squeezed as they walked down the street of the town together.

"This is nice," Arthur said then continued with a laugh. "I think it's the first time we've gone five minutes without an argument since I've been back."

Anna playfully hit him.

Behind them Bess walked on her tiptoes to keep up while she held an umbrella up over Anna's head to shade her from the sun. Arthur could hear Samson's feet kick the dusty rocks a few steps behind him as well.

The street was lined on both sides with tables draped in gingham covered with items for sale like pies and pickles. There was a pen in the center of the street that had been built to display a prize pig that ran in circles on the hay laid out. Each time a person passed, it dashed to that side to see if it would be tossed an apple core or some other scrap or treat.

"That one reminds me of Hattie." Anna pointed and laughed aloud. "She's got the same hips."

Arthur guided her past the pie eating contest, where young men with their hands behind their backs smooshed their faces into pudding and crust all in an effort to win a silly pin.

At the end of the street was a group of musicians on a stand that played on fiddles and banjos. The closer they approached, the louder the music became until at last, when they were nearly upon the stand, a group of townsfolk descended all around them and twirled and danced to the fiddle solo.

"Your father always did love the fiddle!" Anna shouted in his ear above the din.

"Personally, I find it rather low-class and base," she announced with a sneer.

Just then, Gillie ran out from the crowd.

"Arthur." She waved and approached. "There you are!"

Arthur looked to his mother who just smiled and nodded her head.

"Your mother told me I'd find you here today," she cooed. "Won't you dance with me?"

He stammered. "Well, I really don't . . ."

Before he could finish, his mother had unwrapped herself from his arm and propelled his body into Gilllie's.

"Of course he would!" she declared. "In fact, I just was just sharing how romantic I think the fiddle is." Then Anna turned and left.

With nothing to do but the obvious, Arthur took Gillie's hands in his and the two of them danced, promenaded, and swung until they were out of breath. Arthur looked around for Samson but he was nowhere in sight. Gillie grabbed him by the hand and pulled him out of the crowd toward some solitude.

"That was exhilarating!" she declared with panted breath.

She wrapped her arm around Arthur's and walked him to a large oak tree where they sat on the ground under its leaves.

"You know, Arthur," Gillie began. "I've always liked you."

"Well, I like you, too, Gillie," Arthur replied nervously. "It's always good to have friends, especially ones you have known all your life." His eyes scoured the distance as he tried to see where Samson had gone off to. His intention was to have fun with Samson at the fair, that was why he suggested he come along. Now, he was trapped under a tree away from the fair with Gillie looking at him like he was the prize pig.

"No. I mean, I've had . . . feelings for you since we were children," she said in a more serious tone.

"Oh," Arthur replied softly. He wasn't sure how to let Gillie know that this was not going anywhere beyond a friendship.

"I'm just so glad that we are getting to know one another again, but this time in a much deeper manner," she whispered and put her hand on his thigh.

Arthur looked down at her hand. "Gillie, I should probably tell you that . . ."

"Oh hush," she said and put her other hand over his mouth. "No more of your liberal ideas, Arthur. Instead, it's time for some of mine."

Then she leaned over and swapped out her hand for her lips and began kissing Arthur strongly. She slid the hand that was on his thigh up over his groin and across the top of his pants. Then she plunged it below the beltline and grabbed his manhood by the handful.

There was a loud cough behind them, and she quickly pulled her hand out of Arthur's pants.

"Missus Anna been lookin' for you, Artha,'" Samson lied.

"Oh?" Arthur asked.

"She told youse she'd be ready to head home afta the horse pulls and youse know how Missus Anna get if you is late."

Arthur leapt up and dusted himself off.

"Oh! Yes . . . yes," he stammered to play along. "She did say she would want to leave right after."

He held his hand out to help Gillie up off of the ground as well.

"Thank you for reminding me, Samson," he said then he leaned into him closer. "Thank you."

"How unfortunate." Gillie's face was crestfallen.

"I'm really sorry, but I must go. My mother can be quite intractable, as you probably know, if she does not get her way. In fact, I'd worry for any woman if I were to ever take a wife, that she'd like to become my mother's ward and live something akin to a prisoner's life," he said as he started walking away.

"Maybe I could see you tomorrow?" Gillie shouted after him.

Arthur turned back but did not slow his pace. "I'm afraid I'm busy tomorrow, unfortunately."

A Broken Piss Pot

"Ooo, hey, dilly, dilly, bay," Bess sang to herself as she came out of her small room under the stairs. She had a candle in one hand since it was quite early. Each morning, Bess would collect the chamber pots from Missus Anna and Massa Buchana's rooms. It was smelly but she didn't mind much as this house was better than the last one she lived in. There, all the boys come round for a peekaboo near to every day.

What she didn't like though was those big stairs she had to climb up in the near darkness. Bess was frightened by their height, especially when one reached the top 'cause if they looked down, it looked like one was peering into a well like the one Baby Brother Amos fell in and drowned when he was not yet three. Bess could easily imagine losing her footing if one stared too long at the abyss, especially on the next to top step where the brass rod that held down the red and gold carpet seemed wobbly-gobbly. But she had to go up, or as better as this place seemed, that Missus was gonna scream again and send her out with that white piggy-man who tried to put his piddlestick in her hand the last time she was put in the barn. She just laughed at it because it looked like a dead field mouse and nothing like the one Nathaniel had shown her behind the outhouse right before they done sold her to the Buchana's.

"Nathaniel's though be dark and it had a long vein like the one daddy used to get on his head when he yelled." Of course, she then remembered that was before those white men shot her daddy's head off right out in front of her eyes. There went the vein and there went any little protection she had from all them men and their tickle tails.

"Well, 'least Nathaniel's one was not like Piglet's where it be pink and silly looking, almost shriveled up like it hiding 'cause it was as afraid of me as much as I's afraid of it," she giggled.

Wait, why am I out here again? she asked herself. "Oh," she chortled once more then she adjusted the small white scarf she had on her head that was meant to keep her hair out of the bread dough or else that big ole farm dog, Hattie, would be barking at her like she did every time she had to knead for biscuits, just like she would be told to later on.

Bess hiked up her skirt with her free hand and started to walk up the steps one by one.

She counted them in her head. *One, two, then come three, and four,* she said to herself while she sang in a fast beat. Along the wall were lots of faces of dead people. They frightened Bess, so she made a point to just look down at her feet and count them instead of letting all those creepy eyes stare at her. *It be as if they want me to trip and fall,* she thought to herself as she felt them look on out of the corner of her eyes. She then remembered what happened when she tripped on one of the steps when she carried a hot pot of tea for the Missus. Thankfully, it was the bottom step, so she didn't fall far. But damn did that woman holler!

That lady always be mad but she do like her tea with one of them sugar squares . . . not two . . . plus a drop of cream, cream . . . creamy . . . creamy cream soup would be good now that summer was fixin' to be ova in a few months, I think, and it gonna be winter soon, she chirped in her mind as she ascended. *Do they even have winter in Kentucky?* she wondered. She didn't know because in her mind, she had not been in Kentucky before, at least she didn't think Nathaniel's piddlestick was Kentuckian. "Maybe it was since they say I used to live nearby," she shrugged.

"Ooo, hey, dilly, dilly, bay," she sang even softer to herself so as not to wake anyone as she made it to the top then scurried quickly away from that scary place to Arthur's door.

She knocked gently at first. "Massa Artha?" she called out. She knew enough now that you never entered one of their rooms without knocking first to announce yourself.

Bess froze as she swore she heard two voices whispering on the other side of the door.

Naw, she thought to herself. *I must be hearing things.* Afterall, she remembered she thought Nathaniel cried out that he loved her when she pulled on his stick. "There be that fool's piddlestick again in my mind for the third time this morning." She laughed then knocked again.

"Massa Artha?"

"Yes?" came the response from the other side of the door.

"I needs to come in for the pot," she said sweetly.

There was a loud scuffling noise inside the room.

"Massa Artha?" she asked with some concern in her voice.

"It's ok, Bess," came the voice again. "Come on in."

So, she did and she entered only to find Arthur awake and propped up in his bed.

"I put the pot on the bureau for you." He pointed. She grimaced as she usually just picked it up from under the bed.

How strange? Bess thought, but she smiled cause Arthur seemed like he was the nicest white man she could ever remember. *He neva try to touch me*, she thought to herself. *And I feels safe around him.*

She picked the pot off of the bureau and turned to leave.

As she walked away, she could have sworn she saw some black as midnight toes sticking out from under the bottom of the bed.

"Ooo, that almost as creepy as those paintings on the stairs." She shivered inside as she knew for certain there was no barefooted man laid up in the darkness under the Massa Artha's bed . . . no way and no how.

Ooo, hey, dilly, dilly, dilly, bay. Bay dilly, dilly, dilly, hey, hey, hey, was all she could think as she walked out of the room, quickly tiptoed down the stairs, and out the front door.

When she took the pot a few steps away from the house, she poured it out onto the ground; the smell of urine hit her nostrils as it landed in the dewy grass.

She turned around to go back and repeat the same act but this time for the Missus. When she turned around, she briefly looked up at Massa Artha's window as it was no longer dark and now glowed softly with faint candlelight. She could see the outline of Arthur's body in the shadows, but shivered harder than before when she thought she saw another body float by in the dim light.

"Massa Artha's room must be haunted by one of them people with the faces on the stairs." She trembled. "I wish cousin Walla were here. She'd put a pin in a doll and kill those spirits or at least stop them from hurting Massa Artha."

Bess shrugged then went on with her day and off to collect the next piss pot.

• • • • •

SAMSON'S HEART THUMPED WHEN BESS entered the dining room with the morning biscuits.

If she hadn't knocked and just entered the bedroom only a little while ago, she would have caught him naked as nature and Arthur lying atop of him at that. Though he had just barely enough time to roll under the bed, he was still filled with concern that Bess could've seen or heard something. She sang to herself as she put the plate down and Samson's pulse eased as he felt Bess was too plum-headed to keep anything she might have seen to herself.

"Morning," Arthur said as he entered the room. Hattie also came in but from the other door, and her with a bowl of scrambled eggs in one hand and a pile of bacon in the other.

Samson smiled widely at the sight of Arthur then he stepped forward to take the eggs from Hattie's hands. He warmly remembered how last night they changed places, this time he laid on his stomach while Arthur slipped up inside of him from behind. The feeling was a little uncomfortable at first, but once Arthur rubbed a little bit of cottonseed oil on his backside, it be as powerful as fire must have felt when it crackled.

"Would you like some eggs, Artha?" he asked intimately as he moved closer to him with the bowl.

"Arthur?" a voice shouted from the doorway. "You've become too familiar, boy," Missus Anna growled.

In three steps, she was across the room and at his side, where she raised her hand in the air and struck him across the cheek.

Samson froze in shock.

"Mother!" Arthur protested, but Samson's cheek had already been stung.

"You will call your master by his rightful title always or I will slap the dung out of your face each and every time I see it. Do you understand me, boy?"

"Yes ma'am," was all Samson could think to say that wouldn't bring Flicker and Piglet in to drag him off to his death.

"Now, apologize this instant!" she commanded.

Samson looked from Missus Anna's face to Arthur's, which was red with flame.

"This is unnecessary," he heard Arthur call out.

"What's necessary is that this boy knows his place," Anna chastised as she raised her hand in the air again. "Well, boy?"

Samson looked for Arthur to intervene. Instead, all he could see was Hattie's glare out of the corner of his eyes, and it urged him to get this over quickly.

"Sorry, Massa Artha," Samson said softly, but the words stung worse than the slap.

Anna lowered her hand and went to find her seat.

Hattie passed by and put her hand briefly on Samson's forearm, as if to show support.

"Well, that is much better," Missus Anna said while she pulled her chair in closer to the table. "And I'll thank you kindly never to forget to address one of us properly again."

"That's enough, Mother," Arthur snapped. "I had told Samson to call me Arthur in the house."

Hattie came over and started serving Missus Anna some of the bacon. She picked a piece up and took a bite.

"Really, Arthur." She laughed while she chewed. "I don't know why you brought that boorish beast inside to begin with when he's spent a whole lifetime as a field negro."

Samson fumed on the inside. They were talking about him like he wasn't even there.

"I asked Samson to come attend to me, not the other way around," Arthur pointed out.

"No need to get salty on account of his lack of experience."

Samson might as well be the fruit bowl on the table for all they acknowledged his presence and he fumed in his head.

"We could have just bought you one of the more polished and mindful types like we did Nelson after Bevel went and selfishly died on us," Anna lectured as she held out her hand. "Now someone pass me those damn eggs before I have to pitch a fit and slap all of your Black faces to kingdom come this morning."

Hattie rushed forward to attend to Missus Anna. Mother and son ate the rest of their breakfast in silence, but Samson felt anything but silence on the inside.

When he was dismissed, he went into the pantry and loudly stacked the last of the bottles of spicebush jam that had been stored in the root cellar since last fall that Hattie had asked him to retrieve.

He didn't hear Arthur come up behind him, but felt his hand on his shoulder.

"I'm really sorry about that, Samson," Arthur said just loud enough to be heard over the clanking mason jars.

Samson thought it best to continue stacking the jam rather than respond. He knew something was bound to happen and he cursed himself on the inside for going down this path he started with Arthur.

"It all happened so quickly," Arthur explained. "I should have said more and not allowed her to hurt you like that by demanding that ridiculous apology."

Samson whirled around. "What does it matta, Artha?" he spit out. "I's just a boorish beast," Samson said in a mocking tone while he threw his hands in the air and shook his fingers wildly.

Arthur took hold of Samson's hands and he pulled them down by his hips and held them tightly.

"Not to me," Arthur assured him softly. "Never to me, and I'll do better from now on."

"I knows it confusin' for us both," Samson relented. "Hard to know how to act."

"Promise to make it up to you tonight," Arthur soothed him.

Samson could feel all the anger drop from his shoulders straight out his toes.

He laughed. "Only tonight I's get to rub in the cottonseed oil." Then he lifted one of the hands that Arthur held and kissed the back of it.

As he did so, Mae walked into the pantry.

"Oh . . . um . . . 'xcuse me," she said as she moved her eyes off of Massa Arthur's hand that was near Samson's lips.

"Yessuh," Samson said quickly. "I think the splinter is outta there now," he said as he pushed Arthur's hand away from his face.

"I's just comin' for some . . . um . . . some," Mae stuttered as she looked around the pantry. She reached out and grabbed a jar of peaches. "Peaches!" She smiled big. "Yes, that's it. I's wanted some peaches to make some . . . er . . . pie." She grabbed another two jars and left.

Samson sighed. "We best be more careful. I's think no mo' touchin' 'cept in the room, in the dark."

"In that case," Arthur said with a smile. "I'll pray the darkness comes early." He winked at Samson and left the same way Mae had seconds before.

● ● ● ● ●

BESS SCRUBBED THE BREAKFAST DISHES when Mae came in and dropped some jars loudly onto the butcher block.

"My oh my," she huffed to Hattie who stood next to Bess and wiped the dishes dry. "In all my years in this house I's ain't neva seen anything so peculiar."

"Hmm hmm." Bess could see the smirk form on Hattie's face like she done sucked some orange peel that fermented into bitters.

"That young Massa done turnin' things up onside its head," Mae complained.

"You reckon?" Hattie replied with a deep laugh. "Took youse long enough to catch on!"

"I's don't know, but it don't seem too natural," Mae continued. "And now I's done told them all I be baking a peach pie, and I do not have no time to be making crust today," she pouted.

"I wonder, though," Hattie mused. "Is it any less natural than a man be owning a'notha man?"

"Hmm hmm," was all that Mae could now answer back.

I wonder what they be talkin' about? Bess thought in her mind. Then she decided as long as it wasn't about her and she didn't have that fat woman next to her breathin' down her neck tellin' her to hurry up, she would be just fine to mind her own damn business and listen.

"Plus, it'd be you with your dead eyes bulgin' out ya swollen face if youse the one to tell the Missus, now wouldn't it be?" Bess watched Hattie put her hand that held the dishcloth on her hip like she did whenever she wanted to make a point.

Bess hadn't even heard Nelson come in but he chirped up. "Missus Anna sure to kill ya just as fast if we don't tell her somethin' goin' on." He sounded nervous to Bess, so she tried to listen a little closer.

"Lawd have mercy," Hattie exclaimed. "You just figuring all this out, too?"

Mae burst out in a way Bess had never heard that quiet old woman before. "I for one been on the wrong side a' that woman a time o' two over the years and I ain't fixin' to do it again the more I think about it."

She started marching toward the door while she continued speaking. "Not for no one, less some dumb boy from the fields!"

Must be talkin' about that good looking boy, Samson, Bess thought to herself. *I don't know why he hasn't asked me to hold his piddlestick none.* She shrugged.

"Now you hold right there, missy." Hattie threw her towel on the floor and stepped in front of Mae to block her. "Like you said 'fore, it may be peculiar but one thing's fo' sure. We all been a dumb boy from the fields at some point 'fore they brought us inside."

Mae stopped and glared at Hattie in the eye.

"I's too old to go to the barn with Flicker," she pleaded, but Hattie refused to move out of her way. "I's only made it so long by the grace of God, my gift with the skillet, and stayin' out of that woman's way as best I could."

"I rememba you gave me right hell when I moved up to this house because I slept with the Massa," Hattie barked.

"Hah," Mae responded. "And I was right, too. You made a damn fool of yourself without any help from me, and now I been stuck listenin' to your bossy ass for ten plus years on account of it."

Hattie glared down at Mae. "My point is, we all gots to find our way, and that boy deserves every chance to figure it out the same way each of us have." She raised her shoulders as if she was fixin' to strike Mae.

"Now, I's could just as easy slap your wrinkly behind back to the stove." Hattie stepped aside. "But that would be just as bad as you standin' here passin' judgment on that boy the way you passed it on me when I's slippin' with the Massa."

Mae stood there and shuffled her feet.

"So, you just go ahead and tell Missus Anna all about it, and let that boy's neck be on your conscious."

Mae's face fell.

"Youse just as annoyin' as the day Massa Buchana' brought your pig ass up to my house."

"May be." Hattie laughed. "But this pig ass, as you call it, makes sure this whole house runs as smooth as a water mill now and somewhere deep inside that old as Kentucky dirty heart, you love it and you love me."

"I suppose, Massa Artha treat us betta than we e'er been treated, no matter," Mae relented. "So, I reckon makin' a pie is small price," Mae concluded then she reached onto a shelf above Bess' head and she took down some flour and a pie pan.

"It is true," Hattie agreed.

"If Massa Artha likes his tea with a little brown sugga like his daddy, who am I t' judge?" Mae at last teased as she poked Hattie in the ribs with the rolling pin she took out from under the counter.

"You all seem fine with this, but I wonder if it'd be best afta all to let the dumb boy be caught on his own? Maybe without our involvement he could get rooted out by his own actions 'fore he does get us all kilt, though?" Nelson interjected.

Now why would Samson get us killed? Bess wondered.

"Seem like either way, eventually someone gonna get stung and I soon as not be the one to be anywhere near her stinger." Hattie laughed aloud then she headed out the back door.

"Now that I's think on it, me neither," Mae said then she cracked some eggs into a bowl and began beating them.

"Nor I, I's suppose," Nelson responded quietly then he turned and walked out.

I don't want to get pinched by no bees my damn self, Bess thought in her mind. *Glad I don't have to be the one to collect the honey from the hives out back.*

She took the brush and scrubbed off egg bits from a plate as hard as she could. "Ooo, hey, dilly, dilly, bay," she sang out quietly.

The rest of the day she could not help but to see the strange looks the other house slaves were giving each other. *They be really scared of them bees,* Bess thought to herself more than once. *Maybe one of thems like that story I heard 'bout a woman whose eyes swoll so shut after she got zapped by a yellow and black that she ne'er opened them again and went to her grave that way.*

All she knew was she would keep an extra cloth tied at her hip in case one of them got near her today she could kill it with a quick flick of her wrist. But the day went by and she never saw any bees, so she forgot all about the whole thing and went to sleep soon after supper was cleared and Missus Anna was tucked in for the night.

When she woke up, all she could think about was getting those piss pots cleaned up so she could stand by the fire in the kitchen that was sure to be stoked by the time she returned.

"Ooo, hey, dilly, dilly, bay," she sang again quietly as she zipped up all those stairs as fast as her little feet would let her.

I'm gonna ask Mae if she'd let me eat a piece of that cornbread for break-fast, she thought to herself, turning the knob to Arthur's door and walking in.

Imma place it right on top of the stove and let it warm up all ova before I slab some of that sweet butta right down on top of it, she thought as she mouthed the word, "yum" and licked her lips.

She bent down and grabbed the chamber pot out from under Arthur's bed, and briefly thought to herself how full it was this morning and how, *Massa musta drank like two horses yesterday 'stead of one.*

As she stood straight up, she realized that the bed shook violently. So engrossed was she on cornbread that she had ignored all else, but she now found herself looking right at the backside of two naked bodies that faced away from her. They were oblivious to her presence, all twirled up together and humping so loudly they hadn't seen her come in. Arthur was on all fours with Samson behind him putting his diddle into a place Bess didn't know sticks could fit.

The shock of what she was seeing caused Bess to release an ear-popping scream that could have curdled cream.

Arthur and Samson appeared to be so startled with panic that they had been caught doing something of which Bess could not quite understand, but somehow knew it was wrong. She bellowed louder and more violently.

Samson tried to shush Bess as he reached out his hands to put a finger over her mouth, but he did not manage to do this in time to silence her or to catch the overflowing ceramic pot that became separated from Bess' hands in her panic.

Right in the middle of her loud roar, the sound of ceramic crashed onto the floor followed by shards and pieces as well as drops of piss that flew in every direction and soaked everyone nearby, most especially Bess who stood there and blubbered.

•••••

ANNA WAS ALREADY AWAKE WHEN she heard Bess' scream and what sounded like breaking glass. *Oh, good God . . . those shits have finally started a rebellion,* was the first thought that tore through her head.

Her robe was halfway around her body when she rounded the door frame to Arthur's bedroom. What Anna expected to see was one or more of those negroes with a knife to Arthur's throat. Probably that Samson who she should have had strung up last night for his familiarity.

She briefly considered she would not have particularly minded if Samson did have a knife to Arthur. In fact, she might not have minded too much if he cut through Arthur's flesh. It would certainly have made her efforts to regain control of the farm easier. Either way, whether they bled her child or not, she would raise Cain until every one of them that turned revolutionary was dead and buried for this insurrection.

However, when she ran into Arthur's bedroom, what she found instead was Bess soaked from head to toe in urine, pieces of the chamber pot in every direction. Past Bess, her eyes must have lied because she could have sworn she saw her son and Samson naked in bed together.

When she accepted her eyes told the truth, she stood next to Bess and joined in her screams until it sounded as if she and the slave girl shared a mother whom they just found bludgeoned to death. In fact, to Anna, that would have been far more preferable than the current situation.

There's rebellion for certain, she thought in her head. *Only it isn't the slaves.*

Flicker and Piglet, who slept in the small workhouse just off the backyard, must have heard her scream and ran to her aid because they were by Anna's side before her noise had abated.

Without time for thought, Anna commanded Flicker and Piglet to take hold of Samson. Once secured by both arms, they drug him stark naked out of the room while Anna yelled at the top of her lungs. "Lock that boy in the root cellar. He's done a grievous sin here against my house and I need time to think on the proper justice that will be best administered!"

She looked back at Arthur and felt nothing but nausea over the fact that he should be the cause of such great embarrassment to her and to Lanark. This was why she did not want to give up control, but Buck and his will be damned.

The fact that morning porridge looked to have more fight in it than her son with his downcast eyes and limp-wristed response brought on a second wave of disgust. He did not even stand up from the bed to protest Samson's removal. *How can he just sit there like a cornhusk doll?*

"I'll deal with you later," she pointed her finger at him and scolded, and then she took Bess by the arm and walked out of the room.

"Let's go have a little talk in my room, shall we, Bess," she said to her sweetly.

Once inside, she closed the door and motioned to the chair.

"Have a seat, won't you, girl," she invited and Bess obeyed. "You must have had quite a shock."

"Oh yes, Missus Anna," Bess responded; her voice was a slight quiver.

"Now, now," Anna cooed as she came up and put her hand on Bess' shoulder. "I want you to tell me everything you saw this morning. Don't leave any detail out. Ok, Bess, dear?"

"I . . . I . . . don't know what I seen. I walked in to get the pot and . . ." her voice faded.

Anna wanted to do nothing more than slap the hell out of Bess' face, but something inside told her the only way to get what she was looking for was through a kind touch as pathetic as that felt to her.

"Come now," she urged gently. "You went to the room to get the chamber pot. Now take a deep breath and tell me what happened step by step once you entered Arthur's bedroom."

"They . . . they's together," Bess replied cautiously.

"Together?" Anna asked with gentle curiosity.

"Like husband and wife," she said back; her eyes lowered to the ground.

"What exactly does that mean?" Anna pushed, this time her voice raised slightly.

"I saw Samson done had his thing in Massa Artha's backside and they's nekid' and wrigglin' . . . like worms on a fishin' hook," Bess at last let it all out.

"I see," Anna soothed though inside she was ready to spit blood and brimstone. "Did you ever see them together like this before?" Anna inquired.

"No ma'am." Bess looked up at Anna.

She's just a silly frightened simpleton, Anna thought to herself.

Anna crouched down so she could get a good look at Bess' face when she responded to the next question.

"Has anyone else, any of the others ever talked about Arthur and Samson being together in some kind of a different way? A manner other than master and slave? Something like what you saw this morning?" she pressed gently.

She could see Bess using the limited intelligence her kind had to try to conjure up the best answer. *These creatures have one talent, and that's deception,* she said inside her mind. *But this buffoon better tell me the truth or so help me.*

"Not that I know of, Missus Anna," she answered at last.

"So, you are sure, you were the only one that seen them together like this?" Anna pressed once more.

"I think so," she thought aloud. "No ma'am. I don't rememba no one say Massa Artha like to get fucked by his slave boy, Samson."

Anna's veneer of calm was close to its final crack at these words.

"Good," was all she could muster up to say. Then she marched to the bedroom door.

"Now you stay here and rest for a minute. I'll be right back."

She left Bess in her room on top of her chair to rest, but Anna decided her rest would be short.

As she came to the top of the stairs, Flicker and Piglet came back inside the house.

"We did as you said," Flicker called up. "There ain't no way he can get out of that root cellar."

"What you want us to do now." Piglet giggled. "Skin him alive or drag him down the lane by horses?"

Anna thought for a brief second.

"What I'd like for the two of you to do is to come up here for a moment," Anna said, though she momentarily mused suspiciously that not one other slave had come out of their rooms to see what all the ruckus was about this morning.

Once the three were up the steps, she guided them into the bedroom where she pointed at Bess and coolly instructed the men. "Take this girl here to the barn and string her up."

"W . . . w . . . w . . . what?!" Bess cried out in confusion.

"She's been plotting with that boy, Samson, to steal my jewelry and run away together up north," her voice was emphatic.

Bess looked as if she were going to faint.

"When Arthur found out, he confronted Samson about it this morning and that boy attacked him in Arthur's very own bed." Anna's voice now trilled with accusation.

She knew it wasn't just what she said here, but that how she said it that was bound to get around all of Mason County quickly. The walls had ears even if those ears were pretending to still be asleep.

She continued with righteous indignation. "The struggle between them was so fierce that Arthur tore that boy's rags off in the tussle, exposing his shame from every angle."

Then Anna pointed again at Bess. "And this dumm-diddy." She shot spittle from her mouth as she railed. "She just stood by and watched! She wanted to see my son in a pool of blood before they both made a run for it."

Bess let out a loud gasp. As the men rushed toward her, she stood up and tried to back away. "But Missus," she implored. "I ne'er done no such thing. I only saw Massa and Samson in the bed doing . . ."

Anna ran over and slapped Bess hard across the mouth to stop her from saying anything more. "And gag this bitch. I don't want to hear an evil sound more from her mouth. Do you hear me?" she barked at Flicker and Piglet.

Piglet grabbed a handkerchief off the top of Anna's bureau and stuffed it inside of Bess' mouth while her arms were held down by Flicker. She struggled little but whimpered much.

Now alone, Anna sat down on the side of her bed and plotted.

• • • • •

ARTHUR HEARD THE SOUND OF Bess' feet as they dragged across the landing at the top of the stairs all the way from his bedroom. *What can I do though?* he asked himself. He decided there was nothing for it but to lay there helpless.

Why he wasn't more careful, or even better prepared for this moment, were questions Arthur had in his mind, but the sight of Samson dragged from his bedroom left him without the energy or will to even attempt to answer these.

"It'll be all over Mason County by now," he swallowed hard. "Any power I might have had to do something as Master of this place evaporated today like morning fog." Arthur knew once the word was out absolutely no one— anywhere— would want to deal with him and that would be true even within the confines of his own property. His power and standing would be diminished. His mother was probably already plotting how she would use this to her advantage and geld him yet again as she had done repeatedly since his birth.

He sat there feeling sorry for himself but also frightened of the inevitable and terrible ending he knew was to come for his slave friend turned lover.

"I can't save myself, nevertheless Samson," Arthur murmured helplessly. There was no way his mother was going to allow Samson to live. Even worse, Arthur knew his mother would enjoy playing all kinds of games and toying with the slave until death was kindly welcomed.

Arthur's fingers nervously fiddled with the bedsheets.

"Samson was right to worry," he whispered aloud.

His door rattled and he realized that he hadn't been aware someone had locked him inside in all of the morning's chaos. "Not that there was anywhere to run," he mused.

When the jangle of the keys stopped, the door swung open to display his mother, a shotgun in her hands.

"This here's your daddy's shotgun," she stated coolly as she made her way over to his bedside. "He taught me how to use it in case we ever saw an uprising just like the one over at the Clarksons."

Anna held the gun up and pointed it at Arthur's chest.

"What on God's green earth were you thinking?" she growled.

Arthur put his hands up over his eyes. If his mother was meant to kill him, he didn't have the heart to stop her or for that matter, watch her.

"First you came back here with your damn ideas and now these abhorrent deeds under my roof, and I do mean *my* roof?"

He braced himself for the impact of the shotgun's slug that would burst into his chest at any moment, but nothing came. After a few seconds, he opened his eyes to find Anna still there, the gun still pointed, and her face still full of anger.

They stared at each other for what seemed like forever until Anna at last lowered the gun and sat on the end of the bed, the weapon in her lap.

"Oh Arthur," she said this time softer. "Even as a little boy you were overly sensitive. You demonstrated too much kindness toward your inferiors." She paused. "But that don't change what you were born to be, a white man, and a Buchanan at that."

"Let's not pretend. I have always been a disappointment in your eyes," Arthur said weakly.

Her softness over, Anna gritted her teeth. "Word gets around a Buchanan boy likes to lay in the bed naked with Black men and play tickle tail, neighbors are like to set this whole plantation on fire."

Then she stood up.

"And I'll be damned to hell if I'm going to let you and some negro's hickory log take down my own good name," she declared.

Anna sternly reached out one of her hands to Arthur. "Now grab hold of my hand and stand up, boy. You want to finally make me proud? Well, we got negroes to string and gut and you're gonna be the one to make them bleed."

Arthur was numb to her words, but did as his mother said.

"I'll have everyone this side of Mason County know that the Buchanan's brook no African subterfuge." She then reached for a pile of clothes with her free hand and threw them into Arthur's face.

"I will get you out of this mess you created." Her voice was full of resolution. "And when this is finished, you will marry Gillie Clarkson post haste!"

Arthur pulled his shirt over his head and nodded yes.

"But let me make one thing clear," his mother lowered her voice and stared directly into Arthur's eyes. "This gun may have belonged to your father, but I'll shoot you good and dead with it myself this very day for certain if you do not carry out each and every one of my orders."

With that, she stormed out of the room. Arthur was left alone. He slipped the rest of his clothes on and then placed his bare feet into his shoes and followed the same path as his mother.

"That was almost the nicest she's ever been to me," he reflected solemnly.

• • • • •

SAMSON LAY ON THE COLD dirt undressed and vulnerable. It was dark in the root cellar save for the little bit of light that came in between the cracks along the wooden door frame from outside.

What had happened? He shook as he wondered to himself. *It was all so quick.* Samson heard footsteps coming down to the door and steeled himself for death.

"Samson?" a woman's voice whispered. "Samson, are you in there?"

He rushed to the door to find Hattie's face pressed in between the planks.

"Hattie!" he exclaimed with some relief.

"Oh, Samson, why did you have to go an' let the white devil lure you in?" she asked.

"Not the devil," Samson said matter of fact. "His name is Artha, and love don't know one colored devil from the next."

"I suppose so," Hattie sighed. "Truth be, none of us were fully sympathetic to your plight, but I for one, I's been in your predicament. In love. Promised things. Believed the impossible was a come," she said wistfully. "But 'stead I had my baby beat out of my body, dead." Her voice fell flat. "And now, Missus Anna fixin' to do to you worse than she done to me and my baby."

In between the frame and the door, Hattie pushed something inside.

"Ain't nothin' for it now but to take care of youseelf 'fore they do things to you worse than anybody could imagine," her voiced contracted in pain.

Samson reached out his hand. As his eyes adjusted in the darkness, he grabbed ahold of her offering.

"What's this?" he asked, staring at the knife she had passed to him.

"Youse got to end your own life! Don't give them no satisfaction in seein' you swing, boy," she said. Then she turned around nervously to look away and turned back to Samson.

"I's got to go. Be my neck snapped too if they find me here." Hattie put her palm up to the door frame and Samson used his free hand to do the same.

"I's see you the other side of heaven," Hattie said softly then she turned.

Her footsteps receded and he was alone again. Only this time, he held a large knife in his hand.

• • • • •

ANNA ENTERED THE BARN TO find Bess with a noose around her neck that was attached to one of the rafters. She laughed to herself at the sight of Bess' bare feet. Her toes that extended down and stretched out as if they begged aloud to remain in contact with the box that stood between her and eternity amused Anna to no end. She also delighted in the fact that Flicker had clearly adjusted the coarse rope just taut enough to scratch flesh and constrict blood but not enough to choke her dead outright.

This was what Anna lived for. She was born to the hunt, especially of those already corralled. Her artistry was the slow burn of suffering

When Arthur sulked his way into the barn behind his mother, Bess spit the gag out of her mouth.

"I ne'er took no nothing with that Samson," she cried out desperately.

Piglet came over and teased her with a flick to the box from his boot, which made Bess briefly have to stretch even further on her tiptoes to not choke.

"I seen them togetha," she gurgled.

Flicker steadied the box with his own boot and looked up at her.

"Seen who and seen 'em what?" he asked curiously.

"Don't listen to her," Anna ordered with some panic in her voice.

"They's nekid and in bed," Bess gasped in what seemed to Anna to be an effort to exchange information for her release from this noose by the men.

"Get a ladder and put that gag back on . . . now!" Anna yelled.

In her mind, she was unsure who she was more angered by. She expected little from Piglet. Flicker, however, was supposed to be the toughest of overseers. Apparently, he could not even tie a gag tight around a negro's mouth.

Arthur, who stood behind her with sunken shoulders lower than his knees, was just as irksome.

"I'm surrounded by weak men," she muttered inside. "And I always have been."

"Massa Arthur and Samson, they's be doing somethin' with they bodies . . ." Anna's attention was brought back into focus as Bess called out with desperation.

Does this foolish girl really think her words or any of these men will save her from my decision? Anna asked herself in disbelief.

She still had Buck's gun in her hands. She thought about how she could let it rip off and put this negro woman into the ground right now. But then she would deny Arthur the chance to look whole in front of the others. More importantly, this action would ruin her plan to make this morning's tragedy into something of a triumph. *No,* she thought. *Lanark is more important than the temporary joy I'll get from seeing one Black girl bleed.*

Piglet grunted as he picked up a folded step ladder from nearby and approached Bess.

"Massa Arthur and Samson, they's be doing somethin' with they's bodies . . ." Bess called out to Piglet as he made his way closer to her rung by rung.

Anna saw the faces of Flicker and Piglet contort with confusion.

"Do I have to climb up there my damn self?" Anna growled with frustration.

Within seconds, Piglet had secured the gag back in Bess' mouth and Anna sighed on the inside with relief. On the outside though, she laughed aloud. "Damn simpleton . . . She'd not know a naked man's doings from a cock fight."

The men still looked perplexed, so she continued through a chuckle. "Besides, her kind would say anything to save themselves from the fate she brought upon herself this very morning."

That seemed to her to abate their questions, so she came closer to the men. "Now you two go and get that Samson boy. Mr. Buchanan, the master of this plantation, is going to see to this girl himself."

Flicker and Piglet exchanged looks again. Anna could not tell if it was looks of doubt that Arthur would do the deed or of disappointment that they would not get to enjoy the show.

"Don't you worry," she teased them. "She will be halfway to hell by the time y'all come back."

The men followed her orders, leaving Bess alone with Anna and Arthur. Anna saw Bess look down at her son intently as if without the use of words Arthur could still be persuaded to free the slave woman.

She knew she had to act quickly or her son would not execute her plan precisely.

"Here's where you set your legacy, Arthur Buchanan," Anna urged. "It starts right here and right now."

Anna walked over to her Arthur and nudged him forward with the butt of the shotgun.

"Go on," she directed him.

When Arthur didn't move at all, Anna lost her patience. "Do it!" she hollered at him.

"I can't," Arthur replied. His eyes watered as if he were the one strung up.

Anna's eyes widened when her son turned to walk away. *Like hell you won't*, she thought in her mind. She positioned her body as a blockade to his path.

"You will kick that box out from under that bitch right now lest she tell-tale all over this county about how you lay with a Black boy!" her voice thundered with fury.

With no more restraint, she lifted the gun up and aimed it at Arthur. "Be a man!" she exhorted, but her son's slow tears turned to a flood.

"Oh Christ!" Anna yelled to herself then she pulled back on the gun's trigger and a flash of gunfire erupted.

Arthur screamed out as Anna's jaw dropped in disbelief at her own quick action. She looked past Arthur and watched quietly as the blood oozed across the stomach of Bess' dress. The bullet had flown right past Arthur's ear and straight into the slave girl's body. Her hands shook from the kick of the gun, so Anna tossed it onto the barn floor at Arthur's feet.

In a state of delirium, she saw Flicker and Piglet return. Their mouths gaped as they looked at the gun that lay beside Arthur and then at the sight of Bess.

"He really did it?" Piglet asked with great surprise to Flicker and the men stood there transfixed.

"Well?" Anna asked them at last. "Why isn't the boy with you?"

Flicker took his hat off and hung his head. "He's gone."

Pain appeared to register on Arthur's face at the words.

"Gone?!" she asked wildly.

"We went back to the root cellar and he'd pried it open with a knife we found on the floor," he answered.

"Then what in the hell are you doing standing here like a bunch of dumbfounded fools?" Anna barked. "Get the dogs and go get him!"

Flicker and Piglet grabbed whips off of the barn's wall and ran outside.

"And as for you, Arthur Buchanan." Anna turned to her son.

He looked at her and Anna was surprised to find what appeared to be conviction in his eyes for the first time today. "I'm sorry, Mother," he said strongly.

"Perhaps this will all be settled right now." Anna nodded in feigned forgiveness.

Her son came up closer to her and put his hand on her shoulder. Though Anna's instinct was to recoil, she held firm; the taste of owning Lanark ever so close.

"I can see now I have made a right mess of everything," Arthur continued.

"They all think you shot Bess, and Samson will soon be dead alongside her. Then we all can move forward with the rest of our day in peace," she answered coolly.

"I think it best if I go and find Samson myself, don't you?" he questioned.

Do you have the stomach? she wondered.

"I'll take care of all of this once and for good," Arthur replied then he picked the gun up at his feet to follow after Flicker and Piglet.

"Thank goodness." Anna smiled. *He is finally becoming a man.*

She walked over to Bess who still clung to life. The slave girl stared down from above, her with eyes full of terror.

"It's all over now, Bess," Anna said sweetly. She pulled back her leg and swung it hard until it kicked the wooden box right out from under Bess' feet.

Her body dangled wildly but could do nothing to fight against the strength of the rope and the distance between her feet, and the matted, and urine-soaked hay of the barn floor.

"Go straight to hell," Anna's words dripped with hatred then she turned and walked away.

Something unseen before had stirred in her son. He hadn't seemed prior to this moment to inherit any of her grit or determination. But alas, Arthur appeared to be resolute he was going to kill Samson, and set things right. Unknown to anyone but herself, "right" to Anna meant simply that after the deed was done, Arthur would be off to the Clarksons and she would never have to deal with any man's foolishness again.

She left the barn and headed toward the house.

"I think it's best I go and see for myself," she mumbled under her breath.

When she reached the back of the house, she could see from steps away that the root cellar door was wide open.

"Didn't those two mudsills bother to look for anything that could be used for escape before they locked him in?" She shook her head and huffed while she descended.

There, in the doorway she found the knife.

"This is no workman's tool," she said aloud while she bent to pick it up. Anna examined it closer. "No, this is a good kitchen knife for chopping and dicing."

Anna held the knife down at her side then put her other hand on her chin and rubbed.

"Hmm," she hummed to herself in deep thought. "This will need to be returned in good time to its rightful owner."

Bluetick Hounds

Samson's lungs burned from how fast he had run once he broke free from the root cellar. Although Hattie had passed him the knife for other purposes, his instinct to survive kicked in hard. He shimmied that root cellar door open with it as if it had cut through soft butter, then he tore some clothing off the line out back and ran for the woods.

Mason County, though slave territory through and through, was rumored to not be far from Ohio, where the owning of men and women was said to be illegal. But not far seemed like forever when one had to run for their lives. Besides, while Samson had spent his entire life at Lanark, he did not know the distance from Kentucky to Ohio no more than he knew the Constitution from the Franklin Primer Arthur used to sit on the porch and read to him when they were children. Nevertheless, desperation urged him forward to where there was the slightest of hope that he could avoid death and reach freedom.

I's wonder what they do to Artha? he thought to himself as he ran. *All that talk of his and yet he was powerless when his momma came through the door.*

"I'm like to neva see him again . . . or Minerva . . . or any of them folks at Lanark."

Poppa Blue's warnings came to his mind. He told him never to trust, but trust he did. And while Arthur might have been different just as Samson had claimed, he was a fool to think he would end up anywhere other than as cotton fertilizer.

"That's the diff'rence 'tween Artha and me." He considered between huffs. "He's like to now sittin' with his feet up bein' scolded by Missus Anna and I's like to swing by his same momma's hands."

Though Samson's legs had yet to slow down in the thirty or forty minutes since he fled, his body could not keep up this pace much longer. When he cleared a pasture of grazing milk cows, he moved into some trees for cover then slowed his pace to catch his breath.

Think, Samson, he said to himself. *Which way is north?*

He remembered fingers that pointed out how to follow the sun in the day and the moon and stars at night. Though few had been brave enough to ever try it, talk about how to escape was common around the tables of all the slaves' cabins.

The idea of what would finally motivate someone to run for it seemed funnier at the time than now. Samson reflected on how he, like all enslaved people, let folks like the Buchanan's do what they did to them on a daily basis, and it now became a true wonder that more had not risked it all and ran forth day and night for the safety of the north.

"This way," he decided. Then he headed through the trees and he worked to quickly sort through and piece together all of the rumors and whispered conversations he had listened to during his two decades in this world.

The river, he thought through a furrowed brow and he remembered a recent conversation between two slave men about the fast-moving stream they said ran between Ohio and Kentucky.

"Enter that water and you come out the other side baptized anew as your own man," one had said to the other.

"Any kinda man ought to be betta than a dead man . . . save owned. They be almost the same thing," he whispered to himself then he pressed onward in the direction he hoped was correct.

• • • • •

ARTHUR RODE OFF HARD TO catch up with Flicker and Piglet. They were not difficult to follow as the bluetick hounds they had departed with bayed and yipped like they were a Sunday church bell on a tall white steeple. With his thighs gripped to the horse tightly as it cantered and galloped toward their calls, Arthur deliberated in his mind on the best way to join their party.

When I catch up, I will take the show from the front, he said to himself. Arthur knew that Flicker and Piglet would be resistant to Arthur's leadership, but he was certain there was no other way what needed to be done would be handled right if he didn't exert some authority from the jump.

"I was foolish to think this would all play out in silence," he mumbled aloud. "But like mother- I too- can be decisive when it necessitates."

He felt the weight of the shotgun in his hands and held it tightly when the horse landed its hooves on the hard ground. At last, he could see the men across a small field and he yelled out to them to wait until he was at their side.

"Mister Arthur?" Piglet asked as he wide-eyed the shotgun.

"I am glad you have not found him yet," Arthur replied firmly.

He felt Flicker gaze up at him from the ground. He knew the driver tried to ascertain if Arthur was here to help or harm their search.

"We believe he's gone this way," Flicker relented at last.

"Then let's move forward," Arthur commanded. The two exchanged looks, nodding before they fell in line behind Arthur and his horse.

"You mean to take him dead or alive, young Master Buchanan?" Flicker asked from alongside the mare.

"I mean to take him," was all that Arthur replied, though he sounded more resolute than his racing heart let on.

After some time, Piglet yelled out from some trees that the trail ran "this way," and they all tore off in that direction, man and canines alike.

Give me the strength to do what I must, Arthur prayed in his mind. He knew the hour had come and that what he did now would be remembered far and wide. He couldn't make mistakes as there would be no second chances.

Do it! he yelled to himself as if he were once again a captain on the green that led his team in a winning play. "Forward," he urged his horse and she obeyed.

● ● ● ● ●

THE SOUND OF THE COON dogs that bayed in the distance told Samson that he had not run fast or far enough as until he reached the river; he was a hunted beast. So once again, he picked up his pace and ran like his life depended on it.

Every few feet, he turned his head back to look over his shoulders.

How close they be? he wondered to himself, but the question left him vulnerable, for his mind did not ascertain the bigger threat that existed in front of him when he entered a small grove of bald cypress.

As the bawls of the bluetick hounds grew closer, Samson gazed backward while in front of him, the toes on his right foot clipped the knee of a large cypress' roots that grew up wildly above the ground. He fell forward hard, which caused the skin of his shin to rub right off upon its impact with the uneven earth. Not afforded the luxury of pain, Samson dragged himself over to one of the larger tree trunks and sat down with his back against it.

"This is it," he groaned aloud. "I'm good as dead now."

Behind him the barks and ticks increased with intensity.

"The dogs smell something close," he heard Piglet yell from some-where behind him.

"Easy now, Piglet," Flicker's voice grew close. "That boy's like to be like a cornered bear."

Samson sucked up all the breath his lungs could capture and held it. Maybe if he told his body to not exist, if he stopped breathing and slowed his heart rate even, then the dogs and men would pass him by and he would be safe for another moment. Twigs snapped loudly and Samson knew nothing he could do would stop himself from being found if he just sat there, so he leapt up. He could not chance his life to wishes and make believe. Those dogs were about to take a piece of his flesh and that would be the sweetest part because what followed next would be far worse than a bite or even death itself.

With all the might he had left inside, Samson propelled his body for-ward and he ran and ran with abandon. Within a few seconds, he made it to a small field where he pushed his body hard through its long grass as if he were a newborn that pushed to burst through his mother's loins and into the world. Gunfire rang out and dirt shot up into the air where a bullet landed in the ground next to him.

"You can't handle that boy alone," he heard someone yell out over the sound of thundering hooves.

Then the bay-colored nose of a horse passed by Samson's body that sprinted with all its might.

There was no point in running any further now. He could not outpace a horse. No, he must accept it. He was caught.

As Samson slowed his broken body to a stop, he suddenly felt some-one's arm reach down from the horse and grab him strongly by the clothes around his neck. The person then yanked him up so hard and with such force, that Samson's feet lifted off of the ground and his frame hoisted up into the air with the potency of speed from the saddled beast that did not slow. Within seconds, he was in the air no longer but rather his body laid across the saddle as if he were but a blanket, thrown in front of his captor's body with no control over his own.

"Dead," was the word that pounded through his head with each thrust of the charger. But the horse did not slow and though Samson's body jostled about, he could still hear over the sound of hooves the fading calls of Flicker and Piglet who yelled out repeatedly in concern.

"Mister Arthur?"

"Mister Arthur!"

• • • • •

ANNA ROCKED BACK AND FORTH in a chair on the porch with a lantern at her feet. It was late. Later than she cared to think, as Arthur should have been back long ago with that boy's body.

Yips in the distance caused her to stand up and she rushed to the steps and held her light out high.

"Where the hell is Arthur?" she demanded to know as her jaw set firm at the sight of an exhausted looking Flicker and Piglet who dragged themselves into view.

"He ran ahead of the dogs," Piglet cried out as if he begged for forgiveness.

"What does that mean?" Anna pressed.

"I suspect that boy got a hold of Mister Arthur and the gun he had with him," Flicker elaborated.

"Got a hold of?" Anna's voice began to boil in disbelief.

"I suspect he's hostage to that boy now and he's taking him north as a way to ensure the safety of his passage."

"And you two coots simply let him go and came back here with your asses between your knees?" her anger frothed over.

"What else could we do?" Piglet squealed.

Anna's head felt as if it were going to burst.

"Nelson!" she screamed. When the response did not come quick enough, she yelled out louder and this time with a fury even Satan might have run from.

The door to the house flew open and Nelson rushed outside.

"Yes, Missus Anna?" he asked obediently.

"Fetch me some paper and a quill," she ordered.

He was gone quicker than he had come. She turned back to Flicker and Piglet and growled at them. "Tell Ellis, in the stable, to come round with a horse for Nelson."

They nodded as Nelson reappeared from the house with the items Anna had demanded.

"You will take a note over to Mr. Clarkson's for me, since I can't trust these two imbeciles to do anything right," she fumed as she yanked the quill and paper from Nelson's hands.

"Tell him that I'll need more men and his dogs, as they'll be fresh for the hunt compared to ours that have been wasted."

"Yes, Missus Anna," Nelson whispered.

"Tell him also that I will need him to come here and lead Flicker and Piglet back out on their trail tonight."

"Yes, Missus Anna," he said again while she put the paper on the rail and wrote furiously.

"Once they find that son of mine," Anna stormed to herself. "I will make sure that every man, woman, and child from here to Bosley's Station sees that boy hanging from the highest tree." She smiled to herself at the thought. "It will be a celebration like none other, and we will feast under his body while the crows pluck at his flesh."

"Now get!" she commanded. She folded the paper and slammed it into Nelson's open palm.

"As for you two." She glared at Flicker and Piglet. "You best do every-thing that Mr. Clarkson tells you, for I'm not certain there's a place for either of you at this farm if my son and that bastard are not brought back here to me."

Anna did not wait for their response, but she turned and walked back into the house. All of the day's madness left her sleepy. Yes, her son was out there captive to a runaway negro, but maybe that boy would save her the trouble of having to deal with Arthur herself. Though she was angered by the thought of any of the Lanark slaves thinking they could run, she knew all outcomes looked good for her desire to fully claim the plantation.

As she approached the stairs, Anna heard murmurs in the parlor.

"Best to stay clear of her for now," Hattie's whispers carried through the house. "I's never thought he would use it break free from the cella' . . ."

The hushed tones fell silent and then Mae rounded the corner and nearly bumped into Anna.

"Oh," the old woman exclaimed as she smoothed her apron. "I didn't see you none, Missus Anna." There was a nervousness in her voice Anna had not heard before. She contemplated for a second how to respond. Should she shake the slave woman until her frail bones broke with whatever truth she concealed?

No, Anna thought to herself. *That's not enough to reclaim what has been lost here.*

"I'll be goin' this way," the old woman pointed to the back of the house. "'Less you be needin' anything, Missus Anna," she stammered. "Cuppa tea maybe?"

"I'm fixing to lay my head down for a bit," Anna replied coolly. "But have Hattie bring me up a tray in the morning as I don't think I'm fit to sit at the table until my son's been returned to me."

"Yes, ma'am," Mae said then she backed out of the entry hall. Anna stood there at the base of the stairs for a moment. *No*, she thought to herself again as she began her ascent. *A dressing down for one old lady would not be enough.* The balance of power had shifted in Anna's house and she had been blindly unaware. She knew for certain she would need to act decisively to reassert her dominance and the perfect plan began to form in her mind.

• • • • •

GIDEON CLARKSON HAD SURVIVED AN uprising. In fact, he was the only slave owner in Mason County to have hunted down and caught a runaway slave in the last two years. Granted, he had Buck Buchanan's help at the time. Nevertheless, having lived through one successful hunt, he wondered not why Anna Buchanan reached out to him for assistance.

Once Clarkson had received Anna's note, he moved into action. Clarkson feared the news of Samson's escape, especially if successful, could reignite the rebellion he had only recently put down. If he had anything in common with the late Buck, it was his strong belief that slavery was an outright Christian institution. The way God was over man was the same way man was over all other creatures, and the savages of Africa were akin to the lions and leopards he knew the savannah yielded.

There was another reason beyond God that Gideon knew why he must come to the rescue. He had struck a deal with Anna Buchanan that her son would be his son. Gillie was all he had left now that his wife had passed away. She had given him no son of his own to tend the farm when he aged and none to leave the land and his legacy to either.

Clarkson's marriage had been transactional. He took the hand of Prudence for the sum of 1,000 Kentucky Banknotes that he used to buy their estate. True, Prudence was taken with him, but Gideon wanted power that came from wealth and marrying Prudence who came from one of the most actively Protestant families meant he would get money and status. Gideon was prepared to provide at least as much for his daughter Gillie. So, when Anna Buchanan had strangely offered up acreage and her son's parentage in a marital arrangement, Clarkson was determined to do anything to see this deal through and if that meant he had to hunt and murder that damn runaway in order to prevent the loss of this reverse dowry, he would do it twice over if necessary.

Clarkson gathered his two most loyal slaves, Tobias and Cato. Both had helped on the hunt with Buck before and he knew their experience would be helpful. Afterall, who best to tell what an animal will do than another of its kind.

Once his boys had packed his horse with rope, torches, and water bags for the long game, Clarkson mounted the Andalusian Bay he had inherited from an uncle who had died in Texas last year. Rifle in hand, Gideon rode out with Tobias and Cato behind him. They were on foot and held two leashed dogs a piece in each of their hands.

Gideon had few beliefs, but he held those tightly. Those boiled down to these two tenets: God was watching and he was a jealous being. Man's role was to do what was expected. Toil the earth; marry and reproduce; attend Church on Sundays; and preserve the hierarchy, or social order, that had been established. The latter of these he felt most strongly about. It was not for man to counter the will of God.

Black bears, as Gideon often referred to them in his mind, were not quite human. More akin to their namesake animals. They bred like rabbits and their bodies were made for the hard work of the fields, yet they tried everything they could think of to avoid their station. They were lazy and were apt to hibernate more than half the year if given the opportunity. And though he was not known to be as harsh as Anna Buchanan in his treatment of their kind, he understood why she would be inclined to treat them strongly and found no fault in the stories of her actions that had trickled over to his own land throughout the years they had been neighbors.

Flicker and Piglet were in the stables when Clarkson arrived at Lanark. Anna was nowhere in sight. He didn't linger long, as Anna's men, though they looked worse for the wear than Clarkson expected, were ready and mounted within seconds.

Off they headed into the night in an attempt to pick up the trail of the runaway and his captured master.

"The balls that boar has to take one of us hostage," Gideon remarked to Flicker as they rode side by side toward the woods.

"We need to take care of this quick," Flicker urged Clarkson. "We do not know what, if any, news of the boy's actions might have already spread to the cabins."

No more words were needed as the implications were clear, so Clarkson kicked his horse on the sides with his heels. It launched forward with great urgency and speed.

• • • • •

ARTHUR RODE HIS OWN HORSE with Samson sitting upright in front of him. He leaned his head on top of Samson's shoulder and whispered in his ear.

"It's been a few hours. I think we have lost them, for now at least."

He heard Samson exhale with some measure of relief. The moon was full and Arthur saw its reflection twinkle off of a small pond of water nearby. He drew the horse to a stop and slid off.

"Let's rest up here for a few minutes." He led the horse to the water and it began drinking voraciously. "She needs to fill up for a minute before we press on," he informed as he stroked the horse's now extended neck.

Samson slid down next and stood beside him.

"What are you doing?" he asked Arthur with agitation in his voice. Samson's timbre startled him.

"What do you mean what am I doing?" Arthur asked with some measure of surprise.

"I's mean exactly what I's ask," Samson pressed. "Why are you with me? What is in your mind?"

"I'm running north with you," Arthur retorted. "Isn't that much obvious?"

"And then what?" Samson continued pushing.

Arthur sighed. "Freedom."

"For who?" came the reply.

"For us both, if I'm honest," Arthur said softly as he looked away to watch the horse drink.

Samson reached out and put his hand on Arthur's shoulder.

"I's am thankful that you came when you did, but I's don't rightly understand why you are doing this with me, Artha," Samson confessed. "Give me your horse. Then you can turn 'round."

"What?" Arthur could hardly believe his ears. How could Samson be saying this to him.

"You can say I's forced you," Samson continued. "Go home. Get married. Live a rich life as Lanark's master and no one will be the wiser 'fore anything other than a slave that escaped."

"But . . ." Arthur stammered. He turned back to face Samson who was mere inches from him. "But . . . I love you."

The words were out there and they clung to the air like a heavy mist.

Arthur looked into Samson's eyes. He wondered deeply what his response would be.

"Is that enough though, Artha?" Samson challenged softly.

"Yes." Arthur was emphatic. "We are going to get to the Ohio River and swim across together . . ."

Samson put his hand up and cut him off. "-and then what?"

The silence screamed.

"We gonna live happily eva after, like man and wife?" Samson roared.

The horse suddenly stopped its drinking and looked up.

"Easy girl," Arthur said while he patted its neck.

The mare stepped back nervously and snorted. Then after a moment, she calmed down and stepped forward to return to her drink.

"I'm not exactly sure what it will be like," Arthur began explaining. "We will be together. That's all I know." He started to talk excitedly, "I could get a job. We could get a house. You can pretend you are my paid servant, and . . ."

"And we could go on livin' the way things been 'fore youse come home," Samson interrupted again. "I's still be a servant to a white man. Still answering to his needs."

Silence returned.

"I'm sorry, Samson," Arthur apologized. "I didn't really think about it like that."

"Did you eva once stop to ask what it is that I's want here?" Samson admonished Arthur who swallowed hard at the rebuke.

"I only ever meant to . . ." he tried to continue but could not find the words.

"You and your ideas, Artha Buchana' 'bout how we all the same. How we all gots choices. So, I'm makin' mine. I's break north, Artha, and I's ain't neva gonna be no man's servant, white or Black, eva again."

Arthur felt the warmth from Samson's hand on his shoulder.

"Love or no love," Samson finished softly.

"You are right," Arthur whispered. "I can see that now."

"I's make it to the otha side, I'm gonna learn me a trade and earn my own keep." Arthur noticed how Samson's head seemed to stand higher as he spoke and he mused on the fact that even with death in pursuit, the tie that bound all humanity was the belief in tomorrow and Samson still held onto that belief even now.

"I love you enough to know that you deserve that," Arthur said. "A right to own yourself and your future."

Arthur believed what he said to be true, but the lump in his throat at the thought of Samson not feeling the same about him pinched his heart just the same.

As if on cue, Samson answered Arthur's thoughts.

"I feel for you too though, Artha." Samson squeezed his shoulder tightly. "And no matter this side of the Ohio River or that, I's do want to be with you."

Hope rose in Arthur's heart at these words.

"You do?" he asked in surprise.

"Yes," Samson said sternly. "But as a man, not as a piece of property."

Arthur swelled with elation at the power behind Samson's words. Before he knew it, he had leaned forward and pressed his lips against Samson's. Whether it was fear, hope, or adrenaline- they kissed passionately alongside the pond's edge. The kiss was broken when the horse began to stomp her feet loudly between snorts and blows. Suddenly, a large fish broke up from the water and sailed into the air. When it landed back in the pond, a loud splash followed. Spooked, the horse reared back on its hind legs and kicked its front feet into the air then turned.

Arthur dived to the ground in an attempt to recapture the reins that had slipped from his hands in the chaos, but it was too late. He landed with a thud. The horse took off into the darkness with Arthur's shotgun stowed in the pack tied to the saddlebags.

"Shit!" Arthur yelled out into the night.

Samson's eyes stared back at him filled with terror that Arthur now also felt on the inside.

"We best hightail it now," he said with a quaking voice. "Without a horse to run with or a gun to fight, who knows how bad things could get or how quickly."

So, Arthur led their way into the dark, guided by the moon and the stars up above.

"We can be there by sometime tomorrow if we keep to moving," Arthur chirped in an effort to calm them both, but inside he knew the unspoken. "Tomorrow is too far away."

It wasn't long before exhaustion set in, so when they spied a large boulder along a ridge, they decided to sit up against it for a rest.

"You go ahead and sleep for a bit," Arthur said, as he laid Samson's head in his lap. "I'll keep watch and listen for any signs then wake you after a spell."

"Thank you," Samson yawned, and there was the light sound of his snores within seconds.

In the darkness, Arthur considered the path forward. With the moon being so bright, they ought to be able to make it a good distance once Samson had a small chance to recover.

Follow the tree line in these woods until we go through the mountain pass, then we will edge those handful of farms that are left standing between us and the river, he thought to himself. *Might take more than a day now that I think on it, so we just as soon get a move on it.*

But the events of the day, and all that had transpired, weighed heavy on Arthur's eyelids and not more than a minute or two after Samson had fallen asleep, his eyes closed and his head fell forward into slumber.

Baptism

The first signs of daybreak cast the slightest of golden hues across Anna's bedroom. The door rattled open, and in walked Hattie with a tray of food. Anna sat up in her bed and watched her rotund slave place it on the dresser before she walked to the sheer curtains and drew them back fully so that sunlight spilled inside.

"Oh, Missus Anna," Hattie exclaimed when she turned around. "I's didn't expect you to be sat up already. I's figured I'd need to wake you, bein' it's so early and all."

"You thought I'd be asleep?" Anna questioned, sarcasm edging her words. "My son's been kidnapped by a boy who escaped from our root cellar mere seconds before he was about to be killed. Sleep is not high on my list of priorities."

Hattie poured some tea into a cup on the tray and added a dash of milk from a small pitcher and stirred. Anna eyed her as she placed the cup and then a plate of eggs onto a small table in the corner of the room then pulled over a chair for her to sit in.

"I's have your breffus set up, Missus Anna," Hattie said sweetly. "Come on ova and I'll butter your toast for you."

Anna grimaced. She reached under the pillow on her bed to see if it was still there. She felt the inlaid cherrywood against her fingers and smiled.

"I'll take it over here, Hattie," Anna instructed through a smile.

Hattie took up the cup and saucer and began to walk toward Anna.

"No," she barked. "Not only the tea. Bring me the entire tray. I'll have my breakfast right here in this bed."

Hattie placed the tea and then the plate of eggs back onto the tray she first walked into the room with, then she started to walk to the bed.

"Yes." Anna smiled. "Right here."

With her one hand still under the pillow she motioned across her legs with the other. The slave woman smiled and placed the tray down across Anna's lap. Suddenly, before Hattie could withdraw her own hands, Anna pulled her other out from under the pillow and swung it up high in the air. In one fell swoop, the knife Anna had found in the cellar, the same knife that Hattie had given to Samson to kill himself, flew down with enormous force and pierced through Hattie's hand, pinning her flesh to the tray and right through to the bed below.

Hattie screamed in horrible pain into Anna's ear.

Anna leapt from the bed. She felt like a volcano and the tray's contents flew in every direction as if lava and ash from her eruption.

"I should have had you gutted the minute Mr. Buchanan brought you into my house those ten years ago. But in my mercy, I only took that bastard child that you carried from him from you and not your own damn life," she shrieked.

Anna delighted at the sight of the blood that poured out of Hattie's hand. She laughed maddeningly then she moved toward the bedroom door. As she got close, she reached into her dressing gown pocket and frantically pulled out a key.

"Once I saw that kitchen knife, I knew that it was you who helped that boy get free," she hissed violently across the room.

Hattie sobbed. "No."

"All those whispers in the hallways, that skulking about and hiding in your bedroom did you no good, as it was clear as day you knew all along what was happening here but you said naught."

"I's didn't expect him to escape," Hattie protested between tears.

"Spare me, bitch," Anna spat. "When my son is returned to me, I'll see Flicker and Piglet pass you around all the men in the county before they slit you from throat to cunt for crossing me again, you damned ignorant cow."

Anna pulled the door behind her with all the strength she had and it slammed so hard that the walls shook. She put the key into the lock and turned it till it clicked.

"You can rot in that room until then!" she screamed through the door, then she stormed down the stairs, ready to find the rest of the Lanark house's slaves.

Mae was in the kitchen when Anna entered. Her hands were wrist deep in the biscuit dough she kneaded.

"Good morning, Missus Anna," the old woman began to say, but Anna grabbed Mae by her hair from behind and pulled with all her might.

"I'd yank every single one of these gray and white bits out of your head," she hissed coldly. "Except I need you if I still plan to eat." She released

Mae's locs and pushed her forward so that the bowl flew off the counter and smashed into a thousand pieces.

"You've never done much of anything too wrong that I'm aware of up till now," Anna scolded. "Yes, I have had to discipline you on occasion, but that's only because your kind are prone to reverting to your animalistic ways without the stern rod of Christian guidance. So, I'm inclined to believe it was a mistake, and I'll assume this was a momentary lapse of judgment that will never happen again," Anna lectured. "Because if there is a next time, I'm going to have someone chop you up for stew and serve your flesh down at the cabins for all you Black bastards to sup on."

"Yes, ma'am," Mae whimpered.

"Good," Anna sighed. "Then clean up this mess and we will restart our day in this household."

Anna had decided Nelson likely was unaware of the doings of Samson and Arthur. A man of any breed was bound to protest loudly whenever a sodomite was rumored. She could not imagine he would not have told her immediately if he had discovered the nature of that Samson boy. Besides, she couldn't incapacitate all of her negroes at once or she would be forced to tend the house herself, and that was something Anna was just not willing to do under any circumstances.

"Nelson!" she yelled out. He came into the kitchen from his bedroom in seconds. Anna watched him as he looked down at the shattered bowl and then to Mae with tears in her eyes and dough all over her hands.

"Yes, Missus Anna?" he asked cautiously.

"There have been some unfortunate events in this household," she began to lecture. "To put it plainly, Bess is dead."

The two slaves looked at each other.

"There's more."

Tension filled the room.

"Hattie's services won't be needed any longer as well, and you already know about Samson's fate once he is captured."

"Yes, Missus Anna," Nelson whispered.

"What I mean to say is that I'm going to need at least two new negroes for this house and I don't have time to go to market, especially since I want us to plan for a feast."

"A feast?" Mae asked with surprise.

"That's right," Anna nodded. "We are going to have a jubilee celebration that fetes the freedom of Lanark from all rebellion."

"Celebration?" Mae still looked confused.

"Do I need to spell it out, old girl?" Anna chastised. "We will host an engagement party for Arthur to Gillie Clarkson and we will finish the event off with a public hanging and a champagne toast on the front lawn where Samson's body will sway from the big tree in decoration."

Mae gasped.

"No time for sentiments," Anna snipped. "I'll make a list of the dishes I want you to prepare. Nelson will take invitations to the other farms. But first, I need each of you to give me a name of one or two boys and girls we can try out up at the house during the preparations and service."

Nelson and Mae exchanged glances again.

"Don't look back and forth like you are some sort of imbeciles! Give me the names of some slaves you can put to work so Nelson can go fetch them before he goes to town. I'll hold you both responsible that the selected negroes are trained and ready."

The two rushed to come up with referrals and Anna set them both to their tasks then went to the porch to scan the horizon for any sign of the men's return.

• • • • •

IT WAS BALD DAYLIGHT WHEN Samson's eyes opened. His eyes looked up at tree tops and he remembered he was in the woods on his way to the river. He sat up and found Arthur beside him laid flat out in some leaves. He was sound asleep so Samson shook him.

"Artha!" Samson said with alarm. "What happened?"

Arthur opened his eyes and his forehead wrinkled up in a frown.

"I must have fallen asleep." He wiped some drool off his lower lip and sat up quickly.

"I am so sorry." There was great alarm in his voice now and he leapt up and offered a hand to Samson who took it and pulled until he was also upright.

"No point arguin' 'bout it now." Samson shook his head. "It's daytime and we best move."

Arthur nodded and pointed. "This way."

The two men dashed quickly through the trees. Samson wondered if anyone still searched for them at all, and if so, how close they might be.

He stopped and held his hand out for Arthur to do the same.

"What is it?" Arthur asked.

"Shhh," Samson replied and he lifted his ear toward the wind where the sound of a dog's howl carried on the morning air.

The hair on the back of Samson's neck stuck straight up. "They're close," he blurted out, panic on his breath.

"Hurry," Arthur instructed and he followed him down a deer trail that ran through a cluster of pine trees.

Oh lawd, Samson pleaded in his mind. *Please, oh, please let me get to the otha side of that river!*

And their steps became strides and their strides became runs. But the sound of dogs now multiplied.

• • • • •

CLARKSON LOOKED DOWN AT TOBIAS and Cato who struggled to keep hold of the dogs as they strained at their leashes and howled with great fury.

We got that boy, Gideon thought to himself and smiled.

"There is definitely something up ahead!" Flicker shouted and pointed.

Clarkson's eyes strained through the trees and he could make out the shape of something brown moving within them.

"Steady now," he commanded to his two slave men.

Flicker and Piglet broke off, each moved toward opposite sides.

"We've got you surrounded, boy!" Clarkson yelled out. "Let your master go and it will be easier for you," he coaxed.

There was only the sound of the dogs barking as they yearned to be let loose.

"Easy," he ordered the others. "We don't want to scare him into harming the Buchanan boy."

Clarkson got down from his horse and grabbed his rifle. Once it was loaded, he pulled the hammer back and nodded to Flicker and Piglet, who also dismounted and carried their guns.

The trio began to gingerly approach.

"On my signal," he whispered to the other men.

"One step, two steps," he counted quietly before he yelled out. "Now!"

He rushed forward, as did the others, until he burst into a small clearing, as the dogs were released from their leashes and ran to the chase.

"Don't move!" Clarkson yelled as he lifted his gun into the air, ready to shoot Samson on sight. Only, Samson was nowhere to be seen. In the clearing stood Arthur's horse. It barely looked up from the clover it chewed on the ground. The dogs stopped their barking and looped around the grassy knoll then laid down next to the horse.

Clarkson looked at Flicker who looked at Piglet who looked back at Clarkson. All were dumbfounded.

"Dammit to hell!" Flicker shouted.

"That's Arthur's horse," Piglet finally informed Clarkson.

"Hmm," he said as he lowered the gun and released the hammer until it was gently secured once more. "That can only mean they are on foot. And that means it's just a matter of when, not if, till we catch up."

Cato and Tobias soon caught up and brought with them the three horses the men had left behind.

"It's alright," Clarkson said. "We got the upper hand now."

So, Gideon instructed Anna's men to remount and told his slaves to gather the dogs back up.

"We will have this wrapped up shortly so let's just get back on the trail. It should be easy from here."

After a few minutes, the dogs in Cato's hands seemed to pick up a scent.

"Let's keep moving," Clarkson commanded once more, and the posse headed back into the trees.

• • • • •

ANNA SAT BESIDE NELSON IN the wagon. She held her head high. It was topped in a red hat with a white plume that captured the light of the midday sun.

"Pull right in front of Hadler's," she directed him.

When the wagon pulled to a stop, she handed Nelson a long list. "This is just for the dry goods," she stated. "I need to pick up a few other items up and down the main street, so I'll leave you to make sure nothing on this list is missing and it's all loaded into the back before I return."

Anna stepped down out of the wagon and marched off through the dusty road of the town until she reached the dress shop that recently opened.

"May I help you?" a blonde woman in her forties asked as she stepped out from a room in the back, but Anna hardly heard her. Her eyes were filled with such wonder at the beauty of the creations she saw displayed around the small store that her ears were shut down.

"Ma'am?" the woman asked again. "Do you need help?"

"Oh, yes," Anna laughed at last. "I'm looking for some fine fabric for dresses to be worn at a wedding."

"Ah," the woman smiled. "This way, Mrs.?"

"Buchanan," Anna replied with a smile. "Mrs. Anna Buchanan. But please, call me Anna."

"Oh." The saleswoman's face fell. "Are you the Buchanan's with the runaway slave?"

Anna seethed that the news had spread so quickly, and to strangers even at that.

"Not for much longer." She smiled nervously. "Expect all will come to its rightful conclusion shortly, if it hasn't already."

"Is it true that the boy kidnapped your son as well?"

A hot flash crept up the back of Anna's neck. "My Arthur can handle himself. If he couldn't, do you think I would be here ready to spend a small fortune on his wedding clothes?"

At the word "fortune," the saleswoman smoothed the front of her dress as if to say, "I'd rather have a full register than a mind that is full of idle gossip." She took Anna by the arm and led her to a cabinet that was filled with bolts of fine patterned silks and satins.

"I keep these for my most discernible clients," she flattered and Anna cooed with delight.

It wasn't but two hours later that the back of the wagon was filled to the brim with goods and niceties from Anna's venture in town. Anna made a point of securing the most expensive of items from multiple stores, as nothing said, "there are no problems at our home," like the sprinkling of gold coins and the promise of bank notes. *They can all choke on their feigned concerns for my son,* Anna fumed inside each time someone asked her about Arthur's situation. But cool cash and plans for a large wedding were both quick to shift people's attention. No one in Kentucky would be out planning a soiree if things were even half as bad as had been rumored. So, Anna's efforts to turn the conversation ended up a great success, as before she had even pulled away from the town, everyone had the whisperings of the Lanark wedding on their tongues and no one even remembered a thing about any slave headed for Ohio.

At last, Nelson stopped the wagon in front of the Lanark house and Anna's smile that had been permanently cemented on her face all day while she spent much credit on items from wine to flowers, faded from her face at the realization that Clarkson and her men had still not returned with her son.

Yes, I want him gone, she thought to herself while she stepped down angrily. *But the more I think on it, as much as I dislike that child, the implications of a negro killing a Buchanan is far worse for me than my passing him off alive to Clarkson in a groom's bowtie.*

So, Anna went inside more agitated than she had left the house before. She had been successful today, but her confidence in Clarkson matched that of her already tepid thoughts on Flicker, which had hardened since his piss-poor success at tracking down that runaway boy the day before. Once more, men left her wanting.

"If only I could be the one riding," she grumbled to herself. "This shit would be over already."

Mae was there in Anna's face in a jiffy; her face fake-smiling while she took Anna's hat and coat. But Anna had lost all the glow of her shopping excursion and pushed the hat into Mae's hands with great force, then stomped up the stairs and unlocked the door to her room in anger.

Inside, Hattie crouched in the corner on the floor. She held her wounded hand up with her other and looked across the room in great fear as Anna approached and stared down at her.

If she could not go out and capture Samson herself, she may as well deal with this common barn pig that she single-handedly detained. Content that Hattie was still imprisoned, Anna looked down at her for a good minute and thought hard.

"Good." Anna scowled from above. "You just sit there like the wounded dog you are and stew. I reckon I still have not made up my mind what to do with you yet, but I'll be back again soon." She walked away and relocked the door behind her.

It appears that I'm the only one who knows how to keep these beasts in line, she told herself. Anna headed downstairs to make sure the rest of her negroes were hard at work on the long list of items she left for them to prepare. While most of the other great houses didn't teach their slaves to read, Anna found that some simple learning meant that they could do more of the type of work that she required. Her house negroes could follow a list of ingredients or chores that she had spelled out, *but it's not like they can read Chaucer, or even complete sentences for that matter,* she often laughed to others.

• • • • •

IT WAS LATE AFTERNOON NOW and the sun once again dipped behind the trees to the west. Arthur's mouth felt like cotton and he longed for a deep sip of something cool and refreshing like Mae's lemonade.

It had been around mid-day when Arthur had realized he was leading them the wrong way. That mistake had cost them several hours, but he thought that perhaps it would throw those in pursuit into confusion as to why they moved away from the river and not directly toward their goal.

Eventually, after they had doubled back in a zig-zag pattern to keep the people and dogs guessing, they made their way to country Arthur vaguely recognized from his youth. Buck would take him this way on occasion through these backwoods areas, though usually it was to pick up or drop a slave or two that was bought or sold. Had Arthur known that one day he would have need to travel these parts with a life he held precious in his hands, he might have paid better attention. Yet, faint memory served him enough to bring them toward the dirt road he knew eventually led to a crossing point many people used to navigate the river.

"Can't be too much farther now," he said to Samson with some confidence to assure him of the direction and the positive outcome of their flight.

As they passed beyond the cover of trees and into an open path that was unavoidable, seeing that it was bordered on either side by large rocky outcrops, Arthur caught sight of a man on horseback who rode at them from the opposite direction.

"Steady now," he whispered under his breath when he saw Samson ball up his fists as if he were prepared to fight. The man on horseback came closer into view. He was a rustic man in overalls and a straw hat.

"You let me do all the talking," he instructed Samson. Arthur stepped forward as the man's horse drew to a stop.

"How do?" the rustic man said and tipped his hat.

"How do yourself?" Arthur replied.

"Fixin' to be a nice evenin' soon," the man remarked, though Arthur could see he was sizing them up and down from atop his horse.

"I'd say 'tis," Arthur said with a smile.

"Where y'all from?" he finally inquired with a spec of suspicion in his voice.

Arthur could see the man had a pistol on his hip and a rifle in his pack, so he knew they were outmatched if things turned sour.

"We're from over down the river and behind them hills a way back in Mason County," he answered him coolly.

The man said nothing further but sat there as if he were expecting Arthur to say more. The silence became uncomfortable, so Arthur broke it and stepped even closer. "My name is Arthur Buchanan," he declared and reached up his hand in an offer of greeting.

"Ah," the man said then he reached down with his hand in response. "I knowed me a Buck Buchanan before. I got a farm east of Sugarloaf Mountain and we bought a bull and a sow once from him about five or six years back."

"That'd be my father." Arthur relaxed his shoulders.

"Didn't know he had a son," the man said plainly.

"That's because I was away at school in Virginia for these past many years and I only just recently returned after my father, Buck, passed away."

The man seemed to not be fully convinced yet as he looked over at Samson, who after two days on the run looked more than a little bedraggled.

"Hmmm," he considered. "What's your momma's name again then, boy?" he asked, this time the gun on his hip seemed closer to his fingers.

"Anna," Arthur said quickly. "Anna Buchanan."

That seemed to be enough to finally convince the man that they were not a threat as he moved his hands back to the reins.

"Right. Well, watcha doing up this way for?" he asked with curiosity. "Especially on foot?"

Arthur laughed. "Oh that. My horse done run off that's why we are on foot." He thought to himself quickly where else to take this story and his mouth opened to say things even he didn't know it was going to say. "Me and my boy here are heading up to the Ohio River to meet the barge. I got me a new negro child being smuggled in from the north."

"Good on you," the man replied. "It's best to get 'em when they's young so you be able to set 'em in the ways you want and like I always say, a negro up north is a wasted commodity. It's like shitting out a barrel of Liberty half-dollars on the side of the road, then continuing poor pocketed on the road to Damascus." He laughed at his own humor and Arthur pretended to laugh along with him, but really, he used it as pretext to glance over and make sure that Samson didn't pounce with those fists as they had enough to contend with already.

"By and by, that's what my daddy always said, too," Arthur chortled. "We best get to going, lest we miss the barge."

"Keep the mountains on your right the whole way through the valley," the man then instructed. "There be a few twists, turns, and forks on this road but if you remember that you won't get turned around. Once you see the poplar forest, go on through it and out the other side about a mile and a half then you'll see the crossing."

The man tipped his straw hat and trotted forward.

"Much obliged," Arthur called after him. He watched as Samson loosened his fists and the two of them hurriedly headed through the pass and down the country roads just as the man had instructed.

• • • • •

THE DOGS NOW WORKED AT a more hurried pace.

"I reckon it's less than a mile now to the Ohio," Flicker remarked to Clarkson. The men rode side by side followed behind by Piglet who led Arthur's empty horse by a rope.

"Might as well be Egypt, far as that boy's concerned," Clarkson replied.

There was a snort from behind as Piglet found the response to be amusing.

"Mr. Clarkson," Flicker began with a more serious tone. "If I can be frank, sir, I do hope this experience will put some lead in Arthur's belly. I fear he is a bit softer than his daddy, Buck. Now that's a Buchanan that would have never gone off with no runaway slave, either as unwillingly . . . or willingly, be that as it may."

Gideon considered his words. "Are you suggesting Arthur chose to go with this Samson boy?"

"I only bring it up, Mr. Clarkson, as I understand your Gillie has eyes for Arthur," Flicker explained.

"They are in fact engaged," Clarkson informed with a swollen chest.

Flicker continued. "Then my point is best made now." He rubbed his head with one of his hands then pressed on. "Young Mister Buchanan and Samson grew up together as young'uns. While Arthur returned home recently, he has made a point to publicly go out of his way to support his childhood playmate. In fact, some might even say he's looked after him with such care like one might do for their family member or for someone they love, like a spouse."

Clarkson stopped his horse.

"Now it seems as if you are intimating there's some kind of moral defect at play?" There was grave concern in his Protestant voice.

Gideon studied Flicker's face as he appeared to choose his next words wisely. "Couldn't blame the young Mister if he looked on Samson as his pet, given the history, but a pet gets let out to shit and piss in the rain, not brought into the bedroom to sleep at his owner's side."

"Sleep at his side?" Clarkson grizzled at the thought. The thought of any physical attraction between men was repulsive and almost unimaginable to Clarkson. Nevertheless, if that attraction was to a negro. "That would be akin to bestiality." Gideon almost threw up at the thought.

Clarkson was not sold on this wild suggestion as it was frankly too outlandish to even consider.

"Yet the reality is, Flicker, that Arthur seems to have taken a strong liking to our Gillie," Clarkson pushed back.

"I reckon that's more Mrs. Buchanan's doings then not," Flicker answered his volley.

Clarkson tapped his horse on its hind and it began to walk again. His mind swirled. This could explain why Anna was so quick to strike a deal. Send him away from Lanark and make her son Gideon and Gillie's problem instead of her own. He would have to consider reneging on this deal, despite the fact he wanted the acreage, a husband for his daughter, and an heir to his own farm.

Flicker gently came back up alongside him. "Now before you think of canceling any plans, consider this. Let's say Gillie and Arthur *were* to pair off. I mean it is possible that sometime in the near future Arthur, who frankly is not cut out to run Lanark, has an unfortunate accident . . ."

"Well go on," Clarkson pushed. "There's no point in stopping now."

"I just mean to say that this would leave you more or less in charge of two great neighboring plantations that could mighty easily be melded into one. And, I, for one, would be happy to serve under such a wise landowner as you."

When his words were done, Flicker moved his horse off and rode at a distance, which gave Clarkson space and time to think.

No matter if Arthur had a strange affinity for his boy slave, if Clarkson let the marriage go through but insisted that Gillie move into Lanark with him for the first year before they moved over to the Clarkson farm, that would give ample time for them to have a child. And once there was a child, a boy child, there would really be no more need for Arthur. Gideon would have his heir, he'd have his acreage, and most incredibly, he'd have Lanark under his fist, too.

He laughed to himself. "I had to have known that Anna was up to something and I am sure there are layers on top of layers that I can't see. But I've been truly blind not to think her schemes ran so dark and deep. Now, she is found herself to be overly confident and to never think that I might have a scheme or two of my own."

Yes, Gideon Clarkson saw a future for Arthur- a very short future- but he would be an incredibly useful means to an end, no matter if he was in fact a bugger and a pervert.

All I need to get from him is one good potent tumble in the bed with my Gillie, and then he can lay with his slave in Satan's grave six feet under, day and night, Gideon thought. Now this was righteousness in action.

●●●●●

ANNA SAT IN THE PARLOR when Nelson led Gillie into the room.

"Miss Anna," Gillie cried out before she rushed across the parlor toward her. "I am so sorry about what's happened to Arthur."

In her mind, Anna found Gillie's frailty insufferable, but outwardly she stood up and hugged her before she sat back down and patted the cushion next to her for Gillie to sit.

"Fret none, Gillie. Arthur will be alright and he will be returned to us both soon. Your daddy and my men will make sure he is more than okay and then that evil boy will be punished for what he put us all through."

Gillie sat down. "I always did have my suspicions about that boy."

"Well, never you mind all of that for a bit. I asked you to supper because we have much to plan- you and I- for the festivities."

"Festivities?" Gillie asked with great interest. "What for?"

"Arthur told me yesterday that he planned to propose to you this very day!" Anna shouted out at Gillie with joy, who then erupted into giggles from her side of the settee.

"Oh, my lord!" she exclaimed with joy. "Engagement?"

"Yes," Anna smiled. "And I am planning a party for tomorrow night to celebrate the occasion!"

"For a minute, I wondered if Arthur even had interest in me," Gillie wondered aloud through a grin.

"Interested?" Anna gasped. "He's positively in a trance!"

Gillie shot up and clasped her hands together. "This is so exciting! I do not even know what to do!"

"That's why you have me, dear," Anna assured her. "Sit back down now as everything will move quickly. I've been waiting for this day since Arthur's birth. You are the daughter in-law of my dreams, and since your own mother is dead, I will take the lead in all things to make sure you are a bride of great envy."

There was great shock still in Gillie's voice. "Do you really think Arthur will propose? Are we really to be married?"

"Yes, child." Anna grabbed her hands. "Consider the engagement already done, and me Arthur's proxy for the proposal."

"You mean to say, it is actually official? Like, I'm an engaged woman even now, though Arthur has not gotten down on his knee?"

"Gillie, as the daughter of an esteemed family, I can assure you that engagement does not require both parties to be present. I am the ambassador of this union on Arthur's behalf and rest assured, by this time tomorrow, it will be public knowledge to all that you were officially engaged as of this minute. In fact, just know that in short order, you will be Mrs. Gillie Buchanan."

Gillie let out a small shriek of ecstasy.

Once Anna's ears had recovered, she leaned down and pulled a chest out from alongside the couch. She opened the lid to reveal numerous bolts of fabric from the shop she had visited earlier.

"Now what do you think of this for the bridesmaids?" Anna said as she pulled out a pale blue silk. "I have been saving these since Arthur's birth for an occasion such as this. They were part of my mother's mother's dowry imported from the orient itself."

Gillie tittered and cooed while she went through the chest. Anna rang a bell and Nelson returned.

"Have Mae cook dinner for two," she directed him. "Gillie will stay and sup with me as we have an engagement and a wedding to plan."

"Yes, Missus Anna," he replied dutifully.

Anna grinned wide as she considered that perhaps Arthur's unfortunate event wound up being the perfect catalyst after all and Gillie Clarkson the perfect foil for Anna's plans.

• • • • •

THE SKY WAS SCATTERED WITH shades of blue from cerulean to indigo as the sun began to sink beneath the horizon. As the two men broke from the trees, Samson finally caught sight of the Ohio River for the first time. It was incredible in both its scope and in its details. At parts wide and smooth, in places narrow and turbulent. The rush of the water filled his ears and whispered, "freedom."

"Look!" he shouted to Arthur as he raised his hand to point. "It's right there!"

For a second, he was struck by how ordinary it looked on the other side. There trees grew same as they did in Kentucky. The coast was dotted with eddies and still water banks on both edges. Yet, on one side a Black man was his own, and the other, he belonged to another in the same way a man had the right to buy and sell shoes or chicken feed.

"That's the land of self-determination?" He looked at a field filled with wildflowers on the other side and thought to himself. *Funny how it looks just the same. But still, I can almost taste a different air on the wind that come from yonder.* He raised his head to take in the breeze that blew his way from the sloping ground that hugged the river bank.

Samson watched Arthur as he also scanned the shoreline. He was ready to run straight to the first opening and dive right in, but Arthur cautioned that he needed a minute to find the best point of entry and safest passage across. After a few minutes of his head moving this way and that, Samson followed behind, as his master and lover led them downstream.

"The distance over there is not quite as wide as it is back up a way," he explained. He raised his chin toward a narrow piece of water where just past a deep, still pool, the current swiftly rippled over shallow rocks.

"Strip off," Arthur instructed him firmly. Samson watched as Arthur removed his own shoes and clothes first then he curiously balled them up into a bundle and held the clump of clothes over his head. "Do it this way and they don't get wet."

Now that he understood the intention, Samson followed Arthur's orders and it was only seconds before they were completely naked, bundles of clothes lifted high in the air.

They approached the bank gingerly, the rocks nearest the shoreline jabbed into their soles and once they dipped their ankles in, they began to wade out slowly into the water.

"Thank you for comin' with me, Artha," Samson said over the sounds of the river as the water went from their ankles to their knees. The powerful rush of the liquid against Samson's legs surprised him as the river had looked so calm where they entered, at least from his viewpoint above the surface. He did not for one second guess the force that lay under its murky abyss because it was unseen from the land.

While Samson had urged Arthur to leave him miles back, he was grateful for his company now because he did not know crossing the river would come with his knees that knocked together from both cold and fear.

Joy crept into Samson's heart. They were almost there. So close to Ohio, he could hardly believe it. Just a few more minutes. Once they made it past this deep pool, all they would need to do is get over those shallow rapids on the other side and then Samson would finally and fully be free.

Tears of expectation formed in the corner of Samson's eyes. "I neva' dared hope for this moment to be true but now that it's here, I's cannot help but burst with excitement."

Arthur looked back at him and the two smiled warmly at one another.

He noted how Arthur's eyes watered at the sight of the specks spilling from Samson's eyes.

However, the moment and all that it meant was short lived as Samson's own tears did not have time to fall far because at that moment the sound of howling dogs broke over the rustling waters.

"They's a come!" Samson screamed as he turned back around to see the dogs had come out from the trees where Arthur and he had emerged only moments before. The canines began to gnash and foam at the mouth and they seemed to fly the distance that separated them from the shore until the pack was only a few feet away from the shivering river-soaked men. The blueticks snapped and yipped from the shoreline before two of them dove into the water and swam out to Samson and Arthur. The bumps on Samson's arms burst up in panic like the terror that seized his chest.

"There they are!" Samson heard Clarkson yell from atop a horse as he burst into view, and next he watched as Flicker and Piglet, on their own horses, rushed for the river. They were followed by two slave men that Samson did not know.

Samson turned back to Arthur and cried out, "What do we do?"

Arthur, who was just behind Samson, turned his own head back toward the rushing pack of hounds then suddenly he appeared to falter.

Samson looked on helplessly as Arthur, who had lost his footing, fell over head first into the water. His clothes scattered in the wind then rushed right past Samson's legs.

"Sam . . . s . . . on . . ." Arthur yelled out as he thrashed in the water. The current lifted him up and within seconds, Arthur's body was rushed downstream as his arms flailed violently in the air.

Samson stood frozen as Arthur's body was instantaneously carried away. Though his flailing arms flew wildly in the air and his shrinking head bobbed in and out of the foaming current, nothing he did stopped the river's forceful current from carrying him away. Until at last, his body faded into the distance and then around a bend in the river.

All possibility- all hope- vanished in an instant.

"Oh Artha," Samson started to cry, but there was no time left for concern over Arthur's safety. He was gone. There was not a spare second to mourn what could have been. With Arthur already assigned to fate, this moment was Samson's one and only chance to grasp at freedom so he threw his clothes into the water then he dove in head first and tried to swim with all his might toward the rapid shallows on the other side.

It was futile, as within mere seconds, though the dogs retreated from the deeper water and swam back to the other side, Flicker and Piglet's horses rushed into the river, and they were alongside Samson in a flash.

There was no place left to turn as he was hemmed in on both sides. He gave up and his body was dragged back out of the water by his arms until they dumped him hard onto Kentucky's dry land.

Out of breath, his lungs half-filled with river water, Samson laid there naked on the firm, rocky bank while Clarkson's slaves tied ropes around his ankles and wrists.

He lifted his head up one last time to see the land of Ohio that lay across the water just right there on the other riverbank, then Samson cried. He sobbed with as much might as he had tried to swim. He wept for those wild flowers that shook in the breeze as if to taunt him for their freedom. He cried for almost and what was possible. And he wailed for Arthur, who gave his own life so that Samson could fully live his.

Once secured, Clarkson's slaves hoisted Samson up onto one of the horses so that he now hung headfirst over its side. They all marched off in the direction of the riverbend where Arthur had disappeared in an effort to recover his body and bring it back to Lanark.

Sour Wine

Throbbing pain.

   Exhaustion.

It was almost as if he were intoxicated.

To lift his eyelids, it took great effort, but after several feeble attempts, Arthur managed to open his eyes at last. There was a moment of relief in the knowledge that he was alive, though he was unsure where he was. However, the relief was brief. As his focus grew sharper, Arthur realized he was in the bed of his own bedroom at Lanark. He attempted to sit up and was met by the concerned face of Gillie.

"Oh Arthur!" she gasped when she saw him stir.

"My head feels fuzzy," Arthur replied through the haze.

Gillie grabbed a bell off of the nightstand near the bed and rang it twice.

"Doctor said it was for your own safety after such a violent episode as the one that you endured," she whispered to him. "Said that what you went through might produce fits of hysteria and nightmares otherwise. Your mother is nothing if not strict when it comes to your safety. She must really love you!"

She fluffed Arthur's pillow and urged his head back down.

Arthur rubbed his forehead confused. He was groggy— yes— but not enough to know his mother would not be described by anyone who really knew her as caring or concerned, at least not for Arthur's personhood.

He closed his eyes then reopened them again, only this time to find that Anna had come in and now stood there, looking down over him. The glimmer in her eyes scared him even in this state of half awakeness.

"You're safe now, son," she said to him soothingly. She turned to put her hand on Gillie's shoulder and addressed her separately. "Let's allow him to rest a bit now, Gillie," she asserted softly. "He will need his health restored in due time now that we have decided to move the wedding date up."

"Wedding date?" Arthur asked weakly.

Anna gently guided Gillie to the bedroom door while Arthur struggled to sit up again.

"Who is getting married?" he wondered aloud. "Not me?"

With more urgency in her voice, Anna pushed Gillie outside.

"Head on down and ask Mae to put on a kettle of tea for the two of us. We'll take a cup together while we look at the fresh flowers I had snipped from the fields today for you to choose from for your bouquet."

Once Gillie was fully out the door, Anna closed it firmly and returned to Arthur's bedside.

"Now we can discuss things plainly, without having to put on airs or pretend," she noted firmly.

Afraid to hear the answer, he asked his mother anyway. "Samson?"

Anna reached onto the table beside his bed and lifted up a small bottle and a rag.

"Samson can't get anywhere near you now," she replied firmly.

"Please tell me he is alive," Arthur begged.

"Don't you spend another second on that topic," she demanded. "He's out of reach and not even no damn Hattie can make it otherwise," she finished bitterly.

"Did he make it across to safety then?" Arthur questioned. "Is he in Ohio?"

Anna laughed then leaned down and whispered into Arthur's ear.

"He's in the barn," she teased. "I'm going to have him burned alive before everyone's eyes right after you say your vows to Gillie Clarkson two days from now."

Arthur tried to raise himself out of the bed but fell back down. "Burned alive? What are you talking about?" he asked in horror.

His mother giggled. "Oh, I could have had him killed already, Arthur, you know that. But where's the message in that?" She sat down on his bed next to him. "Why would I pass up the opportunity to be bold, to make a statement?"

Acid burned in Arthur's stomach.

"This way, everyone gets something," she explained. "The county gets to see how we handle renegades; Samson gets to see you in your rightful state as a married man, and you," she continued. "You get to see Samson for the creature that he is and then watch his negro eyes as he travels straight to Hades on the devil's flames. After all, I would like to have no doubts that it was he who lured you into carnal lusts and not the other way around. In fact, I might have Flicker warm a hot spike over coals and stick it straight up that boy's ass before I kill him."

A gasp exploded from Arthur's lungs. Even this seemed extreme for his mother's cruelty.

"It will be like a celebratory pig roast for your wedding, turn him on a spit that runs through from his mouth to his anus and have the slaves take turns spinning his body above the fire day and night until his meat falls off the bone. Only no one but the dogs will eat that flesh." Anna laughed heartily as she stood up and tipped the bottle over so that it poured some of its contents onto the rag.

Once it was visibly wet, Arthur watched his mother closely as she returned the bottle to the nightstand.

"What's that?" he asked cautiously.

"Oh this?" she giggled as she held up the rag, "Till the celebrations begin, Doctor Charles has left this little bottle of liquid sleep to help make sure you are unable to awaken long enough to help your little negro escape . . . again."

Arthur lifted his arms to block his mother's hands that rapidly approached his face with the rag.

"Sleep tight, Arthur," she sang. "When you wake next, it will almost be your wedding day."

Then the room went black.

•••••

TWENTY MINUTES LATER, THE TWO ladies sipped Fujian Bohea tea in fine porcelain cups while they sat in the parlor and examined a row of different colored flowers. Anna had personally toured the plantation and hand-picked the assortment to ensure the finest selection for Gillie's bridal bouquet. Anything that pertained to this wedding, and frankly anything that Gillie did from here on out, reflected on Anna and her taste. True, it was Gillie's wedding, but she would guide the young woman to choices that Anna herself had already pre-approved.

"I love these Carolina Spider lilies," Gillie declared while she inhaled the sweet fragrance from a small bunch of pure white flowers with thin spider-like petals that grew out from a large round center. Anna watched Gillie smile as her father, Gideon Clarkson, entered the room. "Oh, Daddy, what do you think of these?" she asked in great anticipation of his response.

She held one long stem up for him to admire.

"Just fine, Gillie," Clarkson replied with disinterest. "Might I have a moment alone with Miss Anna?"

"Oh." Gillie's face fell at his response.

Anna; however, was intrigued by the thought of Clarkson wanting to speak to her privately. *If he thinks to alter our bargain, he had best think again*, she mused to herself.

"Gillie," Anna instructed. "Why don't you head upstairs and take a peek at Arthur to make sure he is resting quietly now that we have re-administered the doctor's medicine. He will need his stamina restored for the honeymoon," she chortled. Gillie blushed then smiled widely.

"Yes ma'am," she impishly replied then curtsied to her father and said, "Daddy," before she exited the parlor.

"Anna," Clarkson began. "I think we need to discuss a few-"

She interrupted him immediately. If she allowed him to continue, he might get the better of her, and this was something she could not allow. "Thank you kindly, Gideon, for taking care of that little problem with the Samson boy."

"'Twas no big thing." He blushed.

"Oh nonsense," Anna cooed then she rang a little bell and directed Nelson to bring another teacup and saucer for Mr. Clarkson.

"Do sit," she insisted as she poured him some of the hot liquid and handed him the cup.

"A few questions have arisen," he petitioned after his first sip.

"Connecting our fine Kentuckian families through marriage will work out very well for both of us, Mr. Clarkson," she reminded him.

"About that . . ."

"Or do I need to rethink that stretch of acreage we discussed?"

"That's exactly what I wanted to talk to you about," Clarkson tried again. "I am a little concerned about what I've heard about Arthur and . . ."

"No." Anna lifted her hand up. "I must stop you there. There is absolutely no reason to be concerned."

"But I-" he tried once more.

"With Arthur living under your care, your expert tutelage will ensure that he walks a fine line, Mr. Clarkson. In fact, I do not see a thing at all to fret about as concerns Arthur and his future as Gillie's husband."

"But I thought it might be best if he remained here, at Lanark with Gillie, at least for the first year until . . ." he blurted out as quickly as he could.

Anna laughed heartily. "That defeats the whole purpose of this arrangement, Gideon. Now let us proceed with what we have already agreed to."

Clarkson tried to interject once more, but Anna simply thought it was best to ignore him and changed the topic.

She picked up a cluster of bright orange butterfly weed. "Let's talk about the wedding," she bantered with an air of excitement. "I think placing some of these around the spice cake Mae is going to make for the celebration will have a beautiful effect, don't you? Or would you prefer something more edgy like a lemon cake with the petals of the swamp agrimony, Mr. Clarkson?" she asked while she pointed to a tall yellow stalk with delicate petals that looked like shaved butter.

Inside her mind, Anna bragged to herself about how easily Gideon had been diverted, but her face remained frozen with a smile of feigned interest in his opinion on the cake and flowers.

Clarkson stood up with his shoulders slumped. "I lived through one wife already and that was enough to know when a woman's done had her say so," he answered her. "As for the cake, do what you like, I should have known all along that you always do."

Anna placed the flowers down then sat back in her seat and sipped her tea while she watched Gideon Clarkson leave her parlor.

• • • • •

SAMSON WAS FASTENED WITH ROPES and tied spread eagle upright to the barn's wall, a foot or two off the floor. They had not even allowed him the decency of clothing, so his backside was raw with splinters as it rubbed continuously against scratchy hickory lumber that had been weathered by years of Kentucky's heat.

Beads of sweat ran over his body as the barn offered little but stale and dusty air.

The barn door rattled. He would have hidden his shame, but the ropes were tight at his wrists as much as at his ankles, so he was trapped there suspended and on display as someone approached.

In front of him gingerly crept in Nelson, who had a wet cloth on a stick. Nelson lifted it to Samson's lips and he felt the coolness of the damp rag on his mouth and sucked at its moisture. An acrid taste passed his lips like something had gone bad and he winced.

"What's that?" Samson asked through a pasty mouth. "It tastes like horse piss." He turned his head away.

"Sour wine," Nelson whispered. "If it was good enough for the Lawd Jesus on the cross, so may it quench and ease your sufferin' here just the same."

"Tis straight up vinegar," Samson spat. Yet, his mouth was dry, so he smiled at Nelson and said, "but I'm in need so I's thank you by and by." As

Samson nodded a thank you, Nelson pushed the rag up to his mouth again. He drank deep from its soaked fabric.

"Youse a damn fool to e'er come in that house," Nelson chastised him while he swallowed. "That's all done though now." He lowered his head in sadness.

Samson finished sucking on the rag and looked down at Nelson.

"I's hate to see you pass your last hours in such a state," he lamented at the young man while he lowered the stick.

"None in the fields gonna mourn you, boy, youse all alone now. Fact 'tis, once youse come up to the house, youse already dead to those who knew you prior. Loneliness done killed you off in the first hours, only youse nor they don't know that. Youse think youse lucky. They figure it be rich and meaty table scraps and lemonade but really it be day and night at the Massa's call and little joy or hope, no neva.'"

He shrugged his shoulders. "I'd give most anything to go back to the cabins. To feel the sun on me for more than a moment. To scrunch my bare toes into the ground. To sit by a fire at night with loved ones. To sup with kin."

He sat down on a bale of hay nearby.

"I'd give a limb to pick cotton by day but have the moon to m'self at the night. 'Stead the call of the Missus keep me up most hours with worry. What she gonna want next? When she gonna beckon?"

There was silence for a moment and Samson couldn't help but feel sorry for Nelson, even though he was not the one who faced imminent death. Samson wondered if Nelson ever really lived much at all. All that haughtiness he assumed the house slaves had at any plantation now seemed null and void. *Haughtiness just be a protective layer, like bran on wheat flour. Rough on the outside, soft powder on the inside,* Samson pondered.

Finally, Nelson looked up at him and spoke again. "Truth is, I's sorry for myself when they brought you in the house. I's thinkin' they'd retire me to pasture or do me like I hears they did Poppa Blue. Not run me into the ground like that Bevel who Massa Buck worked till he was plum dead. No, once they got a young'un like you, they'd sell me off or worse."

Nelson stood up and approached Samson.

"I's sorry now, though. You ain't a bad boy, though I can't say I's under-stand your fascination and interest in obligin' a white man's touch. Neither here nor there after all because I's enuff left in my heart not to see you suffer your last days without a friend, no matta what type of lust you have in your heart," he said solemnly then he lifted his hand and patted Samson on his knee.

Tears flowed from Samson's eyes. "Thank you," he cried out softly.

Nelson turned his head around suddenly toward the door and listened intently. He turned back to Samson and whispered quickly, "I's wish you safe passage to the otha side, wheneva it may come, boy."

Afterward, Nelson disappeared out the back of the barn and crept out of sight.

Samson was alone again.

• • • • •

ALL WAS DARKNESS NOW WHEN Anna ascended the staircase and headed for her bedroom. In her hands she held a candlestick in one and a key in the other. Anna had slept the last two nights in one of the guest rooms. Granted, it was not comfortably appointed like her own suite, but it was adequate. Anna wanted Hattie to be as isolated as possible. Except for the one time she checked in on her, she hadn't so much as stopped by to give her a sip of water or to see if she needed to use the outdoor privy. Hattie could just soil herself and stew in her mess as far as Anna was concerned.

Tonight, though, she decided after much thought that it was time to decide. She had debated back and forth between two options, but while she had walked up the stairs, she reached her final judgment. Now all that was left to do was to let Hattie know her fate and be done with this whole business. She turned the key and stepped into the room, which appeared to be empty. Anna knew better, though. It wasn't like Hattie was as young or as limber as Samson, so the odds of her sneaking out the window and shimming down the siding, or of even overpowering Anna in the darkness in order to make a run, were next to nothing.

No, she thought to herself. *She will be here, cowering as much as she was when I last saw her.*

Anna held the candle up and nodded as Hattie indeed was there as expected. Her wide frame shivered in the same corner where she squatted before from either cold or fear or both.

"Look at you on the floor, like the weak bitch dog that you are," Anna taunted. "I haven't had much time to consider you up until now but I have decided and it's time you knew."

Hattie looked up at her with weak eyes.

"I thought at first that I'd make a sale of you cheap for sport to Piglet so that you were stuck living with him for the rest of your miserable life." She let the threat sink in. "Then, I considered making a spectacle out of you by burning or hanging you with that Samson boy at the same time."

"So, you means to kill me then?" Hattie asked feebly.

Her wilted face looked pathetic.

Anna placed the candle on the bureau then she reached into her pocket and pulled out some crumbs of bread that she tossed onto the floor at Hattie's feet.

"Eat," she commanded her. "You're gonna need your strength."

"What for?" Hattie cried.

"Arthur and Gillie's wedding is going to be held in two days and I've decided to host a small dinner here tomorrow night in honor of the couple before the big ceremony the next day," Anna explained while she began pacing. "Though I'd just as soon turn you into a thing of pleasure for all the hard-working men around these parts, I'll be needing you to serve guests, seeing's that I don't really have time to train up new girls between now and then. I tried, but the ones Mae recommended are all thumbs, and though you broke my platter once, you ain't dropped another of my belongings since."

Relief washed over Hattie's face and Anna watched on as she at last picked up the small pieces of bread with her uninjured hand and shoved them into her mouth. Her other hand was wrapped in a piece of blood-soaked sheet that Hattie had torn from the bed.

"You'll pay for that destruction in time," Anna noted as she nodded toward her bandaged hand.

"Yes, Missus Anna," Hattie said with gratitude.

"Mind you," she continued. "I have not fully abandoned my plans for you and the boys. I'm still considering it, but if you are on your best behavior tomorrow, I perhaps will think about extending my mercy much longer."

"Thank you, Missus Anna," Hattie said through a full mouth.

"Now finish up here and go clean yourself off. You stink like shit," Anna said with a guffaw then she turned to leave Hattie to her crusts of bread.

• • • • •

ARTHUR'S BODY JOSTLED AWAKE. His eyes focused onto the figure of Flicker who held his legs up in the air as someone else slid a pair of black slacks over each of his limbs. Once they were on, Flicker hoisted the pants up over Arthur's hips and then he watched as an unknown slave slipped his feet into dress shoes. Fully clothed, they lifted his body off the bed completely by his shoulders. He could now make out that it was Piglet whose frame pushed up against his right arm, as well as Nelson, who did the same on his left side. Their hands tightly scrunched the suit fabric that had gathered up at Arthur's armpits and pinched his skin.

Out of his bedroom they carried him like this, then through the hall-way, and at last to the stairs, where Flicker went down backward followed by the other two who dipped low so as not to drop Arthur.

Once at the bottom of the stairs, they hoisted him into something of a wheelchair before they went on their way, leaving Arthur close to paralyzed beside his mother.

He wanted to say something, but when he opened his mouth, nothing came out.

"There, there, Arthur," she patronized him with a pat on his shoulder. "You are waking up from a long rest. It will take you a few minutes before you are fully with us, and then I will lead you into the parlor and then the dining room, where a small group of the most important people in Mason County will make merry and toast to your brief engagement."

Arthur tried to protest but all that came out were a few mumbled bits of nonsense. After all, he had been rendered incapacitated by the noxious gas for close to twenty-four hours now.

"Don't strain yourself," Anna said with a smile. "We have quite the celebration planned this evening. You at least have to be present for the champagne toast before I send you back upstairs for more rest."

Anna walked around until she was behind Arthur and put her hands on the chair.

"Everyone will understand that you are too physically exhausted to stay all the way through the dinner, especially if I see signs that you are get-ting *agitated or rambunctious*," she punctuated the last words to make her point. "But they will cheer you on just the same before your next slumber."

As she began to push Arthur's chair, she leaned in close. "You will need to be well rested for the wedding tomorrow, as family and friends are com-ing from far and wide for the event."

All Arthur could do was sit there helpless and let Anna wheel him right into the parlor where numerous guests were gathered. Some sat on couches and chairs, others stood in pairs or small groups, but all had glasses in their hands and laughter on their lips.

"Arthur," an old woman gasped when she spied his entrance. At that, the others rushed closer to examine his invalid appearance.

"It is tragic, yes," Anna cried. "But Doctor Charles assures me that he will make a rapid recovery by tomorrow." She wheeled him through the crowd and into the dining room where she placed his wheelchair at the front of the table, which had been elongated with the extra leaves so that it could now seat close to twenty.

"You better behave," Anna threatened softly in Arthur's ear so no one else was able to hear.

Gillie rushed to take the seat on Arthur's right side while Anna marched to the other end of the table and sat down at its head where Gideon Clarkson sat at her right.

"Gillie . . ." Arthur tried to speak.

Clarkson's daughter put a finger over Arthur's lips.

"Arthur, you silly thing. No need to say anything." She giggled. "I understand you without words. Even though you are under the effects of Doctor Charles' medication, it goes unspoken how you feel about me."

Arthur grimaced as if he had just drunk sour milk.

"I love you, too!" she declared. She kissed him softly on his cheek and whispered into his ear. "And nothing will make me happier than becoming your wife, Mrs. Arthur Buchanan, tomorrow evening, Arthur . . . nothing!"

Anna called out to the crowd to quiet then announced, "Now I happily invite you all to join us at the table. All of the guests entered the room and took their seats. Arthur knew many of the folks though it had been years since he had seen some of them. The high cheek bones of his mother's sister, whose eyes scoured the room to find anything for which she could object. Arthur knew well that high society, as it were, really meant looking down on others as frequently as possible. This was a family trait of Anna's that she took to heart as much as her sister.

Once everyone was seated, a team of slaves rushed in with bowls of consommé. Arthur recognized Nelson, and of course Hattie, whose hand was wrapped up tightly. He briefly wondered what she had done to hurt herself. He surveyed the faces of the others to try and see if any of these new house staff were familiar. One teenage boy and two young women placed steaming China bowls in front of the guests, but his energy started to fade so that the mental connections that would put faces to names failed him.

"I . . ." he began to say with great effort, but Gillie lifted up a soup spoon from his bowl and she shoveled the broth into his open mouth.

"There's a good boy," she sang.

Though the evening seemed to drag on, throughout the many courses —dish by dish— Arthur felt his strength returning. He considered standing up and ending this charade of an engagement, but though his body was coming back to life, his spirit and the will to put his foot down were still asleep. So, he sat there, ate, and smiled at whatever nonsense Gillie said to him in between bites. And all the while, from across the long table, he saw his mother look up at him every few seconds to make sure he was not doing anything that warranted her sending him back to his room.

If there were any hope of an escape from Anna, even if that escape meant marrying Gillie Clarkson, Arthur could not be put back to sleep. There he was even more powerless to act than the freaks he saw chained to their displays last year at the Robinson and Harlow Traveling Circus Do that he and the boys had snuck out to one night in Virginia. There, he saw a woman the size of a sheep who was forced to sing parlor songs under a small tent enclosure that Arthur paid a few cents to enter. She wore irons on her ankles the same way the tall man and the boy with fangs were shackled to their pens where customers came in and out to ogle and make sport with.

At last, his mother struck the side of her glass with a spoon. When she did so, the slaves came around with glasses of champagne for everyone. Anna stood up with her own glass in hand.

"I must thank you all for coming tonight on such short notice," she beguiled the party with her sweet smile. "This is a truly happy occasion and I cannot think of any other people that we would want to share it with than y'all." His mother then lifted her glass higher. "Today we toast tomorrow's wedding, and the many happy tomorrows everlasting for my dear son, Mr. Arthur Buchanan, whom I love with all my heart, and his beautiful bride, Miss Gillie Clarkson."

The guests lifted their glasses around the table.

"To the bride and groom. May they enjoy as many years of prosperity and true devotion as my own dearly departed husband, Mr. Buck Buchanan, did. I'm not sure there was ever a more committed couple in love but if there were to be one, may it be the ones we toast today." There were nods and murmurs of sentimental joy around the table, except for Arthur, who almost laughed aloud.

"Here, here," Mr. Clarkson yelled out. Arthur noted Anna practically cringing at his voice.

"To Arthur and Gillie!" Anna shouted above him.

"To Arthur and Gillie!" the table thundered.

The guests clinked their glasses together and sipped and slurped, then they all sat back down to continue their idle conversations. Anna removed herself from the table and left the room. Arthur saw this as his chance to escape, so he waved Hattie over.

"Would you mind pushing me?" he asked her. Though he was certain he was able to walk himself, he did not want to let anyone else know, especially Gillie. He did not have any specific plans yet, but he knew if he did not want to spend his life like one of Anna's freaks, if he were to do anything at all; he would need to avoid being drugged again. If Gillie believed Arthur was still incapacitated, that would at least be one less person to worry about.

"Allow me though, Arthur." Gillie stood up and rushed to his chair. She pushed Hattie's hands off so that she could take control.

"That is so sweet of you, Gillie," Arthur feigned adoration. "However, I need to relieve myself, and until we share the wedding bed, I think it's best to keep some things about each other a mystery."

Gillie's cheeks reddened. "Of course, of course." She giggled and she left the wheelchair to Hattie then sat back down.

Hattie pushed Arthur through the dining room and parlor, and then into the main entrance foyer where Anna stood on the stairs and stared at Buck's portrait.

Without looking down at Hattie and Arthur, she spoke, "He was a fine-looking man," she said with admiration. "He really had a way with women, too." She laughed. "Just not always with me."

There was now sadness in her voice.

She turned her gaze to Hattie and spat out, "Though I don't suppose I need to tell you that, do I?"

Hattie stood frozen.

Arthur eyed his mother from his chair. He noted how she was ever unpredictably predictable like a poisonous snake. One could never be quite sure when it was ready to strike but had to assume that even when it rested, its fangs were ready to taste flesh if just by reflex alone and that eventually its venom must find use.

Anna turned back to the portrait and smiled again.

"Dinner was wonderful," she conceded plainly. "You did good."

"Thank you, Missus Anna," Hattie answered cautiously.

His mother turned back to them and marched down the stairs until she was in Hattie's face.

"Save it!" she growled. "If you ever cross me again, I'll hold your body down myself while the men use you like a rag doll, do you understand?"

"Yes, ma'am," Hattie lowered her head and said softly.

"Good," Anna snickered. "Then get out of here and make sure everyone's glasses are topped off and they are happy. I will take care of Arthur from here."

Arthur watched Hattie slink off as if the weight of the world were on her back.

"As for you, you can either go back in with your bride," his mother addressed him. "Or I can take you upstairs now for another round of Doctor Charles' medication."

She started to move to the back of his chair to prepare to push him forward, but Arthur had finally reached a point of no return with his mother. His strength returned at last; he whipped his wheelchair around by his own hands and arms until he was face to face with her.

"Why do you always have to be like that," he barked.

Indignation spread across Anna's face. "Like what?" she scoffed.

"Like that." Arthur pointed to where Hattie had exited, as he stood up on his feet. "You are so mean to them all, constantly!" he continued. "You never show any respect to anyone, when all they want is the same as anyone else . . . to be treated like the people they are."

Anna shook her head with fury.

"People?" she bellowed. "Arthur, how many damn times do we need to have this same conversation?"

Arthur glared into his mother's eyes. "As often as it takes for you to see that it's the truth," he vowed.

Anna grabbed Arthur by his arm and tugged at him.

"You want to see people, you ungrateful child," she stormed. "I'll show you people!"

She dragged Arthur to the stairway and pulled him up its sweeping steps.

"These are people," she testified, pointing to the relatives of both Buck and hers who had long since passed away. "The great men and women of your family. These are the people who through great God-given intelligence, through perseverance, and even moral fortitude, shaped your destiny and gave you the privilege to be the opinionated and stubborn little shit you turned out to be."

She stopped in front of a portrait of someone who looked vaguely similar to that of his grandfather whose own painting hung in the dining room. "Look here," she demanded. "This is your great granddaddy, Edgar Buchanan. He crossed the Atlantic Ocean for a chance to stake a claim in the new world. Never once did he dare think to give everything away for sodomy and Satan!"

She pulled him farther up the stairs to the large portrait of a woman with a long nose and high cheekbones. "And my great-great grandmother, Nellie Von Trusdale. She was a baroness, Arthur, a baroness!" she yelled to emphasize her station. "In her household, she molded a generation of aristocracy through her eight children who went off to become all manner of respected gentlemen and women in five different countries!"

Anna appeared to be wild with exacerbation at Arthur. He could never, ever recall her so inflamed and full of fury.

"These are your kin," she lectured. "These are your heritage!" As she continued, she pulled him farther and farther up the stairs and pointed at the various pictures.

"They were civilized," she pointed. "Cultured . . . refined . . . Christian even, yes Christian."

They had reached the top of the steps at last and Anna swung Arthur's body in front of her, while her own back was to the stairway.

"That unclean, Black boy and all those of his kind in the fields and in this house, they are nothing like the family you have on these walls. Nothing like the decent high-born blood of your ancestors!" she shouted. "Instead, they are blood-sucking savages. They come from a land where they chant and shrink heads, Arthur. They are beasts! They are simply and utterly wild beasts!"

Her breath was hot on his face as she leaned in with immense wrath in her voice.

"And you . . . you were just going to give all of that up once you became ensnared by that boy's hedonistic jungle-lust!"

Just then, Hattie walked back through the foyer with a handful of dirty dishes. Anna whirled around and pointed to her. "That there," she accused. "That is nothing but a damn animal!"

Hattie stopped in her tracks. Anna whirled back toward her son.

"All my life I've listened to you and Daddy call them every name imaginable," Arthur's voice began to quiver with anger. "You treat humans as if they are a commodity, something to be bargained for, traded, with no account for anyone's feelings but your own," he returned her rage with his own simmered indignation. His mother was stunned by his response but Arthur knew if he did not speak now and say everything he felt, he might never get the chance again.

"It wasn't just the men and women that work here whose feelings you stepped on, no, you did it to your own son," he continued. "I never asked to be sent off as a boy, discarded. I was alone for most of my youth and though I felt bad at the time, now I thank God for it."

Anna opened her mouth to speak but Arthur cut her off and continued.

"No . . ." he declared adamantly. "You will hear me. I did not ask to be engaged, to be married. That was once again all of your doing. Everyone and everything without any rights, any ownership of any aspect of themselves that is what you demand. You are the most selfish person I have ever had the displeasure to know," Arthur remonstrated.

"Listen here, Arthur Buchanan," Anna interjected with great force, but Arthur was not to be denied.

"You wanted me to come back one day as a man, well I have. I have come back with my eyes wide open. And though you claim people like Samson, like Hattie, are beasts and animals, the only beast I see here in this house is you."

His mother's eyes widened and her lips pursed in vexation. Arthur watched as Anna lifted her hand up into the air and swung it at his face in an effort to slap him with great force and retribution. However, Arthur reached up and grabbed Anna's arm by the wrist before she could land the blow. They locked eyes and he squeezed her arm tightly before he released her with a slight shove.

As he did, Anna fell backward not more than an inch. She gasped in terror as she teetered unexpectedly on the top step for a moment. In a blink, her balance lost, she tipped over and tumbled forcefully all the way down the many stairs until she landed at the base in a pile of plantation dress and limbs. Hattie dropped the dishes and they shattered on the ground with a loud crash. She rushed toward the body and yelled out, "Missus Anna!"

• • • • •

ANNA MOANED WITH PAIN. EVERYTHING hurt from her legs to her arms to her head.

"Oooow," she cried out. But no one answered her. She did not have the ability to say much more so she laid there in agony.

Hattie stood beside her bed while Arthur was over by the door.

She could hear Nelson join them. "That's the last of them," he informed the room.

"They're all gone now, including the Clarksons."

"That's just fine, Nelson." Arthur nodded. "I'll head over and speak to Mr. Clarkson in the morning to let him know that the wedding with Gillie is off."

Inside her mind Anna screamed with hot madness, but with her body, broken as it was, she could not do much else.

"Massa Artha." Hattie turned to Anna's son. "I's just wanted to say thank you." Anna noted the tears in Hattie's eyes and this only angered her more.

How dare she thank my son for anything, she fumed inside. *It was I who let her live, but true to form she's as ungrateful a sow for my mercy as she ever has been.*

"On account of you," Hattie continued. "I's feel like a real person for the first time in a long time. The way you defended me." Her cheeks were wet. "The way you defended all of us. It let me know there is kindness in this world and that not all your kind are cruel to the bitter end."

Arthur came over and hugged Hattie.

Anna could not believe what she saw. If she could get up, she would have found Buck's gun and shot them on the spot here and now.

"I sent Flicker around for Doctor Charles," Arthur explained to Hattie. "But he came back and said the doctor is away until next Tuesday."

Damnit, Anna said to herself. She needed to be healed quickly if she were to set everything right. Inside her mind, she already had a plan to fix things before they got too far off course. Once Hattie and Arthur left, she'd muster the strength to send for Flicker. Then she'd have him kill Hattie, lock Arthur away in the cellar until Doctor Charles returned, and she would have Mae nurse her back to health. In the meantime, she would send Nelson over to the Clarkson's to assure Gideon the wedding was on but it would be delayed a few weeks for her recovery. *Yes,* she soothed herself. *This will all be fine. I will be fine. Just as soon as they get up and leave this room.*

At the bottom of the bed, Arthur reached into his coat pocket and took out the same bottle and rag Anna had used to keep him asleep since his return with Samson.

"Until Doctor Charles returns," Arthur stated. "I reckon we all deserve a little peace around here." She watched him tip the bottle so that the rag filled up with its contents.

No, Anna protested loudly in her mind as her son moved closer to her. When the cloth had almost fully approached her face, she started screaming. Unable to speak before, she somehow found the ability within her to let out a tidal wave of a threat that she meant to keep as a promise. "I will fucking kill you both . . ."

Manumission

The darkness pressed in on Samson from all sides. He had lost track of how long he had been in the barn, but it was still not long enough to feel at ease with the noise of its rats furrowing in the hay. They made their existence known only when all else was at peace, but Samson could not help but feel thankful at least they had tied him up off of the floor, lest they crawl over his feet on their way along the sides of the walls as they made their way outside to search for scraps of food.

At once, their scurries increased in volume as another type of footstep could be heard edging nearer. The barn's door slammed open and in poured light from a lantern held up with Nelson's shaking hands.

"O'er there!" Nelson shouted.

Out of the shadows came Arthur.

"Samson," he gasped in disbelief.

Samson knew he must look a fright, but all he cared about was that people who cared for him were here now. There was warmth in Arthur's touch as he approached and placed his hand on Samson's thigh.

"I'll get you down from here immediately," he heard Arthur say to him, though he didn't have enough left in his voice or his will to respond.

With weak eyes, he watched Arthur pull a scythe from the barn's wall and use it to cut through each of the braided ropes that held his limbs up. Once released, Samson would have fallen to the floor, but Arthur caught him and he threw his arm around his savior's body and let him guide him limply out of this prison.

Once outside, the night air stung at his wrists and ankles where the ropes had bound him. They stung less than the eyes of Flicker and Piglet that watched from nearby as Arthur led him through the dust, though.

Flicker spat on the ground then turned and marched away with Piglet behind him.

Hattie and Mae were on the porch. The bigger woman wrapped a blanket around his nakedness as Arthur guided him to a rocking chair. The old woman swept forth with a cup of something dark and warm and Arthur held it to Samson's lips while he fitfully sipped.

"Let's draw him a bath." Arthur nodded to the three others, and each dashed off to conduct some part of an orchestration.

"What hap . . ." but it would take more than broth and a spell in the chair to recover, so he fell into accepting that in this moment all was okay.

"Right," Arthur said in a soothing tone. "Don't try to talk for now, just rest. Tomorrow, I'll fill you in, but for now, you don't have a thing to worry about. Let's just get you inside, warmed up, and rested.

Arthur helped him back on his feet, then Samson followed him as Arthur guided him up the stairs of the Lanark house and into Arthur's bedroom where the bath was now full.

With shaky legs, Arthur helped guide Samson over the edge until at last, he sat down and let the heat and the steam wash over the past few days. He let his head hang over his chest as Arthur ran a soft cloth and the olive soap across his splintered back.

I's could get used to someone tending to me like this. No wonder the white folk be supporters of slavery, he chuckled to himself on the inside, and with that inner laughter he knew life was still worth the living.

Once the bath was over, he let Arthur dry him and place him in the bed with the help of Nelson.

"Can you make sure they have the horses saddled and hitched to the wagon in the morning?" he heard Arthur ask the older slave. "I have need to head out and to speak to Mr. Clarkson first thing."

Samson let his body go and it fell deep into the comfort of Arthur's bed. The sheets, the pillows- all seemed to cradle him and he let them take what remained of his consciousness until he fell into slumber.

• • • • •

ARTHUR DID NOT SLEEP ALL that well. Too much to sort through. Too much to do. Little clarity on the best way to move forward. Then, there was the worrying about Samson's physical state, not just in the long term, but Arthur felt the need to wake frequently to make sure that Samson was alright. Though Arthur had suffered, he knew it was nothing compared to what Samson had been through and he felt that it was his duty to make sure that, for at least one night, Samson was at peace. That was why he even kept the shotgun next to his bed.

If Flicker, Piglet, or even his own mother had risen from their beds to question Arthur's decision, he was prepared to pepper their backsides with buckshot.

Sooner I get to this, the sooner I get to whatever the next step is after-wards, he thought to himself. He swung his legs out of the bed and kissed Samson, who was still asleep, on his forehead.

"I'll be back," he said to no reply.

Arthur made his way outside where the wagon awaited him, then he climbed up and urged the horses forward down the driveway.

As he rode through the rough roads of his plantation, he saw slaves left and right already picking cotton. It was prime time for plucking before the sun broke high, so though many white folks would first be drinking coffee and eating eggs, the men and women that Arthur himself owned were already part way through their day's labor.

Nearby, Flicker barked orders at a small group of pickers. As Arthur drew closer, Flicker raised his hand and rode his horse over to meet the wagon.

"Morning, young Mister Buchanan," Flicker called as he got closer.

Arthur tipped his hat and replied coolly, "Good morning."

"Any change in Anna's condition?" the grizzled bear inquired.

"No. I expect she will remain in a restful state until Doctor Charles arrives next week."

Flicker grunted.

"What about that Samson boy?" he asked. Arthur felt the tension rise in Flicker's voice.

"What about him?" Arthur questioned back coldly.

"I seen you lettin' him out of the barn last night. Helpin' that boy even. What gives?"

There was suspicion and accusation in Flicker's tone and Arthur contemplated how best to react. To bite back could chance a reaction, but a soft answer now would cement their permanent roles at Lanark.

"I wasn't aware I needed to explain my actions to you, Flicker," Arthur's chest swelled. "Last I understood, it was you that worked for me, not the other way around."

"Well . . ." Flicker began to reply, but Arthur looked up at the sky then spoke over him.

"We'll have to save whatever else you need to say for another conversation. For now, I must make haste, as I have a wedding to cancel before it gets too late in the day."

"Cancel the wedding?" Flicker was incredulous. "If you don't mind my sayin' so, I think not marryin' Gillie Clarkson today would not be just another mistake, it would be a colossal error!"

Arthur looked at Flicker hard.

"Actually, Flicker," he declared strongly. "I do mind." Arthur flicked the horses' reins and continued on his journey.

It wasn't but thirty minutes more before Arthur approached the Clarkson's farm. He heard Gillie yell out from an upstairs window for her father something about bad luck to see the groom the day of the wedding, but Arthur simply pulled the wagon to a stop and hopped off, ready to end this charade.

"Arthur?" Mr. Clarkson said in disbelief as he emerged from his home. "Whatever it is, couldn't you have sent someone over to deliver the message other than yourself? Even with Miss Anna injured, she wouldn't want you to break any wedding day traditions."

"That's just it," Arthur sighed. "There will not be a wedding today."

The front door flung open and Gillie flew out in hysteria.

"No wedding?" she cried. "But why?"

"My mother, of course," Arthur explained. "Her injuries are more serious than we realized and it just wouldn't seem right to proceed given the circumstances." Arthur lowered his eyes to convey remorse.

"Daddy!" Gillie wailed then she threw her ringlet covered head onto her father's breast and sobbed.

"But son," Mr. Clarkson tried to explain. "It's what your mother would want and it's clearly what my daughter wants. I'd hate to see either of them be disappointed."

"But it's not what I want," Arthur blurted out then he softened his words by adding, "Again, given the circumstances and all."

"What if we went ahead with the ceremony today and saved the celebration until your mother was fully healed?" Clarkson suggested. "That would satisfy everyone and in fact, Gillie could come live with you and tend to your mother first hand to nurture her back to her health."

Gillie whipped her head back toward Arthur and smiled through cheeks wet with tears.

"Oh, wouldn't that be perfect, Arthur?" she exclaimed with great hope in her voice.

Arthur lowered his shoulders. "I'm afraid that just wouldn't be possible," he said sadly.

"My mother only has one son and I absolutely could not ever deprive my mother of her one chance to see me wed."

Gillie began to blubber again.

"No, I think it's best that we face reality here and put this marriage on hold indefinitely." Arthur was firm now.

"Indefinitely?" Gillie wailed.

"Too many uncertainties exist to hold you up Gillie from entering into a more fitting marriage arrangement, one that would allow you to start your life as a wife and mother long before I will likely be ready to even consider taking someone's hand. It's possible that my mother could need years of care and I won't put that on anyone else's shoulders, no matter how much they love me."

Gillie ran off into the house and the sounds of her wails echoed above the noise of the front door that slammed behind her.

"Good day, Mr. Clarkson," Arthur said then he turned to leave.

"You know." Mr. Clarkson's eyes narrowed. "There's some speculation been heard about you when it comes to this boy of yours."

Arthur stopped.

"I am loathe to think there's any truth behind people's words, on account of the friendship I had with your God-afeared daddy and, more importantly, my daughter's feelings about you."

As Arthur started to walk again, he felt Clarkson move up behind him.

"I can't allow your actions to negatively affect Gillie," Clarkson warned while he put a hand on Arthur's shoulder. "You understand, don't you son?"

Arthur stopped walking again then he turned to face Mr. Clarkson.

"What exactly are you saying, Mr. Clarkson," Arthur responded.

"You'd do wisely to reign that Samson boy in. Make a point of showing no mercy whatsoever for what he has done to you."

"How so?" Arthur pressed.

"Me and many others around here are going to be watching you," Clarkson menaced.

"We all are going to want to know what your reaction is to his crimes, son. Me most especially."

It was clear to Arthur that there was a threat behind Clarkson's words.

"Thanks for your concern, Mr. Clarkson," Arthur replied. "I have not decided yet what my reaction is going to be, if I tell you truthfully, but by your words I can truly see now that I'm going to have to give a lot more thought to my decision in order to make sure it's one that everyone, everywhere can be clear on."

Then Arthur walked back to his wagon and pulled himself up.

"Good day, Mr. Clarkson," he announced.

"Give my regards to Miss Anna," Clarkson yelled. "Tell her I'll come by and check on her in the coming days. Tell her I still stand by what she and I discussed . . ."

His voice faded as Arthur pressed the horses onward and away from this broken engagement.

The rest of the day was similar to the next few days that passed by in a haze. Things existed in a suspension of time. Everyone carried on as usual, if anything could be called usual. Yet, it was clear that until either Anna was up out of the bed to retake control of Lanark, or Arthur landed on some kind of solution, the storm his mother, Flicker, Piglet, Clarkson, or frankly anyone else would bring continued to gather on the horizon.

There were moments when Arthur wished it could remain as it were in this time. Like when Mae playfully scolded him for taking a quick taste of pie filling as he passed through the kitchen. She slapped his hand with a laugh, something Arthur knew she dared not do if his mother were awake and walked the house. Or when Hattie asked him if she could retire for the evening early due to a cough. Anna would have let her die of typhoid before she allowed anyone to take to bed sick on her watch.

Yet, when Arthur caught Piglet's hand as it struck across Ellis' head out in the barn for his believed to be shoddy work, or heard Flicker growl out justice to those he thought picked too slowly, he was reminded he could not leave things as they were for long. A reckoning was in order and better that he was on the deciding side.

Arthur stewed and stewed until at last something popped into his head. A memory from his time at the Rivington Academy and some of the information he recalled hearing from those in attendance at the Lincoln-Harrington debate. They had something of their own raucous discussion at a pub after the event about some of the laws that existed in these lands. It was only minutes after he recalled this beer-induced conversation that Arthur had saddled a horse up and thundered toward the town.

I wonder . . . he thought to himself as he rode.

• • • • •

THE ROOM WAS FILLED WITH TONES of off-white when Samson yawned and sat up in the bed. He knew it had to be later in the afternoon, but could not recall how many days he had laid in this bed. Across the room he saw Arthur seated. He looked to be bent over some papers at his desk.

"E'erything ok?" Samson asked him groggily.

"Ah, you're awake." Arthur smiled at him warmly as he turned around in his seat. "Your body had been through a lot and needed all of that rest, but you must be hungry by now."

"How long I's been out for?" Samson inquired.

"Days," Arthur said as he stood up and approached the bed. "We've managed to keep my momma asleep, too. Only with her it required a little medication." Arthur winked.

"How's that?"

"When they brought us back here after the river, my mother used some ether on a rag she got from the doctor to knock me out flat. In fact, Hattie's been helping me keep Anna knocked out now by taking turns with me to make sure she stays quiet at the use of the doctor's same ether."

Samson was surprised by Arthur's confession. "Well, I'll be . . ." he gasped softly.

"What?" Arthur asked with a wink. "We are just returning like for like around here," Arthur explained through a giggle. "It can't be expected that we don't go to every extreme to take care of our dear Mrs. Anna Buchanan here at Lanark."

"Seems the whole world gone done turned itself upside down ever since youse come back to Kentucky," Samson said aloud.

"It's what comes next that has all my attention now," Arthur shared.

Samson reached over and touched his wrist where the ropes bound him. His skin was still blistered.

"And that be?" He wondered for a moment if he should take advantage of Missus Anna's slumber and run out the back door one more time for the woods, but though he had rested plenty of days, all of them nights he suffered while tied naked and starved to the barn wall had left him too weak still to make another run.

Samson moved his legs over gently so that Arthur could sit alongside him on the bed.

"Doctor Charles is set to come back into town tomorrow evening, he's been away, and he is sure to look in on my mother before supper's long over."

"Once she's no longer got a taste of that ether and is awoke, she'll call for my neck soon as," Samson predicted. He could almost feel the rope tighten and choke on his airway.

"Truth be told, I'm hoping she's had enough blood lust and lets you be by and by. She has her own physical healing to worry about now, so maybe her hand will be stayed, even just this once."

A laugh burst from Samson's lungs. "Or more like she'll be hotter than the sun on a mid-summer day . . . just itchin' to blister some skin." He reached over and put his hand on Arthur's leg. "It's just not likely she be forgivin' and forgettin' and youse and I's both knows it."

Arthur sighed loudly.

"Reckon, I need to wake her tomorrow and have a conversation with her before the doctor arrives in that case. Perhaps I can get her to see reason."

Samson's muscles clenched. *Reason?* he screamed inside. *Doesn't this man know who his own momma is by now?*

"And what if she can't be reasoned with," he pressed.

Arthur got up from the bed and crossed the room to pick up a piece of paper from his desk. He brought it with him back to the bedside and thrust it into Samson's hands.

"What's this?" Samson asked with some annoyance. "You knows I's can't read."

"That, Samson," Arthur replied calmly. "That paper there *is* reason."

• • • • •

BEFORE SUNRISE THE NEXT MORNING, Arthur woke up and dressed. Samson and he both headed down to the kitchen together where Mae, Nelson, and Hattie were already at work preparing breakfast.

"Did you tell everyone to meet at the cabins?" Arthur asked.

"At first light, just as you said," Nelson replied. "Though not sure how Flicker and his friends are gonna react to slaves not having taken to the fields already."

"Don't you worry about any of them," Arthur insisted, though inside he worried quite a bit more about their reaction to what would happen afterwards.

"Yessuh." Nelson nodded.

"Did you make sure mother will be asleep for a bit longer, Hattie?" he directed his question to the large woman.

Hands on her hips, Hattie shook her head. "Massa Artha, I's let her awake long enough to feed her some soft eggs, then I's did as ya told me and she's already heavy eyed and calling the hogs."

"Then there is no time like now," Arthur informed the group. They fell in line behind him as he led the way out of the kitchen and toward the front door.

"And no hints none on what secrets youse planning to tell us all this morning?" Hattie asked Arthur with a wink.

Mae stepped forward and put her arm into Hattie's and led her on. "Leave that poor boy alone," she chastised her. "Can't youse tell he has enough to handle at the moment without youse prying?"

Off they walked with smiles, and Arthur couldn't help but do the same, as any tension that had existed between all the tenants of the Lanark house in the past seemed to fully dissipate over these last few days. "That is what is possible," he remarked to himself as he listened to Hattie and Mae tease each other.

A few minutes later, the small party broke through the trees to find dozens upon dozens of slaves of all ages there waiting. Men, women, and children stood around or sat on logs in the clearing just outside of the church building. When they saw Arthur, someone rang the church bell, and everyone filed inside. Murmurs of confusion filled the air as they passed their way into pews. Those who couldn't find seats stood up along the walls.

Arthur joined in with them and proceeded through the doors until he reached the front of the church. There he turned to face his property. To his right stood the man who worked cotton for six days but served as pastor on the seventh. To Arthur's left stood Samson, followed by Hattie, Mae, and Nelson, as Arthur had insisted they join him physically at the front of the church.

Poppa Blue was guided to the front pew by Minerva, who Samson had asked Arthur specifically if they could place so he would be nearest to him for this gathering. Once they were seated, a hush grew over the crowd.

Arthur stepped over to the pulpit and as he did so, he saw the door to the church darken with the bodies of Flicker and Piglet, who pushed their way just inside.

Arthur took a moment to gather himself then swallowed hard and looked up. "If ever there was a God, let him be with me now," Arthur prayed silently. His knees felt as though they were about to buckle, but Arthur knew- whatever it took- he must deliver this message clear and with the force of conviction. *Buckle later,* he screamed at them silently. He cleared his throat and spoke.

"Thank you all for coming here this morning," Arthur began. "I know you are probably filled with questions a'plenty, as by now you would already be hard at work if I had not summoned you at first light."

He looked out at the sea of faces and found a mixture of confusion, wonder, and some outright hostility. Arthur could not blame this group for any of their feelings as there was likely never a time that any group of slaves to their knowledge were pulled together without a hard message, so he knew they must be expecting the worst from their master.

"As you all know, I was sent away as a young boy."

There were one or two nods.

"I only recently came back home here to Mason County a few weeks back after my daddy, Buck Buchanan, passed away."

The nods stopped at Buck's name.

"Well, I have come to find out in all the time that I was gone that quite a lot has happened in these years."

Blank stares.

"Only, most of the changes have been with me."

He noted shrugs of indifference interspersed among the crowd in between some heads tilted toward him in wonder at what he was trying to say to them.

"What I mean is that I changed, but nothing around here seemed to change much at all with me. Well . . . except maybe there's some more wrinkles on familiar faces." He continued with a smile, but Arthur knew his audience had not warmed to him as he had still yet to say a damn thing.

Get it together, he thought silently.

"Folks, this set me to thinking what could I do to foster something new on this land since I'd become its owner." Eyes started to widen in curiosity. "Better yet, bring change to an institution that's been in place here ever since the first Buchanan bought this land and its first slaves more than a few generations back."

One man, without thought, rolled his eyes in frustration with the lack of clarity from Arthur's words. A woman next to him elbowed the man in the stomach, and the slave man recognized his error and fear froze across his face.

Arthur looked at him and laughed. "It's ok. It's alright." The others watched with great curiosity as their owner seemed to be soothing the nerves of one of their own.

"I close to rolled my eyes at my own self by now wondering what in Sam Hill I was actually saying."

Some laughter began to ripple through the pews.

"Folks, what I am trying to say to you though is this . . ." Arthur reached into his coat pocket and took out the piece of paper he handed to Samson yesterday. He unfolded it, held it up, and began to read it in a loud, clear voice.

"I, Arthur Buchanan, do hereby on this the seventeenth of July, in the year of our Lord 1860, henceforth emancipate and grant freedom to all 162 slaves to which my family owns possession."

Gasps erupted throughout the church.

"He said what?" Mae turned to Hattie and yelled out over the noise.

Arthur watched Hattie look at Mae in disbelief and replied. "I's think he done said we are free," her voice dripped in confusion.

"It is true," Samson stepped up next to Arthur and proclaimed loudly. "It's true! We's all be free thanks to Artha'!"

There was a loud "hallelujah" from one side, a "praise Jesus," from another, mixed in with hoots, hollers, and shouts of "jubilation," and "can it be?"

After a moment, Arthur raised his hands to quiet the crowd and they all hushed quickly.

"Now this will all take a little time, though not too much, to complete the process," Arthur began explaining. "Each of you will come to the porch of the Lanark house at your given time, where I will hand you a personal letter signed by me that grants you your freedom."

Arthur felt something grow in his heart at the sight of the many wet cheeks and heads that shook with wonder.

"Those of you who want to leave at that time need only show your letter to anyone who asks. That letter is your passage yonder, wherever you choose to go. For anyone afeared of the unknown or who chooses to stay and work at Lanark as they've done before, you will do so as an employee and you will receive a fair wage with fair hours for your labor from this day forward."

At the back of the room, Flicker ripped his hat from his head then he threw it down and shouted, "We will see about all this horse shit!" He spat loudly on the church floor and stormed outside followed closely by Piglet.

Arthur waded through a sea of handshakes, hugs, and hallelujahs for the next moments until at last, he broke through into the sunlight. He felt God smile on his forehead and knew his prayer a little while back did not go unanswered.

As he made his way back toward the house, followed by those he had come down to the cabins with earlier, he could make out the faint outline of Flicker and Piglet on horseback as hooves kicked up dirt before they disappeared beyond the horizon.

• • • • •

IT HADN'T BEEN BUT AN HOUR.

Samson followed Arthur right up to the house immediately and helped him set up his desk on the front porch where Arthur had positioned himself on a chair alongside a stack of papers next to a couple of quill pens and jars of ink.

"Here's some lemonade." Hattie came out with a smile and placed a sweaty glass on the far side of the table. "I's reckon it be thirsty work settin' folks free."

Though Arthur had planned for the slaves to come up to the porch at prescribed times, Samson looked up at the long line that already stretched as far as the barn.

"Can't blames them much," Samson remarked. "If you was the one promised somethin' youse ne'er had before, you'd be anxious for it to be in ya hands as quick as rain, too."

Arthur nodded, but Samson knew Arthur could never understand the magnitude of what was happening for the Lanark slaves, even if Arthur was also about to be tremendously affected.

"In that case." Arthur shrugged. "Let's get it started." He sat down and Samson waved the first ones to come up the porch steps.

Before them stood a man, woman, and two girls, likely six and ten years of age.

"Name?" Arthur asked.

"Zekial," the man said and Samson looked at the man whose eyes were filled with wonder. Arthur put his pen to paper then repeated the same for each of Zekial's family members.

When finished, Arthur folded the papers up and handed them to the man who grasped them quickly.

Zekial's lower lip trembled. "You means to tell me that I's really free now?"

Arthur put his pen down and stood up.

"Free as I can make you." He smiled. "What you do from here is of your own accord."

Zekial's woman cried as well and reached forward and hugged her two children who smiled at their parents.

"Good lawd and thank you, Massa Buchana,'" Zekial beamed.

Samson smiled at Arthur when he heard him reply, "Oh no, Zekial. It's Arthur. Just Arthur Buchanan, and I am pleased to meet your acquaintance." Arthur's hand extended and Zekial grasped it and shook it fiercely.

Applause broke out down the line, and Samson looked up to find the numbers had swelled so that now nearly every slave who had been down at the church by the cabins was here to witness the first of freedom for the Lanark slaves.

Samson called the name of the next group up as Arthur retook his seat amidst the noise.

Yet, the cheers were quickly silenced by the crack of gunfire.

Up the long drive thundered Flicker and Piglet who were followed closely by Mr. Clarkson, and a small pack of gun totting men on horseback.

"Right there," Flicker yelled over the din, and he pointed to where they were on the porch.

The slaves who had lined up broke formation and gathered around the horses who had stopped in a pack in front of the Lanark house.

"You see!" Piglet squealed. "He is freeing them just like Flicker told ya!"

"Writing them all papers for passage, yes indeed." Flicker stared down at them with accusation.

One of the men got down off his horse. He was dressed in a brown sack suit with a derby hat. On his chest he wore a six-star medal with words on it that Samson could not read.

"What have we got here?" the man asked as he walked up the porch steps closer to Arthur who continued writing without looking up.

"And you are?" Arthur asked.

"U.S. Deputy Marshal Young," the lawman responded. Samson felt the wind leave his chest. *Freedom sure is short-lived,* he thought sadly.

"Not you." Arthur looked up at the Marshal. "I'm speaking to the man standing beside you." He pointed at the middle-aged slave who stood next to the Marshal.

"J . . . J . . . Jeremiah," the man practically stuttered with uncertainty.

Arthur went back to writing. Once finished he handed Jeremiah his papers then looked up at the Marshal.

"Now then." He smiled. "How can I help you, Deputy Marshal Young?"

"Got to ask what you are doing here, Mister Buchanan?" Young began. "I happened to be riding through Mason County on slave trade business this very day when I was informed by these folks that something was afoot."

Young pointed to Flicker and Piglet.

Samson was surprised by Arthur's coolness. "Nothing afoot, Deputy," he said simply. "I am handling my own business on my own property." Arthur nodded to Samson who then called up the next slave to his desk.

"I'm told you are granting freedom to all of these negroes," Deputy Young pressed.

"You've been told right," Arthur stated, as he turned and took his seat.

Samson noted the unease of the men on horseback. He saw their hands grip tightly onto pistols and rifles. The slaves came around now so that they fully encircled these men. Faces from all sides were tight. But Arthur's? His face remained still as if he was lost in love thoughts while he floated on a pond.

"Can he do such a thing, Deputy Young?" Flicker demanded. "Ne'er heard anyone freed their slaves 'fore they died. Only as part of a will, and only one or two, not hundreds!"

There was a rustle as Clarkson dismounted and tripped up the porch steps.

"What about his mother?" Clarkson straightened himself up and spat out. "What would she say about this matter? I happen to know Miss Anna had a lot of concerns about her son's judgment, Deputy."

"Say more," Deputy Marshal Young pressed Mr. Clarkson. "What type of knowledge do you have and how did you come upon it?"

But before Clarkson spoke, Gillie rode up alongside the porch on horseback.

"Yes, Daddy." Her eyes squinted in the sun. "Do say more . . ."

Samson closed his eyes tightly.

This was it.

He knew without a doubt that Clarkson would reveal the relationship between him and Arthur. It would be a small miracle if only he were to die, but he could not bear to think that all he had done would now bear down so heavily on all of the Lanark slaves who were now mixed up in this as well.

When he opened them, they looked out at Hattie, Mae, and Nelson on the porch and his heart grieved. These three had laid their lives on the line on account of him and his desires. What would happen to slaves who kept their Missus rag-drunk and abed? He looked out at the people who had been so close to a dream on this morning that they dared not to ever have even whispered to themselves 'fore they went to sleep the night prior.

Next, Samson saw his Aunt Minerva who raised him from a pup and next to herself was Poppa Blue, someone who had likely given more to the whites of this plantation than even Samson himself thus far.

He watched as Clarkson's eyes moved from Young to Arthur to Samson to Gillie and then back to the Deputy Marshal. "She thought this boy would be too soft on these negroes," he said at last. "That's why she and I made a deal to marry Arthur to my daughter."

Gillie gasped in horror.

"What deal?" Arthur shot up out of his seat.

"Miss Anna would get control of the farm and Arthur would move in under my tutelage," Clarkson continued as Samson watched Gillie's body look to almost fall off of her horse.

"You didn't?" Gillie cried. "You mean Arthur didn't even want to marry me?"

Arthur came around from his desk to look Mr. Clarkson in the eye.

"My mother, Mr. Clarkson, as you know, is recovering from a terrible fall, and I can't think of anything more lowly than someone trying to use that to their advantage in a situation."

Arthur looked over at Gillie. "I am sorry for it to be told to you in this manner, Gillie. I like you plenty but not in that way and I really do hope we can stay friends."

Samson saw Arthur turn back to the lawman on the porch. "That said, though," he addressed the Deputy Marshal. "Even if that were not the case, Deputy, the law says a man can do with his property as he pleases. And these slaves are my property, as is all of the Lanark plantation."

Flicker cocked his gun back and took aim at Arthur.

"I thought the Marshal here is the law, young Mister Buchanan?" he growled.

Arthur coolly went back to his desk and pulled a large book out from its drawer that he slammed down onto the table.

"When I was in Virginia, Flicker," Arthur said while he rustled through its pages. "I did a lot of reading and a lot of learning." The pages stopped and Samson's eyes moved back and forth from Flicker's gun to Arthur's index finger that scanned the book. "One thing I discovered was that there was a law passed in 1782 that gave slave owners the right to free their slaves at death, like you said earlier . . . or when they are alive . . ."

His finger stopped.

"Ah yes, right here," Arthur said as he picked up the book. "With a deed of manumission . . ."

Just then the Deputy Marshal reached out and grabbed the book from Arthur's hands and tossed it onto the ground. "I'm aware of the laws, Mr. Buchanan. I am the Deputy Marshal of Eastern Kentucky for a reason. However, you clearly didn't study enough at your school. That there you are reading from is the text of the Virginia manumission law. The Kentucky law says . . ."

Arthur interrupted. ". . . that in order to grant the act of manumission, or freeing of one's slaves in Kentucky, an owner must stand before the county magistrate and declare his intention to emancipate his property publicly at which the court does have no choice but to approve the request post hence."

There was silence.

The Deputy Marshal laughed. "Well, it seems like you got everyone all flustered for naught because there ain't no way in hell the county magistrate is going to meet with you now or ever to hear your declaration after all this shit you pulled here today!"

Flicker, Piglet, and the pack of men laughed hysterically.

Defeat registered on the faces of everyone else nearby. Samson wanted to console them all, but mostly he wanted to comfort Arthur, for though he failed, he had tried, and by trying, he showed his love more deeply than Samson could have ever asked. That was worth dying for.

However, Samson noted that Arthur did not look crestfallen at all. Instead, he stood there and heartily grinned. He watched as his childhood friend, his Massa, and now his lover, bent down and picked the book back up off of the ground. Arthur reached into the large tome and pulled out a sheet of paper from behind the cover that he walked over and handed to Mr. Clarkson.

"And so, duly elected County Magistrate Clarkson," he said as he pressed the paper deep into Clarkson's unwilling hands. "Consider my intentions publicly declared."

No one moved.

Artha' done outplayed them all, Samson thought as he stood amazed at Arthur's move.

Suddenly, a gurgling cry erupted from Flicker's throat and exploded. "I don't give a shit what no paper says! Ain't no nigger walking free while I'm around!" He turned to the crowd of slaves and pulled his trigger.

A blood-curdling scream erupted from the mass of Black bodies and the crowd parted.

Samson looked down from the porch to see the African mother that Arthur had rescued from the auction some weeks back step forward with a blank stare. In her arms, she carried the limp body of her dead toddler son. Flicker cocked his gun back once again and took aim at the woman, but Samson rushed off the steps and stood in front of her. As Flicker's gun squared on Samson's chest, a line of angry men and women came in front of him and they encircled Flicker and his horse.

"We're outnumbered," Piglet wailed to the Marshal.

"Outnumbered or not, it appears Buchanan's got the law on his side now. Let's get," he said to the other men as he headed back to his horse.

"Wait a minute," Clarkson yelled. "Word gets out about this, and next thing we know, all the slaves of Mason County are gonna be expecting a wage. I got a right, too, to ensure order and safety for my own family!"

"Oh pooh, Daddy," Gillie reprimanded him with great force. "Your family'll be just fine."

Samson watched as Gillie turned to Arthur and smiled. "People have got a right to happiness, Daddy." Her head turned and her eyes found Samson's. "All people," she declared.

Clarkson got down from the porch and approached his daughter.

"What do you think you are doing?" he scolded her. "I knew all along that Buchanan bull he was talking in your ears would rub off on your frail female mind."

"Get your horse, Daddy," she commanded, to which Samson laughed to watch Mr. Clarkson obey.

"I seem to remember my momma telling a tale of a time when people thought her mind was infected, too." She laughed.

"What the hell are you talking about?" her father protested, climbing up on his horse.

"She told me the story of how her daddy wouldn't let her near you once he found out your family were secretly Catholics."

Clarkson's face reddened.

"But despite that, she married your papist behind anyway, and you converted publicly to a Protestant. So, you see, men and women have a right to their own lives and not to spend it controlling others . . ." she lectured while they rode away side by side.

"You're a lot more like your mother than I realized, Gillie Clarkson," was the last thing Samson heard Mr. Clarkson say to his daughter.

"Thank you, Gillie." Samson giggled to himself. "Turns out you were the intriguing one after all."

By then, the Deputy Marshal had remounted his own horse and Flicker had lowered his gun.

"What will happen to people like Piglet and myself, Deputy Young? How are we supposed to make a livin' if we have to compete with negroes for farm jobs?" he lamented.

"For now, you just find another farm," Young instructed. "I don't reckon too many folks around these parts will be willing to part with their property like Arthur Buchanan, but he is right by the law as far as I can tell, and it's his choice. Though, I say now that I do plan to go study the books myself and if I find so much as one misstep, I'll make sure to bring all the Kentucky Marshal force back with me."

His threat announced, the pack of men regathered around the Deputy Marshal.

"Now if you will excuse me, I have a lot of writing left to do today," Arthur stated. Deputy Marshal Young and his riders tore away in haste.

When Flicker and Piglet stayed behind, Arthur looked up at them with surprise. "Oh! You two are still here?"

"I'm anxious to hear how Miss Anna's gonna react to her son becoming a bona-fide dick-lover once she awakens," Flicker cussed.

"Well, I guess you will have to find that out from afar, as your services are terminated immediately at this here plantation, sirs," Arthur said sternly then he returned to his writing.

Samson stood in the dirt with the mother and her dead son. He looked on as Flicker and Piglet turned away in anger, slowly riding off together.

By now the sun was headed past its zenith. Samson looked up into the sky and watched a small flock of swallows circle the barn a few times before they dove into a formation and dipped beyond the horizon.

Choices

Anna Buchanan almost looked like an angel the way she slept with her hands folded in her lap. Arthur sat down on a chair beside her sickbed and placed a bowl of water in his lap. He took a rag and splashed some of that cold water on his mother's cheeks to rouse her.

"Doctor Charles is on his way," he informed her as she came to.

"Tell me again why I am in this bed?" she asked with confusion.

"You suffered a terrible fall the night of the engagement dinner," he replied.

It had been several days since the incident on the stairs. But during this time, Arthur had only allowed Hattie to awaken his mother twice to briefly feed her. But Arthur made sure Anna was knocked back out cold before his mother had time to do more than be forced to take a few bites and sips.

Anna rubbed her head. "How many days have passed?"

Arthur moved the bowl so that it now sat on Anna's lap. She dipped her hands in and pulled out a small towel. She rang the excess water from it then used the rag to dampen her cheeks and forehead.

"Four," Arthur stated.

Arthur could see the fog begin to lift from her eyes.

"Four?" Anna's eyes scrunched up. "Then, the wedding?"

"Canceled," Arthur said curtly.

"You mean postponed, don't you?" she wondered aloud.

"No," Arthur responded.

"Samson?" Anna pressed as redness came to her cheeks.

"Freed," he remarked matter-of-factly.

Anna sat up straight and bellowed, "Freed?"

His ears on fire, Arthur knew his mother had fully returned to the land of the living, the effects of the ether gone.

He stood up and took the bowl from her lap. "He and all the others."

His mother balled up the small towel in her hands and threw it into the basin, which caused water to splash up and all over Arthur's face and chest.

"Like hell they are!" she screamed. Anna flung the covers off of her body and used her two arms to push her legs off of the bed. As she attempted to stand up, her knees buckled and she almost collapsed to the ground. Arthur, his hands still filled with the water basin, tossed it aside and grabbed his mother under her arms just as she was almost fully to the floor.

"I don't want your help!" she screamed in his ear, but Arthur lifted her body in his arms. He held her there for a moment and looked at this broken woman and wondered how she had been the terror of so many for so long, including himself.

"There's not been a time of my life that I've wanted more than for my own mother to want me," he said softly. "Why didn't you, Momma?" Arthur then begged. "Why didn't you ever love me?" he asked as he draped her body back down on top of the mattress.

Her chest heaved from heavy breaths; Anna's eyes bored into Arthur's.

"You want to know why?" Bitterness formed on her tongue. "It's cause you've always been a reminder of what softness gets you in this world. Softness with anyone, but most especially with those dark demons we've brought over from across the oceans."

Arthur's brow furrowed. "What does the slave trade have to do with your ability to be a mother?"

"You think you're the only one to ever feel kindly toward one of them Black boys?" Anna barked at him. "How do you think Poppa Blue lost his sight?"

Arthur sat back down in the chair and pressed her. "What do you mean?"

"It was a long time ago now," Anna began. Arthur listened with deep interest because he had never in his life heard anyone talk much about Poppa Blue's story before.

"You see, Blue worked the fields for your granddaddy who took kindly to him and brought him to the house. This was before I married your daddy. He worked inside, a trusted member of the household for a short spell before I turned your daddy's head and become Mrs. Buchanan."

His mother's eyes twinkled with the past as she laughed. "Truth be told, I turned many a head back in those days, but it was your daddy's who turned mine back so I moved into Lanark. With Grandma Buchanan already long dead, I was thrust into the role of woman of the house."

"Again, what does this have to do with Poppa Blue's sight?" Arthur was confused.

"You see, Arthur," Anna continued. "I was beautiful."

Arthur guffawed at her lack of humility.

"No, I was," she insisted. "And your daddy became convinced that Poppa Blue could not keep his eyes off of me. He threatened to beat him, to sell him down river, or once he arranged for him to be sent back to the fields. But I stayed your daddy's hands."

"You?" Arthur was incredulous. Anna had never demonstrated effort toward protecting her own son, nevertheless a slave of either sex.

"It was not Poppa Blue's fault he couldn't keep his eyes off of me." Anna giggled at the thought. Then her smile faded and her face turned to stone. "But it was my own for letting my guard down." Her voice was serious now.

"How so?"

"One night, I strolled down by the pond," she explained. "It was evening and I figured no one would be around. Your daddy was out horsing around doing God knows what and I just wanted to feel the coolness of the water on my toes. My sisters and I used to dip our feet in our own pond growing up and it just sounded delightful. As I sat there in the moonlight, I caught Poppa Blue looking at me from a log nearby. He was harmless in my eyes, just love struck like most men, and even though he was just a slave, vanity likes her admirers no matter their position, so I beckoned Blue over. We sat side by side, our feet in the water . . ."

Arthur noticed there was a serenity on Anna's face again.

"What happened then?" he pressed her.

"Oh." Her face soured. "What always happens if you treat these shits with so much as a drop of humanity . . . Poppa Blue used that negro voodoo on me."

"Huh?" Arthur didn't understand what his mother was saying to him. "His voodoo?"

"He took advantage of my weakness, my niceties, and filled me up with his savage desire. He so confused my mind and my body that before I knew it, Poppa Blue and I were embraced in great and evil passion on that water's edge."

Arthur jumped up from his seat. His face flushed with fire and his head pounded with questions. "Are you telling me that you . . ."

"Yes!" Anna screamed at him. "Yes. Now you know! I fell victim to his devilish ways."

Arthur paced back and forth in front of the bed. "And all of this time you have been furious about Samson and me?"

"Arthur!" his mother yelled. "You are missing the whole point, you dense man-child you!"

His mother's words penetrated and Arthur stopped then turned toward Anna's bed.

"The point is what then?" he begged.

"That on account of that Black creature, I worried fitfully over you in my womb for nine months, Arthur," she lamented. "When you did finally come out, an ivory angel," she clamored, "I had some of the driver men hold Poppa Blue down while I took a hot nail to both his eyes myself."

Arthur gasped. For a moment he even gagged. Then, in shock, he made his way to the chair again and sat back down.

There was silence for a time, then Arthur gently asked his mother. "Why didn't you just kill him instead of leaving him like that to suffer for all those years?"

"I wanted to. But killing him meant the like to raise more suspicions with your father than he already had. Instead, I made sure that Poppa Blue could never look on me or nothing else again . . . that he would live the rest of his life in darkness the way he plunged mine into darkness that night by the pond water."

"And why then have you left me without love?" he asked weakly.

"You were a constant reminder of this white woman's ability to be led astray by those evil beings. It's all their fault. It's always their fault. Should have been left to their tribes and witchcraft but since they're here now, we have no choice whatsoever but to Christianize them with the back of our hands. If I had only done that from the moment I stepped onto Lanark, things would've been different. And you . . . you were always friendly toward them as a boy . . . a constant reminder for me of the sin that I allowed that negro to make me do. So, I sent you away. Wanted to keep you from Samson and the others for as long as I could so that they wouldn't be able to ruin your life the way they ruined mine."

He chewed on her words for a bit.

"So, just to be clear," Arthur inquired, "none of this was your fault?"

Anna sucked air in loudly between her teeth. "Of course not! That's what I've been trying to teach you your whole damn life! It's those God-damned negroes, Arthur and I hate them all!"

Emotion got the better of Anna and Arthur rushed to her side to prop her up as she began to cough up blood violently. Just then Hattie opened the door and stuck her head inside.

"Been told Doctor Charles' carriage is a'come," Hattie shared then she disappeared as quickly as she had shown up.

Her cough settled, Anna stated weakly, "I see that cow stayed behind. Figured she would be the first to turn tail and run the second you mentioned freedom to me earlier."

Arthur looked down at his mother and contemplated.

"I guess you will never feel any compassion for any person other than yourself, will you?" he questioned her.

"That wild dog hasn't got any humanlike qualities about her save her ability to walk on two feet. None of them do. They're just here to eat, shit, work, and fuck," she spat. "If I had been wiser, I would have treated her twice as harshly back when I had the chance. And I would have cut Poppa Blue's balls off and fed them to your daddy."

"Momma," Arthur softened his voice. "What if you tried to maybe change your ways going forward? Maybe it's time to think differently. Time to put aside all that anger and hate since it obviously has not led to any good." Arthur held his hands up and motioned around the room. "I mean, look. You are bedridden, your slaves are freed, Poppa Blue led a life blinded but you took no accountability for the fact that maybe you might have been attracted to him and lured him to make love to you yourself. Frankly, you been filled with poison in your soul for so long that maybe it's time to let in some love and find a new way of doing things."

"New way?" Anna snorted. "It's clear I should have been far more resolute in the old one. None of this would have happened had I killed Blue, had I sold Hattie." His mother's eyes narrowed. "Had I smothered you at birth and said there was a deformity before I'd ever had a chance to see if you were born pure or a mulatto."

Arthur's ears rang. His eyes widened. "Smothered me?" He was incredulous with disbelief at Anna's honesty.

"Better that than to see the day my son been rode bareback by a Black man and then freed more than a hundred and fifty of them savages into the civilized world," she bitterly scolded.

Arthur raised his hands in the air.

"But, it's over now," he pressed her to understand. "All that is gone and done and now there's a chance to start again."

"Nothing's done till I say it's done at Lanark, Arthur," she informed him. "After Doctor Charles attends to me, I have every intention of dragging each and every one of those bastards who dared to leave back from hell if I need to, and I plan to start with your cock-lover first. I've tried to do all, explain all, but you are still blinded and I believe now the spell won't be broken until I have his body dragged behind our wagon all through Mason County, and that is going to happen today," she declared forcefully.

Arthur stood up from the chair quickly so that it knocked over backward. He stepped closer to the bed and studied his mother's face.

"I see it now," he said softly. "I see you speak truthfully, Momma."

Arthur jerked out the pillow that rested behind Anna's head.

"Arthur?" she gasped as her head fell backward.

Arthur clenched the pillow tightly with both hands. He felt his fingers push in between the goose feathers then he pressed the pillow over Anna's face as she let out a muffled, "Arth . . ." before she was silenced.

His face bled from the scratch she landed as she clawed at him for air.

"I suppose none will be free of your hateful wrath this day," Arthur whispered as she struggled. "Least of all you . . . least of all you . . ." his voice softened as Anna's flails reached a fever pitch.

Suddenly, a hand reached out and touched Arthur's.

Arthur looked down and saw its ebony color against his own flesh then he looked up and into the eyes of Samson, who gently helped Arthur remove the pillow from his mother's face.

"We all got to live with our doin's," he heard Samson say to him softly. "Missus Anna and yourself included."

Arthur stepped back in shock at his own actions. Anna lay in the bed; her eyes wide with terror; her hands clasping her neck; her chest heaving to recapture the air that had been lost.

The door opened and Doctor Charles came inside. He approached the bed and examined Anna's body. Though she was alert, Anna was unable to speak; her voice still constricted from the choking. Seconds later, Arthur followed the doctor out of the room where he informed Arthur that Anna would recover only partially; her legs appearing to be in a state of permanent paralysis.

"She'll live," he informed Arthur. "But her life will likely never be the same."

"Neither will any of ours," Arthur replied to the doctor then he led him to the door and waved as the carriage pulled away into the night.

• • • • •

DAYLIGHT RADIATED ACROSS THE FIELDS that Samson passed on his way to the cabins. Though bodies walked up and down the rows of cotton, there were far fewer than usual, and none had any drivers or tastes of the whip to urge them on. Instead, men and women picked the fleecy fibers over a move elsewhere, and their labor was now one of self-determination over subjugation.

Through the trees Samson could see the outline of others who with packs on their backs and small children on their hips, were headed out toward a new life. For these folks, fear of the unknown did not trump the terror they had experienced in captivity.

"Better to take our chances while we can," was a common phrase heard these past days since manumission.

When Samson arrived at Minerva's door, the very cabin that had housed his youth, it was to say goodbye to his aunt. She was headed to Chicago with one of the small groups.

"Imma miss you, boy," Samson heard as Minerva hugged his throat. Through tears she continued, "Fact is, you was already gone, even when I was still here." She stepped back and picked up her bags. "That's what feelin's does to people. When someone takes your heart, ain't no one else you see in the world aside from that person."

His aunt made her way to the door then turned back to Samson.

"You think things be ova, but it's a long and thorny road for a negro, slave or not. In your case, you got difficulties ahead none the rest of us could even begin to imagine. You may be freed, but some will still see you as that man's conquest. Others will not see the color of either of ya's skins but only what they consider the deviances of the flesh. Then there's the simmer that's bound to already be boilin' up across Mason County. Take care, Samson. For you always be like my own child to me and I'll love ya North, South, a cotton-picka, or a cracker's pillow. But I prefers to love you alive than dead, so again, take care. And may the Lawd bless your pathway just the same as he may bless mine. And if youse eva in Chicago, you best come by for your auntie's cookin' or I'm like to tan your hide if I's found out otherwise."

Minerva left and Samson stood in the cabin by himself and let her words turn in and out of his head until at last, he sighed and walked back up to the Lanark house.

When he entered the bedroom, he found Arthur at his desk where he poured over papers.

"Finally," Arthur said as he placed one down on a tall stack and got up from his seat. "It's all settled. Now we can focus on us being together with no one questioning who is in my house, in my bed, in my heart . . ."

He closed in on and pressed his lips onto Samson's.

"I reckon," Samson said softly. "Only, everything you mentioned be yours and I's hear naught of mine in that."

Arthur's eyes studied Samson's face then he stepped back.

"Everything okay?"

Samson hesitated then explained, "We needs to talk."

"You're leaving Lanark as well, arent' you?" Arthur asked through downcast eyes.

"I am," Samson said weakly.

"Oh."

"What you done for me, for everyone, it's mighty fine. Truly 'tis!" he explained more forcefully. "It's just, you rememba when we was runnin' and what we said 'fore Flicker, Clarkson, and the dogs broke upon us?"

"Of course. I remember that we were nearly there and then how it all changed in an instant. You got caught . . . I nearly drowned."

"'Fore that even," Samson pressed. "When we's was talking by the pond 'fore that horse break free."

"I do." Arthur's eyes lifted up. "You said you wouldn't serve no man anymore." He stepped forward and grasped Samson's shoulders. "But things are different now, aren't they, Samson?" he begged. "Everyone's free. You are free."

"Things different only not e'nuff still."

Arthur's hands pulled away and back down at his own sides.

"I's want to do what I's said still. I's want to go north, learn a trade. Maybe I'll be a woodworker. Poppa Blue done taught me enough to whittle over the years that I's bet I'd make a fine cabinet maker or something with my hands."

"You can do all that here," Arthur's voice was now soaked in sadness. "That's what freedom means . . . I signed your papers . . . and I . . ."

Samson approached Arthur and this time put his hands on the young Buchanan's shoulders. Arthur stopped his speaking and smiled weakly.

"Arthur," Samson explained. "Freedom's more than a piece of paper. Freedom about a man being able to walk down the street a man without someone stoppin' him, roughin' him up, or givin' him the side-eye for lookin' or bein' different. Ne'er in my lifetime are the people of Kentucky gonna allow no folks who look like me to truly be free, no matta what no piece of paper say."

They looked into each other's eyes then hugged each other's bodies with all of their might.

"Oh Samson," Arthur said with great passion. "I just want you to be happy, to be safe. You deserve all of that and more. Just promise me that you will write me once you get settled."

When they pulled apart, Samson could see that Arthur's cheeks were soaked with tears. Whatever he knew about Arthur Buchanan, whatever anyone could say about this man, Samson knew that Arthur had a heart of pure gold and that he loved him, and that was all that mattered.

"Arthur," Samson took a hold of Arthur's hands and squeezed. "Don't youse understand?"

Confusion spread across his blue eyes.

"You gave this slave a choice. Now this freedman's gonna give you yours."

"You mean?"

"Wont'cha come wit me?"

Then Arthur nodded yes through tears and Samson grabbed Arthur's face in his hands and kissed him deeply. They fell onto the bed and made love without fear of who might find them in the here and now and without fear of what the future might bring. Samson knew that whatever he faced, Arthur would be by his side and he would be by Arthur's.

● ● ● ● ●

ARTHUR SAT ON THE PORCH and looked out over the Lanark plantation. The air was cool and the leaves were aflame with autumn.

"Peace and possibilities," he heard Samson say aloud as he came out the front door.

"Partings and passages, too," Arthur answered back then he watched as Nelson came up the drive. He escorted Poppa Blue by his left arm to the steps. Arthur got up from the porch swing and went over to help Poppa Blue up the stairs until they were both seated side by side on the swing.

They sat in silence for a moment.

"Are you sure you won't come with us?" Arthur leaned over and said at last.

"I's old and blind." Poppa Blue chuckled. "Most my life been spent on Lanark, and there's no use my movin' now."

"I told ya as much," Samson stepped forward and declared.

Arthur looked at Samson for a second then nodded at him.

"You did." Arthur put his hand on Poppa Blue's shoulder. "Well, in that case, I guess it's a good thing, since I've decided to sign most of Lanark's property over to you."

"Say what?" Poppa Blue's blind eyes widened.

"Sure am," Arthur explained. "Samson's got the deed right here," he continued as Samson took a paper out of his pocket and brought it over to Arthur.

"And Nelson here has agreed to stay on and run the house for you." Nelson nodded from the other side of the porch.

"Sure am," he said with a smile.

"I left Nelson part of the land as well."

"Us too," Hattie exclaimed as the door flew open and slammed against the side. She and Mae rushed outside in laughter.

"This baby Buchana' even made me a property owner," Mae boasted. "But don't youse think cause you own more than me youse gonna be some kind of bossy pants, old man," she teased as she walked over and ribbed Poppa Blue.

"Well, I'll be," he wondered aloud and they laughed at how their fortunes had changed.

Ellis arrived with the wagon and helped Arthur and Samson tie all of their belongings to the top.

Soon, a coach showed up and Hattie pushed a three wheeled chair out onto the porch where Anna, fully dressed in her finest, sat atop of its cushion.

"But I have no desire to go to Boston," Anna protested forcefully. Arthur followed behind her.

"You are going to love it there, Momma," he teased. "I have already made arrangements for you to convalesce in the care home of an abolitionist named Doctor Prim for the next twelve months."

"You son of a bitch," she screamed as Samson came out and helped Arthur carry the chair to the wagon and then helped him load his mother's body into the carriage.

Arthur handed the concerned-looking driver a wad of bills.

"See to it that she makes it all the way there in record time," he said while he pressed the bills into his shaking hands. "The doctor at this ward is expecting her, as she has some type of a rare and fitful mental condition."

The man's eyes filled with terror.

"Yes." Arthur nodded. "She can get quite mean as a result of a suffered brain injury and she will say all kinds of lies in an attempt to skirt treatment. I'm afraid if this doctor doesn't receive her that the only alternative is the asylum, so please make sure my momma makes it to this doctor in Boston . . . please."

The driver assured Arthur that he would get her there "quicker than has ever been done." Then he hopped on board and rode off into the daylight. The sound of Anna's cusses could be heard echoing for minutes before her last. "Curse you to hell, Arthur Buchanan," faded into the sun.

The next moments were filled with hugs and shouts of joy and thanksgiving until at last, Arthur and Samson were both seated on the wagon. Arthur looked over at Hattie and Mae who waved through tears.

Arthur flicked the reins and nodded as the wagon moved forward.

"I'm going to miss this farm in a strange way," he said to Samson.

He watched Samson's smile widened. "Not me," he declared and they laughed heartily.

Epilogue

The hair was white, but his shoulders were still broad. Samson finished chiseling. Then he used the cane to help his creaky knees back up from the freshly churned ground until at last, he could take a step back and admire his work.

The stone that was blank before now read: *ARTHUR BUCHANAN 1839-1910; A MAN WHO GAVE HIS HEART FOR THE FREEDOM TO LOVE*

Samson reached into the gray suit pocket one more time.

He stepped forward and placed an object on top of Arthur's headstone then Samson turned and hobbled away.

Fading behind him stood Arthur's grave. Above the newly chiseled words sat an old stick whittled to look like a copperhead snake that was poised to strike.

In the distance lay the sprawling skyline of a twentieth century New York City.